Praise for Dan Spencer's novels

Four Wheels Good

"… an excellently crafted historical fiction… crisp, clear, eager prose that unfolds in this unique story about confronting challenges head-on. A highly enjoyable read."

- Midwest Book Review

All Eyes Skyward

"Couldn't put it down. It's honest and believable and moving and ingenious…"

- Lillian Ross

All Eyes Skyward – Honorable Mention for Mainstream Fiction 12th Annual Writer's Digest Int'l SP Awards

Loop the Loop

"…an atmospheric novel rich with characters… Dan Spencer has a way with stories and eclectic details."

- Rebeccas Reads

Rule of Existence

"… a good brisk read about a perilous time..."

- BNN Book Reviews

The Acid Diary

Dan Spencer

PREAMBLE

Throughout the 1950s and 1960s, the CIA conducted LSD experiments on the American public as part of a covert "umbrella project" called MKULTRA. Testimony before Congress confirmed that "149 MKULTRA subprojects" covered "research into behavioral modification, drug acquisition and testing or administering drugs surreptitiously" including "6 subprojects involving tests on unwitting subjects."

During the Vietnam War, the U.S. military employed superhallucinogenic drugs against insurgents. CIA documents recommended that one such drug called BZ, which was far more potent than LSD and could be administered as an aerosol, might be used to quell public uprisings.

President Lyndon Johnson ordered the CIA to form a domestic espionage division. Its mission was to spy on, discredit, and destabilize anti-war protestors and other subversives within the U.S.

When he left the CIA in 1973, director Richard Helms ordered the destruction of countless MKULTRA records. Helms testified that the agency maintained "relationships with outsiders" and he made the order "so that anybody who assisted us in the past would not be subject to follow-up questions, embarrassment, if you will."

Although no solid proof exists, some people who experienced San Francisco's Haight Ashbury scene in 1967 still believe the CIA played a clandestine role in the Summer of Love.

1
A Day in the Life

Victim has a dismembered arm, said the dispatcher. The lead detective gulped the last of his coffee, tossed the styrofoam cup out the window, and affixed the blue bubble to the Coronet's dashboard. His partner put the car in gear, hit the siren, and off they sped.

The doorway sleepers scattered along Haight Street dozed through the police siren. August's fog submerged the neighborhood in gray. By midday, when sunlight normally burns away the gloom, crowds would flood the neighborhood. Hippies and tourists and runaways and curiosity seekers and drug dealers and reporters and bikers and cops. They all descended on the Haight Ashbury to trip through the Summer of Love. But at eight a.m. on a Monday, traffic and pedestrians were sparse, so the cop car passed only one homeless teenage speed freak as it zipped straight through.

The unmarked vehicle turned south from Haight onto Cole and pulled up near four SFPD squad cars double-parked in front of a low-rent apartment building at the corner of Frederick. The siren died. The two homicide detectives, both in bland overcoats and fedoras, men as drab as the fog, clambered out of the Dodge Coronet. They trudged into the premises through an open glass door and climbed stairs to a second-story flat. Voices and footsteps echoed off the barren hallway walls.

Two uniformed cops stood in the narrow hallway interviewing a sleepy-eyed, half-clad neighbor in an adjoining apartment. His long hair and thick beard couldn't disguise his youth. The young man's pupils looked permanently dilated.

"No, man, I didn't hear a thing. He's a real quiet guy. Keeps to himself."

"You know his name?"

"Not sure."

Across the hall, four more officers stood inside the crime scene apartment. A police photographer's flashbulbs popped away. An investigator dusted surfaces for fingerprints. The detectives entered and scanned the four-room flat: a walk-in kitchen with aged appliances; a bathroom the size of a janitor's closet; a furniture-free living room where throw pillows covered a dirty carpet. The aroma of incense permeated the flat, a common scent in the Haight. Beyond the living room, the photographer snapped pictures in a claustrophobic bedroom. The detectives slipped inside.

A white male body lay on a frameless mattress. His blue eyes bulged with shock, and his thin lips were parted as if he'd released a final gasp or prayer. His left arm was severed beneath the elbow, exposing jagged edges of the radius and ulna. Blood from the stump had pooled onto the mattress, spattered one wall, and mottled the deceased man's untrimmed beard and shaggy brunette hair. His purple and yellow tie-dyed shirt was soaked in blood, as were his tattered jeans. Only his navy pea coat, which hung from the doorknob, was unstained.

"Helluva way to start the week," the lead detective said.

His partner pulled a pen from his pocket, flipped open a notepad, and began jotting details. "Name?"

"John Doe," a uniformed officer answered. "No ID. Can't even find a piece of mail with his name on it."

"Odd."

"Not for around here, sir."

"Who called it in?"

"An anonymous tip."

"Who responded?"

"Me and my partner. A downstairs tenant let us in. We found the apartment door unlocked. No one in sight. None of the neighbors heard a thing."

"Well, somebody around here must know who he is."

"We're canvassing."

"Get the landlord."

"We're trying to reach him."

"Any signs of forced entry?"

"No, sir. Have a look."

The apartment door had a pristine deadbolt above the handle. The lock showed no signs of tampering.

"So he knew his attacker and let him in."

"Unless the attacker had his own key and let himself in."

"Where's the arm?"

"Can't find it. No blood trail."

"Search the neighborhood. Garbage cans, trash bins, dumpsters, everything."

Two uniformed officers left the apartment. The photographer snapped one final photo, collected his equipment, and departed. The investigators continued dusting. The lead detective removed a handkerchief from his pocket. He used it to protect his hand as he touched and moved the dead left leg. Rigor mortis made the limb stiff. Then the detectives stared at the floor. Blood splattered the hardwood in some places yet was absent in other areas.

"No footprints. But the attacker had to be standing here, and the victim fell backward onto the bed. Looks like he might've raised his arm in defense and caught a blade."

"Somebody cleaned up. See the blood swirls on the floor? Could be from a mop or towels."

The lead detective crossed to the officer dusting for prints. "Whatta we got?"

"Nothing. This place was wiped down."

The two uniformed officers returned with a third cop. "Detectives, this is Officer Delahanty. He works the beat here."

Delahanty stepped forward, broad shoulders scraping the doorframe as he entered. He was guided into the crime scene bedroom.

"We need an ID."

The beat cop nodded. "Known on the street as Tom Tom. A local drug dealer. No priors, no arrests."

"He deals but hasn't been arrested?"

"It's the Haight, sir," Delahanty said with a shrug. "The Narco boys prob'ly know more."

"Thanks," the lead detective said as he escorted the officer out. Then he pulled aside another uniformed cop. "Contact Narcotics. Tell them to get somebody over here who works Haight Street."

The partner inspected a tiny bedside table covered in a tie-dyed cotton cloth. Resting on the table were nickels and pennies, a roach clip, an ashtray recently emptied, a ballpoint pen, chewing gum in wrappers, and a wristwatch. The watch had no inscription. He lifted the tablecloth and discovered a combination safe. The handle wouldn't budge.

"Probably stored his drugs and cash in there," the lead detective said. "We'll need to have it opened. And let's get a toxicology report."

The detectives probed the rest of the apartment. The only natural light came from two windowed light wells, common in San Francisco architecture, that provided banal views of the adjacent building just four feet away. The kitchen was tidy. Cups, dishes, silverware, and utensils were neatly stored and stacked in cupboards. The refrigerator contained bottles of beer, sodas, bread, cheese, lunchmeat, and condiments, most of which looked fresh. The living room had no television or furniture. No books or bookshelves. Recent copies of the *Oracle*, the hippie newspaper distributed on Haight Street, lay in a corner of the floor. A stereo and large speakers dominated the room. Sixty record albums fit neatly into a wooden crate. Rolling papers and ashtrays lay nearby with remnants of joints. The throw pillows on the floor generally matched and were organized in a rectangular pattern. Amidst the pillows was a bongo drum. A lava lamp offered vague illumination. Unlit, mostly melted candles lay scattered around the room like dandelions on a lawn. Two posters were tacked onto the wall, the only decorations. Both were psychedelic prints advertising rock shows at the Fillmore featuring Big Brother and the Holding Company and the Grateful Dead. Not only were furnishings sparse, everything was tidy. The living room carpet needed vacuuming and cleaning, but that was the only sign of slovenliness. Jackets hung on hangers and two pair of boots sat upright in a hall closet. No piles of dirty clothes; three pair of underwear, socks, and T-shirts lay in a hamper in the bedroom closet. The place seemed barely lived in.

"Awfully clean for a pusher."

"In here," the partner said. In the phone booth sized bathroom, he pointed to a cabinet beneath the sink where a box of tampons rested. "A woman lived here."

"No signs of her now."

"I don't know. Some of these hippie girls… They travel with nothing more than the clothes on their backs."

Boots echoed through the stairway. The detectives met two men at the door. Both wore their hair long, dressed in blue jeans with matching jeans jackets, and sported mustaches. One flashed a San Francisco Police badge and said, "Narcotics. You called?"

The detectives led them into the bedroom. "What can you tell us about him?"

"Tom Howard," the narcotics agent said. "He's a local dealer who sells— Christ, they took his arm."

"They wanted the briefcase," the second Narco agent said.

"Briefcase?"

"He walked the streets with a briefcase handcuffed to his wrist."

One of the uniformed officers poked his head in the room. "Excuse me, detectives, we've got somebody out here from the Feds."

The four men stared at one another. "Did you call them?"

The narcotics officers shook their heads.

The men converged in the living room where they found a middle-aged undercover agent in a leather coat and porkpie hat. He flashed his credentials. The Narco agent extended a hand.

"Hey, Dickie. What's up?"

Once the uniformed cops were out of earshot, the Federal agent whispered, "You guys might want to hold off on this investigation."

The lead detective and his partner looked askance at one another. "Oh yeah? Why?"

The federal agent scratched at the back of his neck. "Just pull back. You'll see."

"It's our jurisdiction."

"I know, but…"

The Narcotics officers shrugged, dismissed themselves, and left the apartment. The federal agent removed his porkpie hat and entered the bedroom. He winced when he eyed the body.

"So what's the story?" the lead detective asked.

"I can't really say."

"Off the record, then."

The bald man shook his head.

"Are you Feds involved?"

The agent shuffled his feet and fingered his pork pie hat.

"Hey, if you expect us to back off, you'd better cough up a damn good reason."

The federal agent rubbed his bald pate and whispered, "You didn't hear this from me, okay? But rumor has it your dead guy was CIA."

The homicide detectives glanced at one another with alarm.

Moments later, two somber men in dark trench coats – one with black-framed glasses and the other with a pencil-thin mustache – entered the premises flashing Federal IDs. They approached the homicide detectives. The taller of the two said, "My name's King. This is Menard. We'll take it from here."

Up the trail he climbed with Gina struggling to follow. When he reached the crest, he sat atop a jutting rock and caught his breath. Directly below the sheer cliff was the most stunning sight he'd ever viewed. Sunshine blazed on colorful houses nestled along the verdant hillside. Mediterranean water gently lapped against the beach. A mild breeze swept away all clouds. The Italian coastal town below was a fairy tale setting. He hoped the grandeur would cheer him up, but Evan still felt blue.

Gina huffed and puffed and perched on the boulder beside him. Light perspiration on her copper skin glistened in the sunlight. She arched an arm around his shoulder, tried to catch her breath, and asked, "Worth the climb?"

"It's gorgeous," Evan replied. "Kinda reminds me of your home in Santa Barbara."

"Hmm, yeah, I guess. Maybe that's why Daddy comes back here every year."

They sat in silence and absorbed the picturesque view. Their breathing leveled off. She ran a hand through his blonde hair and rested her head on his shoulder. He slipped an arm around her slender waist.

"Thank you," Evan said.

"For what?"

"For the best summer of my life."

Gina recognized the hint of heartbreak in his voice. She tried to stare into his squinting green eyes. "You're not mad at me?"

Evan shrugged. "You're obeying your father. I guess I understand that."

She rested her head on his shoulder again. "You know I love you."

He didn't reply. Instead, he stared down at the beachfront and burned the radiant view into his memory. Once they returned to the States, he would never see Bonassola again. Gina's parents would never invite him back. That wasn't what he'd originally envisioned. He'd tied his future to her family, and his plans usually came to fruition. He was the golden child of his cursed clan. The young hero climbing toward Valhalla. The all-American with sterling prospects. But recent events derailed his goals, and cynicism subdued him.

Gina nibbled at his ear and repeated, "I love you, Evan Dunne."

"Then run away with me," he said.

She buried her nose in his neck and moaned. "Oh, honey, you know I can't. Daddy would have a conniption fit if I—"

"Come with me to Denmark," he said as he stared at the scenic view below. "I read they don't extradite draft dodgers."

She pulled back and stared at him with surprise. "You're not thinking of…? Oh, Evan."

He turned to her with squinty eyes. "You said you didn't want me to get killed. You cried about it."

Tears welled in her eyes, and she whined. The lissome girl slumped onto his lap and lay there for several minutes. As sunshine burned more freckles onto his pasty skin, he gazed at the magnificent coastline below. The Mediterranean wind and the distant lapping of waves on the shore filled their wordless void. If not for the surrounding splendor, Evan would have drowned in pessimism. As it was, he vacillated between serenity and gloom. The past three months in Italy had been idyllic. Until the marriage proposal. That turned everything sour.

While still resting her head in his lap, Gina muttered, "Maybe we can elope when you get back from Vietnam."

Evan doubted she would wait for him. Declining his proposal at her father's insistence meant she wasn't serious about him. Worse still, he wondered if he would survive the war. But he didn't speak his fears. Instead, he whispered, "Yeah."

Hand in hand, they climbed back down the trail in melancholy silence.

When they returned to the house on the cliff, Mrs. DiGiacomo awaited them on a lounge chair on the veranda. Gina's mother wore a floppy brimmed sunhat and a flowery bikini that exposed too much of her middle-aged flab. A cigarette dangled between her fingers. She rose from her comfortable chair and poured lemonade into ice-filled glasses. "Thirsty, kids?"

"Where's Daddy?" Gina asked as she took a hit from her mother's cigarette.

"Business," Mrs. DiGiacomo said. "Oh, Evan. A telegram came for you." She waddled indoors and snatched an envelope from a table. "They said it was sent about a week ago, but nobody recognized your name, so they didn't know where to deliver it, and nobody knew you were visiting with us. Something like that. I couldn't really understand the delivery boy."

Evan tore open the envelope and stared at the contents. He raised an eyebrow and said, "I need to make a long distance call, please."

"What is it now?" Gina asked.

"I'm not sure. I'll have to call home and find out."

Mrs. DiGiacomo guided him to the kitchen where he could make the call in privacy and spoke Italian to the operator who put him through to the United States. Gina and her mother then retired to the veranda to sip lemonade, smoke cigarettes, and sunbathe.

"How are his spirits?" Mrs. DiGiacomo asked.

"Blah," Gina said after exhaling a smoke ring. "He's getting on my nerves."

"Your father's right. He's beneath you."

Mother and daughter donned sunglasses, stretched out on lounge chairs, flicked their cigarettes into ashtrays, and let the blazing rays sear their caramel complexions, even though darker skin tones seemed impossible. Evan was of no concern to them. All problems were disregarded for sun worship.

Moments later, Evan appeared on the sunny veranda. The women removed their Raybans and squinted at his ashen face.

"Everything okay?" Gina asked.

"I need to return to San Francisco as soon as possible."

"What's wrong?"

"My brother was murdered."

2
I Just Wasn't Made for These Times

Fog suited his mood. With summer's end, the fog usually crept back into the Pacific. Autumn brought flawless California sunshine with only occasional clouds that had lost their
way, but now the gray blanket lingered over San Francisco.
From the backseat of the cab he could barely make out the red
and white communications tower, the sentry that stood atop
Twin Peaks. The familiar briny scent of the bay evoked
memories of the Mediterranean coast, and that made him sad.
Italy and Gina's dazzling body were two things he would lust
after but probably never experience again. He tried to shut out
those cruel thoughts. The cab wound its way from the airport
along the city's back routes, up and over steep hills, and
through familiar neighborhoods. The driver sped along as if he
suspected his passenger was in a rush to get home. Not so.
Homecoming held no joy for Evan Dunne.

His heart ached with memories of Bonassola, the
yacht, the water skiing that he failed so miserably at, the veal
piccata, the sunshine that burned his pale Irish skin, Gina's

sexy complexion that turned chestnut brown with exposure to the rays, and making love in mysterious places throughout the huge house. Then his daydream gave way to sad reality. Returning to San Francisco should have consoled Evan, yet even that didn't fill his spiritual hollow.

The cab sped up Eureka Street and screeched to a stop. Evan stepped out of the taxi, grabbed his two hard suitcases from the trunk, and paid the driver. Then he stood before the aging Victorian house, his childhood home.

As the cab sped away, a man in a crisp khaki Army uniform marched down the street toward him. Evan did a double take and recognized his neighbor Harry Perryman. He cut quite a figure, which was odd since he had grown up a doughy lad. Evan marveled at his old classmate's chiseled appearance.

"Look at you, Harry," Evan said.

"Hey, Evan," Harry said as he extended a hand and shook with a firm grip. "Sorry about your brother."

"Thank you." Evan bowed his head and changed the subject. "Headed overseas?"

"Just finished basic. I ship out for the Philippines next week." Harry pointed to the luggage that sat on the sidewalk at Evan's feet. "Where've you been?"

"Italy. My girlfriend's parents have a place."

"Must be nice. So you came back for the funeral?"

"That and my induction notice."

"You got drafted? But I thought you were two-S. Loyola, right?"

Evan nodded. "This would've been my senior year, but... well, money is tight and I got the offer to go to Italy, so I didn't register for college this semester. That voided my deferment. And before you could say Vietnam, my draft notice came in the mail." Evan eyed Harry's uniform. "So what's it like?"

"All I know so far is basic training. Fort Ord is rough. But you'll fly through without a bruise, knowing you."

"How are things here in the old neighborhood?" Evan asked.

"Different," Harry said with a shrug. "Too many long-hairs, if you ask me. When we graduated, you never heard the word hippie. Now they print it in bold letters on the cover of Time magazine. I don't know what to make of it." Harry realized his faux pas and added, "Sorry, no disrespect to Patrick."

"No problem," Evan said. They both bowed their heads, and Evan changed the subject again. "How's the Kraut?"

"Haven't seen much of him or the guys," Harry said. "I sorta lost touch."

Evan nodded. "Same here."

"Well, gotta go. My condolences to your mom." Harry shook his hand again, which seemed to Evan more formal than old school chums needed to be. Then the soldier marched on and turned the street corner. Evan wondered if he would look as sharp and confident after he entered the service. He doubted it. Ambivalence about the war made him shudder.

Dolores greeted Evan at the front door with a hug. His sister's strawberry blonde hair had grown halfway down her back and was frizzier than he recalled. A peasant dress hung from her full hips, a madras top covered her plump torso, and black-rimmed glasses perched on her button nose. She was nineteen now, he realized. Although her face looked more mature than when he'd last seen his kid sister, freckles still stood out.

"Welcome home," Dolores said.

"Hey, Dolo. Where's Mom?"

Alice Dunne wiped wet hands on her apron as she strode out of the kitchen. With moist eyes and a lump in her throat, she held out inviting arms to her son. She examined his angular face and soft green eyes, and then pecked him on the cheek. She whimpered when they hugged and clung tight even when Evan tried to pull away.

"God, Mom, I haven't gone off to war yet."

"Come, sit down, honey," Alice said in her croaky voice.

Evan abandoned his luggage beside the front door as she guided him to the living room. The plush chair and ottoman awaited him - his deceased father's throne, the family seat of honor. Evan sunk into the soft cushion and propped his legs onto the stool. He removed a pack of menthol cigarettes from his shirt pocket, dug out a fresh one, and lit up. The smoke gave relief as it slid down his throat.

"You look good, Mom," he lied.

In the months since he departed for Europe, Alice had aged a full decade. Crow's feet filled her face and pointed toward bloodshot eyes. Age spots marred her hands. Her mother hips seemed even wider, and varicose veins formed spider webs on her chunky legs. Gray streaks made her red hair the color of pale wheat. So aged in appearance, yet she was only fifty. Fate had not only stolen her mate and now her oldest child, it had also robbed her health and wellbeing.

"I've made chicken and dumplings for dinner," she said.

"My favorite," Evan said.

A quick look around the room proved that nothing had changed. All furniture still faced the black-and-white television. The TV rabbit ears were splayed at an odd angle with tin foil over the tips for better reception. Framed photos of family members Evan had never met still adorned the wallpapered walls, as did the Dunne family's Irish coat of arms and the framed San Francisco Chronicle article about Evan's teenage heroism. He still squirmed at the goofy photo of himself in his Eagle Scout uniform. He wished they hadn't printed that in the paper. Elsewhere in the room, the wooden coffee table displayed the same cup rings and scratches. The only noticeable difference was a layer of dust that Evan knew his mother would never normally permit. But with normality a thing of the past, only a cruel person would point out minor lapses in housekeeping.

Alice sat on the sofa, the springs squeaking as her bottom hit the cushion. Dolores sat cross-legged on the floor despite the carpet being in need of vacuuming.

"How was the flight?" Dolores asked.

"Long. Too many connections and layovers. So, when's the ceremony?"

"A week from Friday," Dolores said. "Sandy agreed to wait until you came home. We've rented a boat."

"Spreading his ashes on the bay, for God's sake." Evan shook his head, exhaled a plume of smoke, and stubbed out the cigarette in an ashtray.

"I know," Alice said. She, too, shook her head with melancholy. "If your father were alive…"

"Patrick wanted cremation," Dolores said. "We have to respect that."

"Still," Evan said, "no church service?"

"Sandy's Methodist," Dolores said, as if that explained everything.

Then Evan asked, "So where's this draft notice?"

Alice rose from the sofa and crossed to the old rolltop desk in the adjoining room. She dug through a drawer and returned with an envelope. "I wouldn't have opened it, you know, except it says it's from the Selective Service. I would never go through your mail."

"Don't worry about it, Mom." Evan removed the thin sheet of paper from the envelope. The wording was concise and impersonal. *Selective Service System*, it read, *Order to Report for Induction. The President of the United States.* What a joke, he thought. As if LBJ had personally selected him. *Greetings*, it read. *You are hereby ordered for induction into the Armed Forces of the United States.* The date listed was October 7, 1967 at 7:00 am. Evan shook his head with disappointment. In only nine days, the U.S. military would possess his life. His stomach gurgled at the thought of it. Evan stuffed the notice back into the envelope.

"When's dinner?" he asked, even though he wasn't the least bit hungry.

✧

"How do you like working at the Castro Theater?" Evan asked as he shoveled dumplings into his mouth. Dolores sat at her seat across the table, and Alice was in her customary chair. Everyone sat in the same spots since childhood, while two empty places at the table left memories of their diminished family.

"It's okay," Dolores said. "We sell popcorn and candy and soda for, like, an hour before showtime. Then we just stand around until the next showing. The pay's not that great. I'm looking for something else."

Evan tried to ease into a discussion of Patrick. "How are Andy and Matt?"

"Confused," Alice said. Creases formed in her brow, and a faraway look clouded her eyes. "Would you care for a beer, sweetie?"

He did. He could've guzzled a six-pack. He wanted to get and stay drunk. But that wouldn't suit any purpose. "Maybe later."

A lengthy silence followed. Alice and Dolores had finished eating, and Evan chewed the last dumpling before setting down his fork. Then he sighed with satisfaction. After three years of college chow and despite a summer of linguini vongole, his mother's cooking still tasted best.

"Let's retire to the living room," Alice said. Evan took the seat of honor and stretched his legs onto the ottoman. Everyone avoided the number one topic as if discussing it would further curse the family. A tiny rivulet slid down Alice's cheek and she spoke in a cracking voice. "I wish you weren't leaving so soon."

Evan bowed his head. "Me, too, Mom."

"I hope you don't... I mean, I hope you come back without..." Alice's voice quivered and quit. She wiped tears, even as more escaped. Then she rose from the sofa. "I need to clean up the kitchen."

"No, Mom, leave it," Dolores said.

"You two talk," Alice said as she staggered out of the room. "Catch up with your brother."

"Mom!"

Too late, Alice was already out of the room. Dolores rose to join her. Evan reached out to his sister.

"Let her go."

Dolores flashed a frown at him and whispered, "She's not going to clean the kitchen. She'd going to have some remedy."

Evan's heart sank. He knew the code word meant booze. While Dolores stormed off to prevent her mother from soaking her grief in bourbon, Evan stayed in his father's chair. Woe the Dunne family, he thought. How had so many calamities befallen them so quickly? Neil Dunne was a good provider and a respected firefighter. His sudden death in 1963 opened a chasm that swallowed his wife Alice. Surely, the mysterious and grisly murder of her eldest child buried her deeper into that fissure. Evan couldn't bear the thought of his kindly mother numbing her pain with booze, but he couldn't blame her for it, either. Escaping from reality seemed the most natural thing to do.

Dolores returned moments later and flopped onto the sofa with a look of disgust.

"She locked herself in the bathroom. I think she's been drinking since noon."

"Leave her be."

"You won't be saying that after you find her passed out in the back yard."

Evan blinked. "She's done that?"

"While hanging laundry. I had to ask Mr. Martino to help me drag her into the house. So embarrassing. She has a boy deliver bourbon from the package store. Whenever I find it, I dump it down the drain. But she hides the stuff everywhere."

Not wanting to hear any more disturbing news about his mother, he changed the subject. "How's Sandy?"

Dolores sighed, ran her hands through her frizzy hair, and adjusted the glasses on her nose. "Coping. She's pretty out of it. She caught him dealing drugs on Haight Street, y'know. In broad daylight."

"I can't fathom that. I mean, Patrick was straighter than straight."

"People change."

"Not that drastically."

"He got into some heavy stuff. And now he's gone... Sandy's barely keeping her sanity, but she has to for her kids."

"What about you? How are you doing?"

Dolores gave him a weary look and shook her head. That said it all. She had always been mature beyond her years, but now she appeared haggard.

"How are you and Mom fixed for cash?"

"She says not to worry. I guess with Dad's pension and Social Security... I don't know how, but we're staying out of the poorhouse."

"How's my car running?"

"I haven't driven it since you left. With all the shit hitting the fan around here..." Her face sagged, and a tear escaped down her cheek. A rockslide of troubles had fallen on Dolores, and Evan pitied his kid sister.

Alice appeared in the doorway. She teetered in place and averted Evan's direct gaze. "Would you mind, honey, if I went to bed and saw you in the morning? I'm just so exhausted."

"Sure, Mom. See you tomorrow." As Alice trudged upstairs to her bedroom, Evan whispered to his sister. "She's not well."

Dolores narrowed her eyes in disdain. "It's a martyr act. She blames herself for Patrick. I'll find her loaded and she'll say things like, 'I don't deserve God's forgiveness.' Or 'Christ himself would have me stoned for my sins.' At first, I laughed. I mean, that's such a goofy thing to say. But then it made me angry. Like Patrick's death is all about her. 'Oh, if only he had told us the truth, boo hoo hoo.' What bullshit."

Dolores's venom towards their mother surprised him. Each word carried a snake hiss of resentment. She could be cutting and sarcastic about anyone, but rarely was his sister so acrimonious. It pained him.

"Has Mom had company?"

"Aunt Helena was here for a weekend, but she had to go back to Nevada. With her bad arthritis, the fog was killing her. Sandy brings the boys by, but Mom is so depressed that Sandy doesn't stay long. Uncle Stu calls all the time. Mrs. Martino came from next door twice, but the only company Mom really keeps is with Johnnie Walker."

Evan let out a sad sigh.

"I don't know what else to do for her," Dolores said. "She never seems to shake it off. I mean, I understand. There are moments when I feel like smacking myself for having a laugh or a smile when I know I should be mourning Patrick. But we have to move on, right? Like with Dad. She was the one who told us to keep on living. That was the best way to honor him. Well, Patrick is gone and his killer is already in prison. At some point you…" She rose from the sofa. "Let's talk outside. I need a smoke."

After grabbing a can of beer from the refrigerator, Evan joined Dolores outdoors on the front stoop. The temperature had dipped. Evan dug an old jacket from the hallway closet. Dolores was already halfway through a filtered cigarette when he sat beside her.

He accepted a cigarette from her pack and a light. "All this business with the biker… I'm unclear. Did he confess or not?"

"It's so freaky." Dolores took another long pull on her cigarette before beginning the tale. "The highway patrol found the guy in the car staring out at the beach. He was tripping his brains out and mistook the cops for giant seagulls, they said. They ran the license plate and discovered it was Patrick's stolen car. Then they found his bloody arm in the back seat."

"Patrick's arm was just lying there in the open?"

"No, inside a briefcase. I went with Sandy to the Hall of Justice for the sentencing. Mom stayed home and got drunk. I wish I had, too. Anyway, the biker made a confession to the court. An allocution. Part of his plea agreement. He said he didn't remember killing Patrick, said he barely knew him, and he had been tripping for, like, three days straight before they arrested him. But since he was in a stolen car with a dead arm in the back seat, he said, 'I musta done something bad.' Those were his actual words. The bastard kills my brother, carries his arm around like it's a leg of lamb, and says, 'Duh, I musta done something bad.' No shit, biker asshole." She flicked her cigarette into the air and watched it land in a sidewalk collection of other discarded butts from previous smoking jags.

"The man barely knew Patrick," Evan asked, "yet he killed him and chopped off his arm? Are things that screwed up in the Haight?"

Dolores stole a sip from the can of beer before answering. "I've been over there about once a week since last spring. It's a pretty groovy scene. Crowded as hell, but it never felt that dangerous. On the other hand, Patrick was into some heavy stuff. He used a phony name. Sandy got a call saying Tom Howard had been murdered and they needed her to identify the body. And she said, Who's that? Then somebody corrected the cops and told them he was Patrick Dunne. Turns out he used the fake name so nobody would know he was pushing drugs."

"Does Mom know all this?"

She nodded. "Couldn't hide it from her."

At that moment, a teenage brunette strolled up to the house. Like Dolores, she wore a peasant skirt and a jeans jacket. A cigarette dangled between her fingers. She waved hello to Dolores.

"Oh, Carlotta," Dolores said. "This is my brother, Evan." She flushed and turned to him. "Sorry, I forgot I was supposed to go out tonight."

"We're going to the Avalon Ballroom," Carlotta said with a smile and a wave. "Wanna join us?"

Evan frowned. He'd never heard of it. "A ballroom?"

"Quicksilver Messenger Service are there tonight," Carlotta said.

That made no sense to Evan, and it showed in his blank stare.

"The Avalon is a rock club," Dolores explained. "Quicksilver is a band."

"I'll stay here and look after Mom," Evan said. He stubbed out his butt on the sole of his shoe and flicked the remainder onto the sidewalk.

Dolores stared at her feet and said to her friend, "I better stay, too."

"Oh, honey," Carlotta said, "you've been so down in the dumps. And you promised."

Dolores crooked a thumb at her brother. "He's only home for a few days before he goes into the Army."

Carlotta's face fell as if she had just announced his death sentence. Evan turned his gaze but appreciated the sympathy.

"Don't stay home on my account," he said. "I won't be up much longer anyhow. Jet lag, you know. So go ahead. Have a good time."

Still, Dolores sat motionless with eyes to the ground. She bit her lip. Evan rested a hand on her shoulder. "You deserve it, Dolo."

Her lips trembled and her eyes watered. "I'll see you tomorrow, okay?"

"You bet."

Evan sat on the cement steps and drank the rest of the beer as the girls wandered off into the night. He grinned and waved as they departed, belying anguish for his little sister. Until that moment, he hadn't considered the burdens she carried. Tending to their drunken mother and dealing with their brother's murder while holding down a minimum-wage job… Dolores deserved more than just one night of fun. He felt guilty for having spent months away on a hedonistic holiday when he was needed at home.

He entered the house and crept upstairs to his mother's bedroom. The door was ajar. Evan peeked in the darkened room and spotted his mother dressed in a bathrobe and curled up in a fetal position atop the blankets. The sound of gentle snoring convinced him not to bother her. He then tiptoed down the hall.

His bedroom was unchanged from when he left for college years earlier, except that clothes weren't strewn on the floor and the bed was made. The space seemed tinier. Despite the room's claustrophobic feel, Evan looked forward to sleeping in his own bed. He stretched and yawned and pulled summer clothes out of his suitcases and placed them in drawers. They wouldn't be needed where he was going.

A neat stack of mail rested on his wooden desk. His mother respected his privacy and left it all unopened. At the bottom of the pile he found a dozen copies of *Boys' Life*. He smirked and shook his head. Why did Mom continue his subscription? He hadn't read the magazine since he left the Boy Scouts. Other mail was junk not worth saving, let alone opening.

A small package rested amongst the mail, however. It measured the size of a slender Bible. Crumpled brown paper was wrapped around the contents. Cellophane tape covered the entirety. It was addressed to Evan Dunne at the Eureka Street house, but no return address was added. A haphazard mosaic of first-class stamps covered the wrapper, more than enough to pay the postage and applied in haste. Evan ripped into the wrapping, which required his pocketknife to tear off. Four layers of brown paper covered the contents.

A book.

No dust jacket. No pictures or words on the all-black cover. Nothing printed on the spine. When he flipped open the book, a lined piece of notepaper and a business card fell out. He grabbed them from the floor, sat on the edge of the bed next to the bedside lamp, and read the handwritten note.

MOM! Put this down right now! Don't touch it!

Dolo or Evan, if you're reading this it means something happened to me and I wasn't able to come home to get it myself. If I'm in jail, give the book to my lawyer. If I disappear, give it to Carl Burnblad. His card is inside. Don't involve Mom or Sandy. I'll explain later.

Patrick

Curiosity made his skin prickle. Here was his brother calling out from the grave. Whereas he'd been sleepy from jet lag moments earlier, Evan jolted awake with an adrenaline rush. He flipped to the first page and began reading.

December 25, 1966

A new diary for Christmas. I wonder why the boys chose this gift. Sandy probably suggested it. Makes me a bit suspicious. Is she trying to spy on me? Can't say for sure. Maybe I'm getting too paranoid. Seems innocent enough. Besides, I thought about writing down notes in the event I need to cover my ass. My assignment is knotty, and I'll need to protect myself as best I can. I'll just have to keep the diary out of Sandy's mitts.

As I write this, she is in the living room listening to the Beach Boys on the stereo, my Christmas gift to her. I hear the song Don't Worry, Baby, which echoes what I've said for years. Although I've always told Sandy not to fret, I lately find myself concerned and agitated. Can't help thinking bad things are on the horizon.

The boys deserve a happy Christmas. I've been distant during the past few months, literally and figuratively, but I'm home now and making every effort to focus on family during the holidays. Sandy insisted on it. She's right. I've got to pull myself together for the kids' sake. Be a dad, she said, not a cigar-store Indian. Don't just sit there staring at them with stoned eyes. Absolutely right. Gotta stay clean for a while. Don't touch the merchandise.

Today, we played a board game together for the first time in ages. Sandy wouldn't let the boys win. I thought it was a bit cruel, but she said losing prepares them for the cold truth of life. As if she knows what that is. Since the experiments at Lemoore and now this operation, I've shed all naiveté about truth. Reality shifts. It's subjective, malleable, easily distorted. It can hide in plain sight. It can be bent to meet needs. If she thinks winning or losing is predicated on truth, she's just a gullible little girl.

Enough cynicism. It's Christmas.

December 30, 1966

All quiet on the street today. Not many sales. Too much rain. Most kids probably went home for the holidays. Good. They should all go home. I overheard some-one at the Drogstore talking about a free concert with free acid on Christmas Eve. Owsley, no doubt. None of the other dealers would give their stash away, not even for Christmas. Who's sponsoring him? He gets the raw materials somewhere. Where does his bankroll come from? Can't be from the bands. From what I understand, he supports them, not vice versa. Somebody must be backing Owsley. Can't shake the notion that he works for our side.

December 31, 1966

Another year over. Maybe the next one will be better. I doubt it. Somebody said Walt Disney died recently. I mentioned that to GH. He laughed and said old Walt was about to miss out on the real Fantasia. I figured he meant tripping, but he said, Keep reading the papers. You'll see. Riots, protests, anti-war. Given the souring of the national mood, I'd say GH's pessimism is on target. Feels like this country is teetering on a precipice. Once we plunge over the edge, just a matter of time now, we'll long for Disney's innocent world.

January 1, 1967

Poster said, Bring whale meat. More Digger street theater nonsense, I presumed. So I checked it out, a big happening on the Panhandle. Bunch of bands: the Dead, Big Brother, etc. Somebody handed me a beer, no charge. Tried to sell my wares, but one of the Diggers pressured me into giving away the stuff for free. They always want shit for free. Free food, free love, free music. So what's the event? He tells me the Hell's Angels are throwing the party for the Diggers as a thank you for springing them from jail. Christ, just what the Haight Ashbury needs, getting in bed with the bikers. Pretty soon they'll invite the Black Panthers to move in from across the bay, and then we'll have a regular hootenanny on the street. Hell, send in the Klan, too, why don't you.

The Diggers. I really can't fathom their angle. They're not political as far as I can tell. They don't protest the war. Never heard or read about them blasting the Man. No anger or vitriol. They just dress up in weird puppet heads and stop traffic or make people pass through a picture frame in order to get a free meal of bland soup and stale bread. Can't call it anarchy because they're nondestructive. It's all just street theater. And to what end? They get off on creating public nuisances, but what does it amount to? Do they really expect to change the world with their stunts?

Wrote about them in my weekly report. If there's anticipation of violence and anarchy, I'm not sure the Diggers will be instigators. They'll pull pranks and act out psychedelic trips for some esoteric purpose that even they can't explain, but the result will be more satire than unrest. They're strictly a phenomenon of the Haight. Not a national group like SDS or the Mobe. Not even a traveling gang like Kesey's Merry Pranksters. The Diggers remain in the Haight. No aspirations beyond this neighborhood, as far as I can tell. Plus they have no apparent leader. Ask a Digger who's in charge and he'll respond, You are. An amorphous group of like-minded acidheads with no discernible agenda. I don't think they're any legitimate threat. Not now, anyway, but in the long term, who knows? Worth keeping tabs on, I suppose.

January 2, 1967

GH read my report and gave me his take on the Diggers. He thinks they're a bunch of dangerous radicals. They tip the applecart, for sure. But dangerous? He didn't back down. Listen to their agenda, he said. Possession is wrong. Everything should be free. Everyone owns everything. Food is free because it's yours. They operate a free store with secondhand clothes, no money exchanged, because ownership is bullshit in their minds. I asked, Where's the harm in that? He's seen them burn money. GH says when rioting breaks out the Diggers will steal anything and everything. They pose a clear and present danger, he says. Told him if he wants to add his opinion to my report before I send it off to TSS, that's okay with me. Naturally, he already did without asking, the prick.

January 4, 1967

Rumor on the street of a big event in the park on the Saturday after next. They're calling it a Human Be-In. Some political speakers, some bands, maybe Timothy Leary. Sent off warning to SG. Asked how he'd like us to proceed. The police know. Permits were filed with the city. Thousands of people anticipated. Supposed to be a peaceful love-in. Even so, GH smells trouble. A big crowd event like that is exactly what our covert operation was designed to tackle.

3
Shapes of Things

Ten-thirty a.m. by Evan's standards was late. Despite jet lag, he had stayed awake reading the entire diary until past three, so he forgave himself for oversleeping. The information he'd read haunted him. Patrick had indeed been into some heavy stuff, as Dolo said. She had no idea how heavy.

Addressing the package to Evan was an odd action designed, it seemed, to keep the secret diary hidden in plain sight. Patrick must have mailed the book with the notion of retrieving it long before Evan's return from Italy, but he was murdered before he could fetch the package. Or so Evan surmised. The diary gave vague answers.

Evan grabbed the princess phone in the hall and carried it into his bedroom. The cord was just long enough to reach inside his door. He sat on the floor and focused on the business card in his hand. Carl Burnblad, Associated Press. He lifted the phone receiver to dial the number. But he heard a voice on the line. Alice was having a conversation. Evan hung up. The information was too explosive for his mother to overhear. That made calling from home problematic. Safer to reach the reporter from a public pay phone, he thought.

After a quick shave and shower, Evan bounded downstairs. His mother was no longer tying up the line. Instead, Dolores sat on the sofa and jabbered away on the telephone. Alice sat at the kitchen table with the morning edition of the Examiner. Reading glasses hung from her nose. She erased entries in the crossword puzzle and tried again. A stack of pancakes rested on the table beside a bottle of maple syrup and grilled sausages.

"Where are my car keys, Mom?"

"Hanging on the key rack. Breakfast is cold, but I can reheat it."

Evan snatched his old key ring from the rack near the back door. Then he grabbed a pancake and two sausages and rolled them into pigs-in-a-blanket.

"I have to meet someone," he lied. He pecked his mother on the back of the head and kept moving.

Outside, Evan lifted the garage door and inspected his kelly green 1962 Plymouth Valiant Signet 200. Sunlight exposed the car's disuse. Cobwebs ran from the side rear view mirror to the driver's window. Dust covered the hood, roof, and trunk. Animal footprints tracked through the dust, probably those of a neighbor's cat. The tires looked soft. Uncle Stu helped him buy it from the city impound, a real steal. The key turned in the ignition to no avail. The battery was dead. The interior light didn't even come on. The Plymouth needed a jump. He slumped in the driver's seat with disappointment.

Alice appeared outside the garage, arms folded across her chest. Lines creased her face to spell out her guilt. "I'm sorry, dear. I should've…"

"Don't worry about it, Mom. I'll take the train."

"Where are you going? Let me give you money for a cab." Before she could scamper inside, he stopped her.

"No, Mom. I'll be fine."

Evan ambled down the street without looking back and lit up a cigarette. The smoke felt good as it glided down his throat. He walked several blocks to the busy corner of Market and Castro. Phone booths lined the sidewalk outside the bank. He pulled out Burnblad's business card, pumped coins into a machine, and dialed the reporter's long-distance number. A woman answered.

"Hello, how may I direct your call?"

"Carl Burnblad, please."

"This is his answering service. Would you like to leave a message?"

Unprepared, he fumbled, "Oh, uh, yes. My name is Evan Dunne."

"Message, please?"

"Tell him this is regarding my brother, Patrick Dunne." He wondered what else he should say and whether that scant message would suffice, but he also didn't know how much private information to entrust to the answering service operator.

"Telephone number, please?"

Evan hesitated. The only number at his disposal was his family's home phone, and he was reluctant to give it out. Doing so might involve his mother.

"Where can Mr. Burnblad reach you, sir?"

"Please tell him I'll call back." He hung up.

Evan pocketed the business card and walked away. Later in the day, he could call again. Next time, to save long-distance charges and to make sure he spoke to Burnblad instead of an answering service, he would call person-to-person.

When he marched back into his mother's house, he found her seated on the sofa watching a TV game show. She hid a small bottle underneath a throw pillow. Evan saw it but said nothing.

"Back already?" she said.

"I rescheduled."

"Who did you say you went to see?"

"Just an old pal."

"Tim Leiber called."

"Yeah? How's the Kraut?"

"He heard you were back in town and wants you to meet him tonight. I wrote it down." She handed over a slip of paper on which she'd written the address of a bar on Market Street. "Anytime after nine, he said."

Evan grinned and pocketed the note. He looked forward to seeing long-time pals, but there were more pressing matters.

He found his sister in her room upstairs. She lounged on her bed in bare feet and flipped through Life magazine while listening to a Laura Nyro record on her turntable. Dolores mouthed the words to "And When I Die." When Evan spotted her, she stopped and scowled at him for interrupting her privacy.

"Wait here," he said. Then Evan slipped down the hallway to his bedroom, lifted the mattress, and retrieved the diary. Making sure his mother wasn't in earshot, he tiptoed back into Dolores's room and quietly shut the door. Then he handed her the book. "Read this."

Dolores turned it over in her hand. "What is it?"

"Patrick's diary."

"Oh, yeah? From when he as a kid?"

"From the last few months."

She opened the cover, flipped through the handwritten pages, and blinked with disbelief. "January, March, April… What the hell…? Where'd you get this?"

"He mailed it to me. It's been sitting untouched on the desk in my room for weeks."

"Holy shit. What does he write about?"

"Read it for yourself. Then we need to talk. But don't show Mom or Sandy. I don't think either of them are ready for this yet."

"Okay," she said. "I've got a job interview this afternoon, but I'll get to this."

"Where's the interview?"

"Playland at the Beach."

"That old dump?" The aging amusement park at Ocean Beach had fallen into disrepair in recent years. "What job?"

"Concessions. Selling popcorn. That's about all I'm qualified for."

A notion struck Evan. "Tell me about the biker."

Dolores rolled over and rubbed her face. "Ahh, I don't wanna talk about him."

"What's the guy's name?"

"Jack Pulasko."

"Do you remember his lawyer's name?"

Her face twisted with disgust. "No. Why?"

"Do we have transcripts from the trial or anything like that?"

"No. He just appeared in court, confessed, and—Why do you care, Evan?"

He scratched his head. "Was anything written in the newspaper?"

She rose from her bed, reached for a three-ring binder on her dresser, and handed it over. A faded photo of Patrick as a ten-year-old boy was glued to the cover. Evan flipped open the binder. Inside were page after page of memorabilia: photos of Patrick throughout the years; crayon drawings he'd completed as a tike; school essays marked with high grades; photographs from Sandy and Patrick's wedding; a formal portrait of Patrick in his Naval dress uniform; a picture of the proud father holding baby Andy in his arms; a Polaroid of the young family on a picnic with Patrick's hair grown long. Evan's eyes welled.

"In the back," Dolores said.

He flipped to the final two pages. On one side was a typed poem, which Dolores had written about Patrick. On the opposite side was a newspaper clipping from the San Francisco Examiner. The headline read, *Confession In Haight Murder*. He scanned the short, three-paragraph story. The article noted the victim as Patrick Dunne, Pulasko's guilty plea, and the information Evan sought – the name of Pulasko's attorney, Richard Friedman.

He handed back the binder. "This is real nice, Dolo."

She shrugged. "Probably too sappy for his taste."

"Read the diary," he said. "And not a word to Mom."
Then Evan slipped out of the room so his mother wouldn't become wise to their secret.

✧

Half an hour later, a service truck towed the Plymouth
to a local garage. A mechanic looked over the dirty car. A new
battery was required. So were brake fluid, steering fluid,
washer fluid, gas, and oil. The bill would make him cringe.

For the remainder of the sunny afternoon while his
Plymouth was in the shop, Evan wandered the streets to reacquaint himself with the old neighborhood. Things hadn't
changed much since he left for college: the camera shop, the
candy store, the Chinese laundries, the family hardware store,
the dingy pubs, the old drugstore, and looming over it all, the
Castro Theater's marquee. Like the Dunne house, most of the
working-class neighbors' Victorians showed various states of
disrepair. From all exterior signs, the neighborhood seemed
the same, but Evan noticed more men on the streets. Before he
left for college, rumors swirled about deviant men's clubs in
the area. He didn't want to believe that gossip, though. Not in
his Irish Catholic neighborhood. Some people had begun calling the district the Castro, but to him it would always be
Eureka Valley.

By four p.m., like clockwork, fog cascaded over the
top of Twin Peaks. In two more hours, the gray mist would
also envelope Eureka Valley, which seemed unfazed by the
wild scene in the Haight Ashbury. The hippie district was only
a mile away, but it might as well have been in another state.

With cigarette in hand, Evan walked back to the pay-
phones at Market and Castro and dialed the Associated Press
reporter. Again, the answering service picked up the line, but
because he'd instructed the operator to make a person-to-
person call, the connection was dropped. Did Burnblad ever
answer his own phone? Maybe not. He made a snap decision
and dialed direct.

"How may I direct your call?"

"Please take a message for Carl Burnblad. This is Evan Dunne." He then gave his mother's telephone number. "I'm in San Francisco. Please tell him to contact me after six p.m. Pacific time. I'll wait for his call."

"Is this urgent, sir?"

"Um, yes."

Leaving his family number seemed chancy, but he had little choice. Off he went to retrieve his car. To Evan's dismay, the bill for towing and auto service came to a staggering ninety-three dollars. Filling the gas tank cost over four bucks, leaving a paltry two-fifty in his pocket. At least his Plymouth was operating. He drove it to Eureka Street. A sedan blocked his driveway, so he parked his car at a curbside spot halfway down the block and walked home.

Inside his mother's house, just beyond the open door, stood two men in trench coats. Alice wrung her hands. As Evan climbed the steps, the men turned to greet him. Both were middle-aged with square jaws. One wore thick glasses. The other sported a pencil-thin mustache. They wore matching suits and ties and patent-leather shoes.

"Mr. Dunne? I'm Agent King. This is Agent Menard. Federal Bureau of Narcotics."

Evan closed the door behind him. "What's this about?"

"We're just following up on the case. We wondered if—"

"My brother's murder?"

"Actually, we're tracking his activities. If you have any information regarding that, we'd appreciate your cooperation."

"His activities?"

Agent King pushed the thick glasses onto his nose and cleared his throat. "As you know, he trafficked in narcotics. We're trying to track his suppliers and rid the streets of all these drugs. I'm sure you understand. Is there anything you can tell us?"

"I've just returned from Europe, so…"

"Did your brother write to you while you were overseas?"

"No, sir."

"Phone calls?"

"No."

"He never talked to you about his activities on Haight Street?"

Evan didn't like their questions. Suspicion welled up in him. "Can I see some ID?"

The agents looked askance at one another. Both hesitated. King motioned to his partner. "Show him yours..."

While Menard patted down his pockets, King kept talking. "Maybe Patrick mentioned something to you, Mrs. Dunne?"

Alice trembled. "Like what?"

"Did he ever discuss any new friends? Did he bring anyone here who you found suspicious?"

"No. He only came here with Sandy and the boys."

Menard searched through all of his pockets but came up empty. Evan glared at him. The agent shrugged to his partner and said, "Musta left it back at the..."

King faced Evan and looked down upon him. "Since you've returned, have you noticed anything peculiar? Something in Patrick's room? Anything at all out of the ordinary?"

"Patrick hasn't lived here for years," Alice said. "He rents a house in West Portal."

"Do you mind if we have a look through the house anyway? Just to see if there are any leads whatsoever."

Evan stood tall and said, "Two federal agents and neither one of you has identification. How do I know you're legit?"

King glared. "I know you don't want to obstruct justice, sir."

"Until I see some ID..."

A tense pause ensued. Menard deferred to King. Their bluff was called. Evan knew these men weren't who they claimed to be.

"Well, maybe Mrs. Dunne wouldn't mind if we—"

"You can go now," Evan insisted.

King tried to charm Alice. In a soft tone, he said, "Ma'am, if you want us to leave…"

Alice swallowed but found her courage. "Yes, please go."

The men said nothing as they exited. Evan's heart pounded. He watched them stroll down the steps to their sedan. Neither man looked back at him, but Evan never blinked. Once their car drove off, the tension melted away.

"Ever seen them before, Mom?"

"No."

"Don't ever let anyone in unless they show ID, okay? Where's Dolo?"

"At a job interview. Then she has to go straight to work."

Evan panicked. Where was the diary? Had the strangers sought the book? He darted upstairs to his sister's room. Patrick's diary sat in plain sight on the nightstand beside the bed, and he snatched it. Leaving the dangerous book out in the open was unwise. A safe hiding place came to mind.

Once his mother occupied herself with dinner preparations, Evan slipped into the garage. He didn't know how much of the diary Dolores had read, but she could finish it another time or he could fill her in. For now, the explosive book needed to be secured where suspicious strangers like Agents King and Menard couldn't get their hands on it.

January 9, 1967

J has returned. Found her crashed in the doorway. I told her not to come back and to stay in San Leandro, but she insisted home was a house of horrors. Showed me the bruises on her arms from her old man's brutality. Couldn't let her spend the night in the rain, so I invited her in. Big mistake. No self-control.

I felt guilty afterward. Plus, I was stoned. So I blurted it out. I'm married. Two kids. J didn't blink. So what? Free love and all. She gave me that Haight Street pabulum about marriage being possession and should be banned. Couldn't tell if she actually believes it or if she's in denial. She insists it won't change a thing between us. If I didn't worry about this chick, she'd be out on the street with all the other lost urchins, scrambling for a warm, dry place to sleep, searching for a morsel to eat, and taking any chance to get high in order to forget their miserable lives. So for now she stays. Besides, she complements my cover.

January 11, 1967

SG has instructed us to lay low and observe. The Human Be-In is not the event officials fear. It's a precursor to bigger things on tap for summertime. Low chance of rioting, they predict. GH doesn't understand how they reached that conclusion and thinks we should be prepared anyway. He's bringing an aerosol can of BZ. I didn't know we had it in a spray. He says TSS has all sorts of crazy James Bond gadgets for drug dispersal. But two ops couldn't dose a thousand-man mob with spray cans. That's nuts. GH is hard core for this gig that sometimes he scares the shit out of me.

4
For What It's Worth

While his mother prepared dinner, Evan sat in the living room and read the afternoon edition of the newspaper. The war in Vietnam dominated the front page. General Westmoreland declared that the U.S. was winning. If so, Evan wondered, then why were more men necessary? Why did he need to be drafted? He dreaded the thought of basic training and whatever misadventures he might face after that. He wondered if Gina would cry for him if he died in Vietnam. She promised to write, but he doubted her sincerity. Hell, she probably already had a new Italian boyfriend by now. Evan tried to shake away his black mood. Accentuate the positive, he thought, although a dark future was all he saw.

The telephone rang. Before Alice could react, Evan rose to answer. The wall-mounted phone was in the kitchen, but its long cord could reach to the bathroom in the hallway. Alice stared with suspicion as Evan took the phone there for privacy.

"This is Verne Klaussen, Associated Press, returning your call."

"Actually, I was trying to reach Carl Burnblad."

"I'm his editor. Is this about a story he was working on?"

"You could say that."

"Well, I assume you don't know... Carl died a couple of months ago, so I'm reassigning his work to other reporters."

"No, I didn't know. How did he...?"

"Auto accident."

"When?"

"Back in August. So, what can I do for you?"

The information surprised Evan. Patrick had specifically requested Burnblad. Now he was dead. In August. The same month of Patrick's murder.

"The 415 area code, that's San Francisco, right?" Klaussen asked. "Is this a follow-up to Carl's Haight Ashbury piece?"

"What piece?"

"The Summer of Love, the hippies, all that. You a hippie?"

The conversation didn't feel right and made Evan's stomach quiver. Revealing Patrick's secrets to this stranger - over the phone, no less – set off Evan's alarms. The information was poison. To divulge it so casually...

"You still there?"

"Yeah."

"Carl was a good man. Did you know him well?"

"No."

"Well, he's missed around these parts. Look, it's late here in Washington, so..."

"Then I won't keep you."

"What were you calling about?"

"I, uh, I just wanted to touch base with Carl."

"But your note says it's urgent."

"For Carl."

"Hmm, I see. Goodnight, then."

"Wait." Evan wondered if he was too mistrustful. Patrick had requested Burnblad but, under the circumstances, did it really matter which reporter received the facts? "I have some information that I was supposed to give to Mr. Burnblad."

"Information? About what?"

"My brother." Evan ran the tap and flushed the toilet to prevent his mother from eavesdropping. "He was murdered here in San Francisco in August. Just before his death, he contacted Burnblad."

"Hold on a second while I get a pen... Okay, go on."

"My brother worked for the CIA."

"Really? In what capacity?"

"He was involved in a top secret operation in the Haight Ashbury district. He posed undercover as a hippie drug dealer in an effort to flood the neighborhood with a variety of narcotics."

Klaussen hesitated on the other end of the phone line. Evan wasn't sure if he was suspicious or just writing down the information.

"So, your hippie brother was murdered because he was really a CIA drug pusher?" His skepticism poured over the phone line. "Did Carl buy that?"

"My brother wanted to expose the illegal activity to the press, but he was murdered before he could speak to Burnblad."

"Hmmm." Again, momentary silences and grunts framed Klaussen's doubt. "Look, I'll give it to you straight. That sounds like a pretty whacko story to me. So I don't know if I would assign manpower to—"

"My brother left a diary. It details what he did for the past year."

Klaussen snickered. "A diary? Like Anne Frank?" His cynicism cut Evan's ego. "I dunno. Still sounds pretty thin to me."

"You should read it."

"What do you want out of this? What do you expect the press to do for you?"

"First of all, the public should know this information. Secondly, it might help reveal my brother's true killers."

"What does that mean, true killers? Is the murder unsolved?"

"A man confessed and is serving time, but I don't know for sure if he's responsible. I have reasons to believe the CIA might be somehow to blame for—"

"Whoa, okay, I've heard enough. Look, if you want someone to investigate this, go to your local newspaper. Okay? Try somebody at the Chronicle. Good luck." With that, he hung up.

Evan slapped his forehead with self-disgust. I must have sounded idiotic, he thought. Until he heard the words flowing from his mouth, the idea never occurred to him that the entire story sounded like a lunatic's wild fantasy. Ever since JFK's assassination, conspiracy nutjobs flourished, and the CIA got blamed for everything under the sun. If he wanted to be taken seriously, he'd have to establish a more plausible explanation. What he really needed, though, was someone to step forward and tell the truth. Someone who knew Patrick's alter ego. Someone written about in the diary. But how would he find those people?

He needed help. A face popped into his mind, someone he could trust.

Evan stepped out of the bathroom to replace the phone on the cradle. As he entered the kitchen, he spotted his mother hiding what looked like a pint bottle of booze into a cupboard behind a canister of baking powder. She slammed the cupboard door, wiped her mouth, and turned her attention to peeling potatoes over the sink. Evan felt both pity and shame for his sorrowful mother, but he didn't know how to deal with her drinking. Instead, he ignored the situation.

"I'm going out," he said. "I'll be back for dinner."

"Where are you off to?"

"I'm going to see Uncle Stu."

January 14, 1967

Today was the Human Be-In in GG Park. All fears allayed. At noon, J and I joined the flock of hippies leaving the Haight for the Polo Grounds. A gorgeous afternoon for a walk in the park, the first dry day in weeks. All we had to do was follow the aroma of weed carried on the wind.

What a freak show. Stoners and acidheads by the boatload. Rough estimate: 9,000. Hard to tell, though. Might've been more because people drifted in and out all day. GH had a cow wondering where the cops were. Hardly any police to manage such a large crowd. Fortunately, they weren't necessary.

J and I found a dry patch of grass and plopped down. Hundreds of doobies passed around. If you didn't get stoned directly, you couldn't avoid a contact high. Allen Ginsburg chanted some bullshit, Timothy Leary preached his LSD hype, and the sound system kept shorting out. There were a couple of rabble-rousing political speakers, but the crowd mostly ignored them. Then the bands took the stage, all the usual suspects: Grateful Dead, Quicksilver, Jefferson Airplane, and a bunch of unknown hippie acts. The lousy sound system kept cutting out. Something about a generator. The audience was too high to care. Somebody was passing around free sandwiches – might've been the Diggers – and they were supposedly dosed with acid. That would explain why so many people were lying in the mud.

GH showed me some clean white tabs of acid that were going around. Excellent craftsmanship. Scary. Word spread that it was Owsley's handiwork, the most potent LSD he'd ever concocted. I gave it to J to try. She's good for that: sampling products so I don't have to. Another reason to keep her around. When she peaked, J agreed it was a super trip. In typical conspiratorial fashion, GH insists we need to find Owsley and take him down. I argued that he's doing our job for us. With everyone tripping, there's no violence. Isn't that our directive? GH backed down, but he still sees Owsley as public enemy number one.

January 15, 1967

Last night, I cleaned up and went home to Sandy and the boys. Naturally, we fought. She's getting tired of me spending so much time away from family. I warned her I had important work. Doesn't seem to get through. She worries that Matt and Andy are growing up with an absentee dad. I complained about the nature of the job, how it wouldn't last, and promised to make it up to everyone.

Deep cover is a bitch to maintain. Successfully, that is. The FBN cowboys on the street don't fool anyone. Take Dickie Trussdale. Everybody knows he's a Narc. Nearly forty, bald, and he wears that stupid porkpie hat. In a way, that helps my ruse. Most buyers avoid the idiots like Dickie, men with suspiciously well-trimmed mustaches and too much cologne. But no one seems to suspect me. Plus, Narcs arrest people. I've never made a bust — don't even have the authority. I just deal. The shit I peddle isn't top shelf, which adds to my cover, too. If it were quality LSD, questions would arise. Does he make his own? Does he have a lab? Is he as good as Owsley? That would draw undue attention. Can't have that. Gotta keep to the shadows. If buyers find out I'm a fraud, word will spread across the Haight Ashbury like napalm. And if they hear I'm CIA, I'm a dead man.

5
The Fool on the Hill

When Evan's firefighter father was alive, smoking indoors was punishable by endless Irish bellyaching. By contrast
and despite battling emphysema, Uncle Stu couldn't care less.
His house smelled like a tenement. Cigarette smoke covered
the odors.

Retirement had changed Stuart Dunne. Or maybe divorce had. When Evan last saw him, his only uncle was a
paunchy beat cop who said little, grunted while his wife prattled away, rarely smiled, drank sparingly, fell asleep at family
functions, and smoked like a campfire. Now, at midday, Uncle
Stu rested a cold can of beer on his expansive gut as he
coughed up a lung. Due to disease, his once-omnipresent cigarettes were replaced with unlit cigars. An oxygen tube ran
from a metal cylinder beside his recliner, circled his head,
looped over both ears, and fit inside his nostrils. Gin blossoms
sprouted from his nose, purple veins lined his cheeks, and
stubble covered his jaw. The man who ruled the roost from his
recliner looked fifteen years older than his actual age.

"No more patrolling the Tenderloin. No more rousting drunks at two a.m. No more busting trannies and queers. My uniform stopped fitting right ten years ago. Now I can let my gut grow all I want. Sleep till nine. Shave if I feel like it, don't if I don't. And with the ex-wife off to Connecticut with her new husband, I'm livin' the bachelor life. Which ain't all it's cracked up to be. For Hugh Hefner maybe. Not for me. But it beats the hell outta nag, nag, nag."

Aunt Lucy's absence was obvious from the apartment's general mess. Crumbs littered the furniture and the hardwood floor. Previously read newspapers lay scattered on every table, every chair except the recliner, and other random places. Two *Playboy* magazines lay in plain sight. None of the furniture matched and every piece looked secondhand. The window shades were drawn, perhaps to obscure the clutter. The apartment smelled of stale socks. It wasn't quite squalor, but Evan remembered his uncle living in better conditions.

"I don't suppose anybody told you yet about Shirley," Stu said with a frown, referring to his eldest daughter. "She's shacked up with a Puerto Rican in Los Angeles. Just to spite me, no doubt. Christ, it makes my skin crawl just thinkin' about my little girl and some spick... Y'know, your dad was real proud of you, son. Saving that little girl, getting those commendations. He's looking down on you from Heaven with a big ole smile on his fat mug. I guarantee you that. I never saved nobody in twenty-five years on the force. Oh, sure, I helped get some pregnant ladies to the hospital, but nothing to brag about. You, on the other hand... What was that little girl's name?"

"Carmen Rodriquez."

"She ever talk to you or write or anything?"

"No."

"Hmph," Uncle Stu said with a scowl, as if that proved something about Hispanics. "So, our hero is going into the Army."

"Yes, sir."

"Well, you get over there and win this thing for our team. Don't pay no attention to the pinkos here at home. Give 'em hell over there. I'm with you all the way, for as long as it takes."

Evan withheld a grimace. Uncle Stu's only concept of combat was what he'd seen in John Wayne movies. He had been a kid during the First World War and was 4-F for the Second. Despite the hollow clichés, Evan couldn't refuse his support.

"Hey, you still drive that car I got you from the impound?"

"Yeah, it's right outside."

"You made out like a bandit on that one, my friend. Charlie Garrison was eyeballin' that little number for himself, so you were lucky to get it. The guy who owned it is doing a stretch in Lompoc. Charlie busted him personally, and he told me how much he wanted that sporty little Plymouth. But then he saw this shiny blue Chevy…"

As Uncle Stu blathered, Evan's mind drifted. This chatterbox wasn't the man he remembered at all. Stu was usually mute while his wife prattled on and dominated conversation. Maybe he'd changed, or maybe Evan's judgment of Stu was dead wrong. People weren't always who they seemed. Like Patrick.

"I need some advice, Uncle Stu."

"Okay, shoot."

"When Patrick was stationed at Lemoore Naval Air Station down in the San Joaquin valley, he served with Navy Intel. That lasted about two years. Then, don't ask me how, the CIA recruited him."

The old man stared. The oxygen tube slipped from his nose. Evan had his undivided attention.

"Right up until the time of his murder, Patrick was working undercover. He was no drug pusher, Uncle Stu. He was a CIA operative. But for some reason, the agency seems to have disavowed his—"

"Patrick told you this?"

Evan hesitated. "Not personally. But I know."

"Who told you?"

The brusqueness of the question jarred Evan. The narrowing of Stu's eyes suggested he already had the knowledge and was suspicious of what and how his nephew knew. Evan felt hesitant.

"I have documents."

Stu squinted with confusion. "Where'd you get 'em?"

"You already know what I'm talking about, don't you?"

"Patrick consulted with me. Just once, but in strictest confidence. So tell me. Where'd you get these documents?"

"From him."

"How could that be?"

"Not important. The point is, Patrick wanted the documents leaked to the press in the event of his… disappearance. I think he intended to expose the operation. Now I have them, and I'm wondering what you think I should do with—"

"Get rid of 'em." The ailing man sat upright in his recliner. "Whatever you've got, it's hot molten lava. Destroy it before it destroys you."

"But my brother's wish was to—"

"Patrick's sworn duty was to maintain secrecy. National security business. What you know you need to forget. But quick. Whatever material you have is top secret. Either turn it over to the Feds or burn it."

"But he seemed to—"

Uncle Stu held out a hand to silence him. "You wanted my advice? There it is. If you want, bring the documents to me. I'll get rid of 'em. You don't wanna be caught destroying government property. Better they throw an old coot like me in prison than a young man like you."

"Actually, it's personal property. I don't think the government has a right to it."

Stu leaned forward and slammed his can of beer on the armrest for emphasis. "You think you're gonna win that argument? They got teams of lawyers who'll tell you that red is green and the moon is made of plastic! Don't mess with those people! If you do, you'll be wearin' a straightjacket in a prison cell, shittin' in your undies, and wishin' yer Mommy would come read you bedtime stories! Now, I'm tellin' you, son! Whatever you got, burn it!"

Evan sat in silent shock. He'd expected different advice, nothing so vociferous. Although Stu's counsel worried him, Evan felt compelled to ignore his pleas. "Do you think Patrick was murdered because of what he was doing?"

The old man trembled. "Where'd you come up with that crap? The official record shows a drugged-out biker did it."

"So you believe the official record...?"

Stu's scowl deepened. He chugged the remainder of his beer and then reattached the oxygen tube to his nostrils. "Don't go dancin' around that volcano, son. You might fall in."

Minutes later, Evan left the shabby apartment feeling just as confused as when he entered, if not more so. In his decades with the SFPD, Uncle Stu had seen and heard ugly truths. Most people would've heeded his judgment. Yet if Patrick's death was the result of chicanery, he deserved justice or at least exoneration. Evan read words of regret in his brother's diary and sensed that Patrick sought absolution. Destroying the truth would reduce Patrick's life to a fire-gutted house to be demolished and forgotten. Evan's conscience wouldn't permit that.

January 20, 1967

GH suspects my misgivings about the assignment. Today, he asked me if I had any questions about Operation Shunpiker. I said yeah, I didn't know what it meant. He flipped out. Don't question orders, he bellowed. You were Navy, he said. You know better. Whatever the operation is ultimately about is for the brass to understand and for us to carry out. Calm down, I said. I meant I didn't know what the word shunpiker meant. That barely cooled his jets. You're getting too close to the subjects, he said. Stay neutral, remain impassive. I assume he meant J.

Then he talked about career advancement. No matter how this op turns out, GH insists the agency will hire us permanent in order to keep us quiet. I asked what the hell the CIA would do with us. They'll need analysis of all these subcultures, he said, and radical elements keep springing up. Analysts make good dough. That's his motivation. The guy really wants to get ahead. I suppose it's something I'd consider, but I don't know if that path is for me. Maybe. Don't know what else I'm gonna do.

He also warned me not to share operational details with anyone and asked about pillow talk. Are you kidding? You think I'm going to share this stuff with my wife? Divorce would strike lightning quick if I said one word about the shit we're pulling off. Yes, Sandy suspects I'm involved in Naval ops, but that's it. She doesn't know about the alter ego or the drug deals or the crash pad or even who really hired me. Not going to tell her either. Not ever, probably. Not going to tell Mom, Evan, Dolo, or the boys. Not telling J. Maybe Stu. The guy barely talks and he's an ex-cop so I figure I can trust him. Come to think of it, with his connections to SFPD, Stu could probably pull me out of jail if the need arises. Okay, he's one person I might trust. But nobody else.

Of course, if anyone ever discovers this diary, I'm screwed.

6
Within You Without You

Evan pitied his nephews. Their heads bowed and shoulders slumped as if their dad's death intensified gravity. Evan knew that heartbreak; he coped with his own father's passing as a teen. But he couldn't fathom the psychological scars on a pair of young kids. Andy and Matt had grown into pudgy fire hydrants. Both boys had blonde brush cuts and blue eyes. Some of their teeth had surrendered to the Tooth Fairy. Each wore blue jeans with rolled-up pant legs and baggy plaid shirts, the better to grow into. They showed their mother polite obedience and clung to her sides. Evan sensed their youthful buoyancy deflated.

"You look good, Evan," Sandy said.

"Italy is a healthy place," he said with a hint of melancholy in his voice. "You look good, too."

Sandy had aged, but he was too courteous to say so. Straight, long blonde locks replaced her once prominent bouffant and fell stylishly beyond her shoulders. The young wife and mother who once preened with lipstick and hairspray was now a widow with minimal make-up. Instead of knee-length skirts, she dressed in blue jeans and a loose blouse. She'd always been a tiny woman, even after mothering two children, but now her hips and waist were fuller. Hardship showed in the dark rings around her eyes. Despite widowhood and raising two kids, Sandy's good looks hadn't completely abandoned her. She just appeared more mature than most twenty-seven year old women. Evan saw in his sister-in-law the same change he'd seen in his mother when she became a widow. Tragedy ages a person fast.

Dinner was a quiet affair with stilted conversation. For the sake of the boys, the adults avoided serious matters. Small talk was the extent of things. Andy and Matt pushed food around on their plates. They missed their Aunt Dolo who was at work. Alice had raided the liquor cabinet before the kids arrived, which showed in her glassy eyes, but Evan chose to ignore her behavior.

"How's your brother Mel?" Evan asked.

"He enlisted in the Marines," Sandy said.

"You're kidding."

"He already shipped off to Vietnam."

"A Marine, huh? I didn't pick Mel for the type. Isn't he over thirty?"

"Twenty-nine. To tell the truth, I was pretty stunned. He had such a good job at the butcher shop."

"Why did he decide to join?"

"A snap judgment, I guess. Said he really wants to serve."

"Protesters, all over the country," Alice said out of the blue. "Shameful. Disgraceful."

Alice's drunken outburst made Evan squirm, but Sandy and the boys showed no reaction.

"Did you read about the protests when you were in Italy?" Sandy asked.

Evan shrugged. "A little."

"It's the damned hippies!" Alice blurted, her face crimson with anger.

"Bad word, Gramma," Matt scolded.

"Sorry, Matty," Alice said without conviction.

Andy tugged at Evan's shirtsleeve. "Were you in the war?"

"Not yet."

The boy frowned with confusion. "But isn't that you in the picture?"

Evan knew the boy was referring to the framed newspaper clipping that hung on the wall in the living room. "Yep. That's me when I was sixteen. Just before you were born."

"You weren't in the Army then?"

Now Evan understood the child's confusion. The photograph showed him in his Eagle Scout uniform shaking hands with Mayor Christopher and receiving a commendation. "No, I was a Boy Scout. I'm going into the Army next week."

"Then why did they take your picture?" Andy asked.

"Your uncle is a hero, that's why," Alice slurred.

"I was walking down Market Street one day and I saw a car accident. A mother was behind the wheel and a little girl, about your age, was trapped in the wreckage. I pulled her out, gave her CPR, and resuscitated her. Do you know what CPR is? It's a way to save people's lives. I learned it from my father, your grandpa. He was a fireman."

"You saved her life?"

"Yes, I did." He said it as a statement of fact, not with pride or false humility. Over the years, Evan had grown accustomed to telling the tale of that April morning, as if it occurred to someone else long, long ago. Andy and Matt stared at their uncle with wide-eyed admiration. Evan had spent most of their young lives away at college, so he had never shared the tale with them before. But he felt somewhat surprised no one else had ever told the boys.

"Now you're going to the Army?" Andy asked.

"That's right."

Then the boy whispered, "Are you going to kill the bad guys?"

"You mustn't ask that, child!" Alice blurted.

Andy cowered. His eyes bulged in fear of the old lady. Blood drained from his face.

"Calm down, Mom," Evan said with anger in his voice.

Sandy leaned toward her sons and addressed them in a singsong cadence as if tempers had never flared. "Don't you like Gramma's cooking? Your Uncle Evan does. That's how he got big and strong. They wouldn't let him in the Army otherwise. So eat up, my good little soldiers. Okay?"

The boys didn't heed the advice and instead pushed meatloaf and lima beans around their plates. Their blank eyes stared into an imaginary distance. Young Matt looked ready to burst with tears. Then, with a disregard for the truth that Evan found odd since neither boy had finished their meals, Sandy said, "You guys ate so well! Okay, you're excused from the table."

The lads leaped from their chairs and trampled to a hallway closet where Gramma kept their Matchbox cars and G.I. Joe dolls and Rock'Em Sock'em Robots. In no time, they were at play and ignored the adults. But even then they looked uncomfortable, as if visiting Gramma's house was punishment and they needed to be on guard for the old woman's outbursts.

While the boys played, Andy's simple question rolled around in Evan's mind. The paradox became so obvious. He'd been hailed as a lifesaver; a teenage hero who had saved a child's life. Now the Army wanted to turn him into a killer. The irony made him queasy. He tried to wipe the notion from his mind.

"How late does Dolo work?" Evan asked.

"Usually till midnight after the last show," Sandy replied. "There's still some coffee, I hope."

"I'll get it," Alice said. She struggled to rise from her chair, nearly slipping her hands off the dining table. His mother's drunkenness pained Evan.

"Sit. Let me." Sandy crossed to the kitchen and poured herself a cup.

"Mom, what were you thinking?" Evan whispered between gritted teeth.

Alice tried to focus an indignant stare, but her eyes wouldn't cooperate. Instead, she appeared even more sloppily drunk. Despite a defensive glare, words failed her. She wagged a finger at her son, which only made her look foolish.

After returning with her coffee, Sandy cleared dishes off the dining room table.

"Leave those," Alice griped. "Sit and have your coffee."

Sandy ignored her mother-in-law's drunken demand and removed the dirty dishes. Evan helped. He followed her into the kitchen while Alice remained at the dining table watching her grandsons play. Sandy ran the tap, waiting for the water to get hot enough for dishwashing. Evan sidled up beside her with glasses and silverware.

"Is Mom usually this drunk at dinner?" he whispered.

Sandy shrugged. "Sometimes."

"Doesn't it disturb you? The boys…?"

"They can't tell the difference. To them, she's just an old woman with bad breath."

Evan's brow wrinkled with doubt. Even he could see how his nephews feared their grandmother. Couldn't Sandy see that?

She sipped her coffee. "Don't worry. Dolo keeps after her."

"You, too, I presume."

"Me too what?"

"You keep after Mom."

Sandy squirted dishwashing liquid into a cloth and began washing glasses. "She just snaps at me. I've got the boys, y'know. They're more than I can handle without having to deal with…" She stopped herself from saying anything impolitic. "Plus, we usually leave earlier than this to catch bus connections, so we rarely see your mom this snockered."

Alice staggered into the kitchen and pointed at Evan. "You're driving them home, remember."

"I know, Mom."

"I'll write down the directions." She reached for a pen and a paper napkin.

"I've been there dozens of times, Mom."

"Don't meddle, Alice," Sandy said as she washed plates.

"Don't talk to me like that!"

The harsh exchange stunned Evan. He'd never seen his sister-in-law and his mother bare their fangs. The boys ceased playing and little Matt appeared on the verge of tears again. Sandy showed no reaction; she kept washing as if the woman's tone meant nothing to her.

"You're not the only one hurt!" Alice blurted out.

Finally, Matt cried. Andy tried to ignore his Gramma's outburst and his bawling brother, but his weak attempt at play belied his anxiety. Sandy ignored the situation as if reality was too much burden and kept washing dinner plates.

Evan glowered at his mother and lorded over her with arms akimbo. "Say goodnight to the boys and go to bed."

Doleful bloodshot eyes stared back at him. The rebuke nearly scared her sober. Alice bowed her head with puppy dog remorse and obeyed. She slithered into the den, kissed each grandson on the top of the head, even as Matty continued crying, and staggered to the staircase. She blubbered as she climbed the steps to her bedroom.

Evan's stomach grumbled, bile burning inside, and self-loathing struck him. He'd never scolded his mother before. For one chiding moment, he'd become his father. Now he came to appreciate his kid sister's bitterness. Coping with their mother was hard enough, but Deirdre had to nurse two women psychically crippled by death.

While Matt cried, Sandy stood oblivious and towel dried the plates and placed them in a cupboard. She then sipped her coffee and showed no sign of fret or concern, as if all the misfortunes of recent months had lobotomized her.

Sandy caught Evan staring and asked, "You okay?"

"Yeah. Are you?"

She scowled as if he'd asked a silly question. "Of course." Then she turned to her sons. "Put the toys away, pumpkins. Time to go home."

✧

Patrick's home looked familiar, except for his absence. The walls were still painted utilitarian white, the only color the newlywed couple could afford when they moved in. Evan recalled the painting party when he slathered two coats on the bathroom walls. As homemaker, it had always been Sandy's house. Her framed photos and paintings and knickknacks decorated the place. Patrick led a Spartan life; she filled it.

Once the kids were put to bed, Sandy joined Evan at her dining table. She brought two cold cans of beer. Weariness showed on her lined face, in her leaden eyelids, and in the way she slumped into the chair.

"I heard Italy didn't turn out the way you hoped," she said as she yanked the ring tops off the beer cans.

"Gina's a dream, but… Well, it was time to wake up." He sipped his beer and said nothing more.

"Please, tell me about it," she said.

Evan winced. "You don't want to hear my heartaches. You've got your own."

"No, it's okay. You proposed, right?"

Evan nodded. "I asked Dr. DiGiacomo for permission to marry his daughter and he hit the roof. 'My little girl is only nineteen! She's too young to marry!' Then he calmed down and told me, 'No offense, son, but you're not Italian.' And I said, 'But I'm Catholic.' Then he made some crack about how the Irish are still considered the Negroes of Europe. I explained that we're third generation Americans – just like Gina – and that marriage between different nationalities doesn't matter these days. I mean, the Second World War changed all that, didn't it? That really pissed him off, me giving him a history lesson."

"How did Gina take it?"

Evan sipped his beer and then continued "She cried, but... It felt phony, to tell the truth. And she wouldn't disobey her father. So that was that. It made the rest of my stay in Italy pretty awkward."

Sandy drank her beer and stared at the can. "Then you learned you'd been drafted."

Evan shook his head. "No, I knew a week prior to the proposal, which is why I popped the question. Maybe if I hadn't been drafted the old man might've given his blessing. But when he said no and Gina sided with him, I turned into a zombie. It's like the stars aligned into a pentagram over my head and cast an evil spell on me. I wish I had never left college, I wish I had never gone to Italy, and I wish the war would end tomorrow." He took another swig of beer, hesitated, and then said, "And then, as if all that wasn't rotten enough, I got the news about Patrick."

Sandy stared into her beer can as if she wanted to crawl inside. "Yeah."

The ten-mile stare returned to her eyes. She looked anesthetized and adrift inside her own mind. He wanted to tell her about the diary and how her husband's death was more catastrophic than she knew, but he sensed her fragility. Admitting what he had learned might drive her into catatonia. Then again, he thought, maybe she already knew more than she was letting on, which might explain her numbness. He asked, "What did you know about Patrick's last few months?"

"Not happy memories." She swallowed another gulp of beer.

"Do you know what he was doing on Haight Street?"

"Stop." She held her fingertips to his lips to stop the flow of words. The thinnest sliver of anguish showed on her face, and her eyes watered. "Please. I'm barely keeping my act together as things are. For the boys. For my sanity. So let's not go there right now."

The information would have to wait until Sandy recoiled from the shock of Patrick's death. Evan wondered how long that would take; he hoped to tell her before he set off for

Fort Ord. On the other hand, Patrick's request – the note he left with the diary – was to keep Sandy in the dark. Evan could see why. The poor woman was buried alive beneath an avalanche of bad tidings, and she seemed snow-blind to reality.

At that moment, Matt toddled down the hallway in his pajamas, all tears and wailing. He cried for his mother with hard, heaving sobs. A yellowy stain soiled the crotch of his pajama pants.

"Did you wet again?" Sandy asked.

The boy nodded as he wailed.

"But I just put you down," she said with exasperation. "Okay, let's get you changed." She turned to Evan and said, "This won't take long."

"Actually, I'm going to meet some pals, so… Thanks for the beer."

Her grin belied disappointment. Evan sensed her loneliness. There she was, a young widow raising two kids on her own, no money and few friends. He owed his sister-in-law more, it seemed. But he felt compelled to leave.

"You're around for a few more days, right?"

"Until a week from Saturday."

"We'll see you before then. The spreading of the ashes."

"Right."

He saw himself out. He would've stayed longer out of pity, but Matt needed his mommy and Evan didn't want to interfere. Besides, Sandy had turned to cardboard. Any talk of Patrick would probably crush her. Later, when her eyes weren't so hollow, he would explain everything. For now, though, he moved on without revealing the secrets he knew.

January 24, 1967

Read in the Examiner about Haight Street teens filling SF General Hospital after bad acid trips. I hope I'm not selling to anyone under eighteen. Can't tell. Can't ask for ID. No way of knowing whether or not the tabs are being resold or given away to younger kids. GH has no reservations about it. We can't control the situation, he claims, so we just have to accept 'collateral damage.' Sorry, that's bullshit. When I signed on for this op, I didn't agree to harm innocent kids. We're supposed to stave off radicals. GH points to the soldiers in Vietnam who are dying for a cause while the punks on Haight Street wander about in LSD stupors, and he asks whom I have more sympathy for. Frankly, I feel sorry for all of them. Wish I'd have thought of that at the time. Instead, I sided with the military on impulse. But it was an apples-and-oranges argument, and I was stupid to fall for it.

Take J. I feel real sorry for her. She'd have been much better off in a happy home, staying in high school, working toward college. But her life wasn't on that track. Kids run away from home for a reason. It's not just rebellion. Some have no family stability, no family structure. They take drugs to escape their shitty realities. The tales J tells of her father's abuse chills me. She recounted the soda bottle incident without emotion, like a doctor discussing a tonsillectomy. The street is full of kids like her. That's why I harbor guilt about this assignment.

January 28, 1967

This is some bad acid they gave me. I had J trip with a couple of buyers yesterday, prove my stuff was worth buying. I hate that part. A necessary evil. J thinks the LSD might've been laced with speed. TSS warned us that what we're dumping on the street is less than pure. I kept J mellow, talked her down from the bad trip. We listened to groovy music, lit candles, and stayed cool.

Worst of all, the buyers suffered bad trips, too, and refused to deal. They say Owsley's acid is far superior and a better price. Can't argue with that. If Owsley's product is as good as they say, it makes our mission increasingly unnecessary. Makes me wonder how much thought has really been put into this operation.

February 2, 1967

The street is buzzing with rumors about a massive drug sweep. Governor Reagan made campaign promises to clean things up once he got into office, and the neighborhood is on edge now that he's in Sacramento. Good. A little paranoia should keep the peace. On the other hand, it might lead to irrational behavior. Better be on guard.

February 5, 1967

GH sent a memo to SG. He'd heard rumors of a major bust through the entire Haight Ashbury. We requested advance warning of any police action so that GH & I could avoid arrest. SG got back to him pronto. No bust planned by Narcos. He'd get back to us regarding other agencies, but so far it looks like we have nothing to worry about.

Even so, GH brought up a good point. The plan is that if he's busted, I bail him out. And vice versa. But what if we're both busted simultaneously in a drug sweep? How are we to be sprung from jail without giving away operational information? We can't identify ourselves as CIA ops. SG suggests that we alternate workloads so we're never selling at the same time. Have GH deal on even numbered days, and I sell on odd numbered days, therefore there's less likelihood of concurrent arrest. Seemed like a piss-poor solution to us. So then GH asked, What if there's a sweep and I'm busted for dealing while he's arrested for possession? Who comes to our rescue? SG hemmed and hawed and then assured us that he'll address our concerns with his advisers. Answers forthcoming.

GH is pretty clever about operational hazards. Got to hand it to him. He knows how to cover his ass. I also think he doesn't trust our employers. Or anybody else, for that matter. Yet he's loyal to the cause. Overzealous at times. He's a contradiction. Hard to figure out. Someone to be wary of.

7
My Back Pages

A haggard waitress and a crew cut bartender served Evan and his buddies, the only patrons in the establishment. Enough cigarette smoke hung in the air for a platoon of smokers. The Kraut and his pals all lit up, as did Evan. Even the waitress had a menthol dangling from her lips. The four friends held cues and hovered beside the pool table. Vernor lined up a shot and failed to drop a ball into a pocket. On the jukebox, the Association's *Windy* gave way to *Happy Together* by the Turtles. The bartender with his handlebar mustache washed glasses behind the bar. The rouge-slathered lumpy waitress brought four draft beers. The Kraut handed her two bucks. "First round is on me, fellas. Keep the change, honey."

"Mr. Big Spender over here," O'Hara said. He grabbed a glass and gulped.

"Hold on, you dumb mick, hold on." The Kraut raised his mug in toast. "To Dunne. For duty to God and country and e pluribus unum and all that crap."

"Here, here," Vernor said. They all chug-a-lugged their cold brews.

Nobody had more enthusiasm, more energy, more ribald derring-do than Tim Leiber, the Kraut. His high school pranks were legendary: plastic wrap on the toilets in the teachers' private lounge; letting field mice loose during an assembly; building a mountain of shave cream on the principal's desk. The faculty knew who the culprit was each time, but a campaign spread throughout the school – Don't Rat Out the Kraut. Leiber got away with everything through roguish charm. It was infectious and alluring, and Evan hoped that by falling in with the Kraut's crowd he might acquire even an ounce of that devilish charisma and shake off his goody-boy image. That never really occurred, though. He would forever be seen as the Eagle Scout hero. After high school, when he departed for college in Southern California, the old group splintered. Evan still had fond memories, though, and he looked forward to reminiscing over beer and billiards.

"My turn?" Evan asked. He sized up the two ball in a corner pocket and just missed.

"So tell us about your travels, Dunne," Vernor said.

"Aw, you know…" He tugged at his ear and stared at the floor. Evan's reticence to discuss it couldn't have been more obvious.

But Vernor wouldn't let it lay. "How's that Italian pussy? Did she taste al dente?"

Evan blushed. Gina's image flashed through his mind, and his heart pinged at the thought he'd never be with her again. Boasting about bedroom endeavors wasn't in his nature. He wasn't some drunken soldier on leave. Not yet, anyway.

The Kraut slugged Vernor in the arm. Vernor's face went slack.

"A little respect," the Kraut said. "The guy's brother passed away."

Vernor rubbed his arm and muttered, "What's that got to do with it?"

Evan had hoped to enlist his pals' help in uncovering the facts of Patrick's death. No sooner had he entered the sleepy barroom and clasped hands with his high school buddies than he realized what questionable allies they would be. Although each had physically matured and gained weight - the Kraut sported a paunch - their sophomoric personas hadn't changed at all. Evan wondered what aged Tim Leiber and Joe O'Hara and Mark Vernor beyond their twenty-one years yet kept them foolish boys. When he left Sandy's house, Evan looked forward to the camaraderie, the classic sense of mischief, even if he felt in himself the sobriety of adulthood that only large amounts of beer could quash. But on being reunited with the guys the old esprit de corps felt anachronistic and the thought of employing them for something as serious as exposing Patrick's undercover operation seemed unwise, like hiring teenagers to fight a war.

"Let's go bust up some fags," Vernor said. "I seen 'em on Castro Street. They all go into this one house."

"Wouldn't surprise me if it's *your* house," O'Hara said.

Vernor slugged him in the arm, making O'Hara's beer slosh onto the floor.

"It's pretty sickening what they're doin' around here," the Kraut said. Then he shot the cue ball against the nine ball.

"Are you talking about what I think you're talking about?" Evan asked.

"Fags," Vernor said. "Like cockroaches. They're infesting the neighborhood."

Evan frowned. "Yeah, I saw some today."

O'Hara chuckled. "How do you know, Dunne? You got special homo glasses?"

"You can tell," the Kraut said in Evan's defense.

"They got private clubs they all go to," Vernor said. Then he pantomimed fellatio with his fist up to his face and his tongue pressing against the inside of his cheek.

"And you probably got a life-time membership," O'Hara said. That earned him another slug in the arm and spilled beer.

"I don't wanna talk about that," the Kraut said. "Turns my stomach. Hey, didja read about our boy McCormick?"

"The Cy Young award," O'Hara said.

"Let's see if he can match it again next year," Vernor said with a sneer.

"What, you don't think he can?" O'Hara asked.

"Nobody can pitch consistently in Candlestick."

"Hmph. Listen to the expert," the Kraut griped. He then knocked the ten ball into a corner pocket.

"Nobody's gonna top the Cardinals," Vernor said. "Not as long as they got Gibson."

Talk of baseball and homosexuals was lost on Evan, just as tales of Europe or college would surely bore his pals. He felt disconnected from his friends, and their trite high school escapades seemed lost to nostalgia. His life shifted gears when he left for Loyola. Theirs hadn't. Moving away helped him to view the world through a new prism while his pals lived beneath a protective bubble. Evan felt like a sprinter among these sleepwalkers. Even three beers didn't lighten his mood, and the inexplicable discomfort made him want to bolt.

"Pretty weird about you getting drafted," O'Hara said.

"Yeah," Evan said.

"You can get out of it easy," Vernor said. "You're the only son now."

Vernor's insensitivity made Evan cringe, but he let it pass. "That only applies if you've already served in the military."

"Oh," Vernor said.

"Look at us three idiots," O'Hara said, pointing his beer mug at the Kraut, Vernor, and himself. "We're all registered, no real prospects, no college, just working stiffs. Yet you, Joe College, the world traveler, the guy with the wind in your sails... you get called up by Uncle Sam. Don't seem fair."

"Wanna take my place then?" Evan said with a grin.

"Not on your fucking life," O'Hara replied with dead seriousness. He finished off his beer in one swig.

O'Hara hit a nerve. Evan wondered what he'd done to roll snake eyes. Neither Leiber nor O'Hara nor Vernor had ever accomplished anything beyond class clown status. The Kraut got a job with the postal service. Vernor fixed commercial refrigerators. O'Hara worked at his family's warehouse. None were married or even engaged. How had they avoided induction? For that matter, why hadn't they *enlisted*? Because few young men wanted to fight in a strange land for a murky cause. Again, Evan's gut quivered, and he felt sick.

"I've gotta go, guys."

"What're you talking about?" the Kraut said. "The night is young."

"I've got to look after my mom. She's taking it all pretty hard, y'know. About my brother, I mean."

"My folks wanted to send flowers," O'Hara said, "but we couldn't get any info on the service."

"There isn't going to be one." When they stared at him for an explanation, all Evan could say was, "Cremation."

Judging by their silence toward the matter and knowing their tough working-class backgrounds, the Kraut's crew didn't approve of Patrick's hippie lifestyle. Surely, they had read or heard about how Patrick died as the result of dealing drugs. Evan couldn't blame them for any silent condemnation.

Handshakes, pats on the back, and goodbyes were shared, as well as one last toast. Evan feigned a brave indifference for impending Army life when, in fact, he feared the year to come. Then he slipped out of the mostly barren barroom into the quiet night and imagined what cutting remarks they were dishing about him or his brother or his family.

He wondered why he ever ran with that crowd.

On a whim, Evan detoured his Plymouth to the crest of the hill where Portola becomes Market Street to partake of the dazzling view of the city below. Dense fog often draped San Francisco at night, especially at the top of the peaks, but that

September evening was clear. Lights shone along Market Street and the Bay Bridge. Downtown glowed. For one moment, his woes and worries vanished, and he was glad to be home.

Evan wondered if the Kraut and his cronies would ever awaken to the world beyond their neighborhood. Probably not. Their experiences were black-and-white while his were in technicolor. Most people lived within simple parameters, he reckoned, and maybe that was enough. Maybe he just felt bitterness because he was going off to war and they weren't. Better for them to drink beer, shoot pool, and talk sports. They wouldn't survive the military. The Kraut and his cronies were slackers. They probably couldn't even comprehend what Patrick had been doing. If he wanted assistance in exposing the truth of his brother's death, he'd have to look elsewhere. And he would have to be prepared for the likelihood that some people wouldn't believe him.

Within minutes, his Plymouth turned onto Eureka Street. A curbside parking spot was available two doors down from his mother's house, so he glided the car into the space.

Then he saw a flashlight beam dance across the lower floor window of his mother's house. He stared, waiting for the light to return. There it was again. Even if she were drunk, why would Alice need a flashlight when she could just turn on the lights?

Someone else was inside.

Evan cut the engine and climbed out of the car. The beam darted again through the window. He rushed up the steps but then stopped on a dime. If burglars were in the house, he had no weapon to fend them off. Going in alone was a foolish notion. He then clambered to the neighbor's house and rang the doorbell.

A teenage girl with long brunette hair answered the door. He couldn't remember seeing her before but assumed she was the Martino's daughter.

"I'm from next door. Evan Dunne. Call the police. I think we've got burglars."

The girl turned away from the door. "Dad, this man says Mrs. Dunne is getting robbed."

Evan had already descended the stairs when Mr. Martino stepped outside. "What's this?"

Evan said, "Mr. Martino, it's Evan Dunne. We've got burglars. Please call the cops."

Martino frowned with skepticism and pulled his daughter back indoors.

Evan dug keys from his pocket and unlocked the small garage side door. Once inside, his eyes adjusted to the deeper darkness. He tiptoed along the garage walkway and listened for noises overhead inside the house. An old baseball bat rested against a wall. He grabbed it and slipped out the rear of the garage into the back yard.

The back door opened without creaking, and he crept into the mudroom. He tried to control his breathing. Lights were off throughout the house, but Evan knew his way around perfectly. He crept through the kitchen to the living room and then the staircase.

Without warning, two men were right beside him.

In the darkness, he couldn't make out their features, just vague silhouettes skulking through the house. He heard their heavy breathing and their footfalls on the floor. His adrenaline spiked.

He swung the baseball bat. It thudded against flesh. One of the men groaned in pain.

When Evan raised the bat to swing again, an aerosol spray hit him in the face. He drew a hand for protection and backed away with fear. But he felt no immediate effect. It wasn't pepper spray. Whatever they'd shot at him seemed to be a dud.

A flashlight beam in the eyes made him flinch. The bat missed its targets and slammed against the staircase banister. On recoil, the bat smashed a table lamp. He flailed away, whiffing through the darkness, and kept swinging. The bat connected with an arm, and a man in the shadows let out a woof of pain.

"C'mon!" one of the burglars said.

"Give it another second," came the casual reply.

The beam was still aimed at his eyes, so Evan lashed out at it, missing twice. The bat thumped against a wall, and the impact sent a framed picture crashing to the floor. Evan wondered why the noises weren't waking his mother. Was she harmed? Or was she hiding?

"Mom! Call the cops!"

Then dizziness hit him. Evan stumbled as he raised the bat over his head. Time slowed. A surge ran through him that turned his body into liquid, waves crashing against the shore of his torso, legs rubbery and moving without moving. Lights danced across his eyes and through his brain, even in the absence of light. The blackness of night swirled and commingled and bounced in rhythm with his increasing heartbeat. The flashlight beam bore a hole into his retinas, so he closed his lids. In doing so, the universe spun and glowing spheres filled his vision. His heart pounded. His skin felt sunburned. Sounds were magnified; he could hear a dog barking somewhere in the neighborhood and the burglars' heaving breaths. But the noises were discordant, out of pitch, and too slow of tempo. His mouth felt filled with sand. An armchair swallowed him, and he melded into the wood. When he opened his eyes, the sun burst through his mind and low voices sang a funeral dirge and a potato face in a fish-eye lens leaned toward him with questions.

8
White Rabbit

The world detonated into a blinding white light. All around his body burst spirals and stars and purple globes and swirling moons and neon glows of soaring eyeballs and swarms of pink fireflies and concentric circles and sparkling bees in flight. The clear light shimmered and he soared toward it without moving. Collapsed on the floor, his body felt squeezed from every angle, and his head felt like a lemon in a juicer. Carpets undulated and lapped against the floorboards, and he melted into the ground. His skin felt slippery and cold while the floor beneath him burned. Tingling crept from his fingertips and toes up his arms and legs and back again in perpetual motion. A volcano erupted from within his tailbone and sent lava up his spine. It turned into vomit in his gut and neared the point of explosion. Blood chugged through his veins in a steady thump, thump, thump. His pancreas produced a dripping sound, and his kidneys sloshed and gurgled.

All around him a field of energy glistened, a cloud of charged atoms dancing and sparking, spirits of the dead floating on air and miraculously made visible to the naked eye. He followed the reverse flow of electricity from wall socket to wires to street poles to electrical grids to dams to waterfalls to mountaintops to heavy clouds to the souls of the dead, the source of all power in the universe, straight from the heart of the sun, and he wept for the dead babies who sacrificed their souls for the sake of incandescent light.

Before him appeared a potato face bearing craters of the moon sworn to flesh. Fiery carrot eyes stared. Questions in Sudanese or Arabic or Korean or Martian. Words bounced like pinballs in his head. A voice dripped with lemony snot. Potato Face grew reptilian gills and swam through the thick air to reach him. Lacquer covered his image. More questions in Russian or rabbit or hyena. One word echoed in his mind: diary, diary, diary, diary. The word then morphed into a crow's caw and then a cow's moo until it faded away.

Then came the barrage: flaming bats in flight, crucified scarecrows, cars melting in motion, maggots on green cheese, ruby red cats chasing headless mice, mountains of skulls, black ants the size of tanks that devoured children, cadavers floating on bloody rivers, neon trees that burst into flames, storks laughing as they dropped babies from their beaks to the ground far below. Colors and images and faces and sounds attacked him. Then came Patrick's disembodied arm. It chased him, fingers dancing across the floor, a trail of blood in its wake. When it grabbed his ankle, a scream emanated from the seeds deep inside his scrotum.

Waves of electric nothingness washed over him and took him under. Oh, for solid footing. His tears made the tide rise higher. He drowned on the waterless ocean and succumbed to fear. Colors that had shone so vividly now turned muted and dull.

I am no more, he thought.

He was alone. Darkness. A tunnel. A third eye shone from his forehead to guide him as he sloshed through the muck. The darkness stretched on to eternity. Miles of labyrinthine paths. The malodors of piss and pig's blood. Then a shaft of light. Blue sky shining through a keyhole. Too tiny to fit through. He dug and scraped, wrestled the earth, naked and sweating. Gasped for air. Then he climbed up and out of a womanly passage. Before him stood his mother. Tearful, grateful, presenting her teat. Replaced by his thumb. He suckled and sighed and calm washed over him as she cried.

His sister's face appeared and metamorphosed into the likeness of Laughing Sal. Gyrating to and fro. Buckteeth and a devious cackle. Welcome to Playland-at-the-Beach. Come one, come all. Feast your eyes. Only a quarter. Cackle, cackle. Ride the Big Dipper. Enter the Dark Mystery, the winged skull invited. Inside, pirates and haunted mansions. See the Funhouse! He took aim and threw grenades at milk bottles. You win, young man! Name your prize! Home, sir. No, you haven't even entered the Funhouse yet! Ride the merry-go-round! The machine gun in his hand roared and bullets picked off Asian children on the Ferris wheel. Laughing Sal cried and hid her face in shame.

Dolo sang lullabies from a vinyl record. Musical notes marched from speakers with the G clef as drum major, baton twirling. The electric bass pounded a hole in the wall. The notes slipped through the gap and submerged beneath the layer of wallpaper that rippled with the intruders. They transformed into tiny insects that crawled through woodwork and then burst out, sprouted wings, and filled his ears. He tried to swat away the musical notes to prevent them from controlling his mind, but they were too numerous and sinister. Fireflies danced in daylight and made him giddy. They flitted across his field of vision. Pop! Like flashbulbs, they disintegrated before his eyes. Dying fireflies begat newborns, a constant supply of bursting lights in the air. The color green on his shirt tasted sweet and salty. No matter how much he rubbed, the green wouldn't vanish. The thinnest thread on his sleeve demanded its freedom, yet the tugging and unraveling produced tiny cries of anguish that turned red from bleeding. Green and red melded with skin and felt dry and cold. Sunlight brought flames. Burning yet not destroying. Intensely hellish. Flying in streams, crackling fingers of fire.

His father's disembodied face appeared amidst the flames, crying out for revenge against the arsonist who caused his demise. His dying rant. The sofa became his father's open casket with the old man resting inside for all to see. Third degree burns had melted his skin. Evan wailed with more grief than he displayed at the funeral. His father's ghost rose from the sofa and pointed a finger of blame. Honor your brother! He shares your blood! Find his truth! Demand justice!

Shiny strands of spider web hung in a corner of the bedroom ceiling. The spider had run off to find its chicks, lost in the forest, hiding in tunnels dug beneath the earth. Evan saw his brother's face trapped in the webbing. He cried out, "I'll free you, Patrick!"

Every speck on the linoleum floor was a piece of dead flesh left to accumulate and reanimate. He tried to collect them all in his hands in the hope that microscopic fragments of Patrick could be rebuilt. But their father's atoms might be in the mix, too. And Mom's and Dolo's and bits of aunts and uncles and cousins. No, he left them on the floor and implored his mother to never sweep again.

The discordant sound of the color yellow hurt his ears, only to be drowned out by the roaring chirps of griffins outside the window. Morning fog carried ghosts of gold miners that seeped into fabrics and lay dormant. He scratched at his skin for fear that spirits were trying to invade his body against his will.

He was a cog in the universe, a dot of light burst from the sun, bringing life to blades of grass, the dance of photosynthesis, dying and reborn into a cow's stomach, used for muscle, slaughtered for food, and eaten by children. He refused to be chattel. No one would ever claim him body and soul. Like the fire consumed his father. Like the phantoms devoured Patrick. Like firewater controlled his mother. He grew porcupine quills to prevent being eaten. And he vowed to find whoever had swallowed up and spat out his brother's life.

The Kraut appeared with fire in his eyes and took him in his mitts, shaking and hollering. Vernor exposed fangs, swept up Dolores in his arms, stuck his forked tongue down her throat, ripped off her clothing, and they copulated on the floor. With rage and flailing fists and gnashed teeth and scraped knuckles against bone, Evan lashed out. "Not with my sister!" Flash a garlic braid to ward off the vampire. Climb the wall to grab the crucifix and jam it into the monster. He struggled against their grasps, expending every calorie to be free.

In short order they stuffed him into a cage filled with swirling whirls and harsh sunlight. Planet Earth rolled and tilted and then froze in place as the Sun collided with the Moon in an explosion of stars that spun around his head.

✧

Twelve hours after his sister discovered him huddled in a corner of the dining room, Evan still hadn't returned to normal. For most of the night, he lay in bed, giggled, and stared at his arms, which he wriggled about like charmed snakes. Any attempts Evan made to get out of bed resulted in falling to the floor. His muscles didn't obey. His slurred words made little sense. Dolores kept him mellow, sat with him through the night and into the next morning, and played soothing music on her record player to keep him calm.

"Don't go, Dolo!" he said during panicky moments.

"I'm right here," she said.

"I'm dying!"

Alice kept her distance and cried in private. Evan's condition made her frantic, and Dolores had her hands full keeping both her brother and mother from going batty.

By two o'clock in the afternoon, when Evan hollered at full lung capacity that his mind had fallen into quicksand, Dolores knew that he suffered more than just a bad trip. She contacted Tim Leiber for help. The Kraut arrived with Vernor. Evan made bizarre accusations and brawled maniacally. Getting him under control required a team, so O'Hara arrived with his brother. While Alice bawled, they stuffed Evan into a car and rushed him to San Francisco General Hospital.

9
Down on Me

Despair tried to pull him straight through the soil and into a grave. He fought gravity, though, and hovered at ground level. When he was fully awake, he discovered he lay in a hospital bed in a sterile tiled room. Depression and irritability conquered him. Bulldozers rumbled in his head. The other patients in the ward spooked him, especially the screamers.

"Where am I?" Evan asked a nurse who showed him only vague concern.

"San Francisco General."

"What day is it?"

"Tuesday the third."

Panic rippled through him. Three days! Where had the past three days gone? What had happened to him? He recalled the darkness and the spray in his face. The strangers who assaulted him in his home. What had they done to him? Why was he hospitalized? Burglars had come to steal something specific. What, though? He wracked his scattered mind, gradually pushed through the mud and muck that filled his skull, and came up with the answer: Patrick's diary.

San Francisco General's psych ward was the ninth circle of Hell. He wanted out. In the bed next to him was a skinny man with a face constructed of sharp angles. At first glance, Evan couldn't tell if he was a longhaired male with feminine features or an ugly woman. The patient sat up in bed and spoke in a deep voice. "Dig it, man. Two hundred mikes to heaven. Eight hundred mikes to hell."

Evan just stared. Then the stranger lay back down and mumbled to himself.

Dolores's arrival gave him the first sprig of hope. A deep black and purple bruise scalloped her left cheek beneath the rim of her glasses. Worry lines wrinkled her forehead. "God, I thought you were never coming down. How do you feel?"

"Lost," Evan said. "Empty."

"You scared the hell out of Mom."

"Scared the hell out of me, too. Are you okay?"

She dabbed at the bruise on her face. "No big deal."

Evan hadn't noticed the black eye until she touched it. "How did that happen?"

"You don't remember?"

He shook his head. Recent memories were vague at best. The hallucinations were a blur. A patient screamed across the ward, a sound somewhere between terror and ecstasy.

"Get me out of here, Dolo."

Dolores sought out the attending physician and returned minutes later guiding a young man with two-days' growth of stubble and greasy hair that fell below his ears. Aside from the white coat and stethoscope, the doctor would have blended in well on Haight Street. He reviewed the bedside chart to reacquaint himself with Evan's case.

"You took some powerful drugs, my friend," the doctor said. "By choice?"

"No."

"A sugar cube?"

Evan frowned with confusion. "What?"

"Somebody gave you a sugar cube?"

"No."

"How about a piece of paper, like a postage stamp, in your case, probably several, with cartoon characters or colorful designs printed on them? Did you swallow something like that?"

Evan shook his head.

"Maybe something was slipped into your drink or your food."

"I was sprayed."

The doctor grimaced. "That's a new one by me. Well, I believe you were given a drug called STP. Nasty stuff. Just showed up in the Haight this past summer. Very serious. Untreatable. Normally, we offer Thorazine to LSD victims, but that doesn't work with STP. Only makes it worse. That's why I didn't prescribe any for you. We just had to let you ride it out."

"Does it come in a spray?" Evan asked.

"What, STP? I don't think so."

"How about BZ?"

The doctor arched an eyebrow. "I've never heard of that one. You're sure?"

"No, but… I have suspicions."

"Hmm. Okay, hang on a second." The young doctor disappeared for a moment and returned seconds later with another physician with graying temples, more mature and presumably more experienced.

The older doctor approached Evan and, without even saying hello, asked, "You mean the incapacitating agent? That BZ?"

"I think so, yes."

The older doctor narrowed his eyes and asked, "What's your MOS?"

"Excuse me?"

The physician hesitated. "You're not in the military?"

"Not yet."

"That's a military grade drug. How do you know about it?"

Evan wasn't about to divulge the secrets of his brother's diary to the doctor, but he saw no reason to lie, either. "I read about it."

"What makes you think you were given BZ?"

"An educated guess."

The doctor cleared his throat. "If you're telling me that BZ is out on the streets, then we need to know all about it, son. You're talking about some highly dangerous stuff."

Evan felt the weight of his allegation and knew he had no proof to substantiate the claim, so he backed off. "I really can't say for certain. It was just a guess."

The older physician took his colleague aside, muttered a few words, and then went about his business. The younger doctor then sidled up to Dolores.

"You have a way to get him home?" he asked.

"Yes," Dolores said. "By car."

He then stood at the bedside. "Okay, Mr. Dunne. We're going to release you. You seem well enough, but take it easy for a couple of days. No more tripping, okay?"

Evan frowned at the doctor's condescending, accusatory tone, as if he chose to be dosed with a severe drug.

"Oh, I should warn you," the doctor said. "This drug might recur."

"How do you mean?"

"You might have other hallucinations days, weeks, even years from now."

"The drug stayed in my body?"

"No, but it might have altered your brain chemistry. We're not sure how these things work. But don't worry over it. The flashbacks might never happen. If they do, remain calm. The recurrence usually doesn't last too long."

✧

Evan changed out of the hospital gown and into fresh clothes that Dolores had wisely brought for him, since the shirt and slacks he had arrived in were soiled with vomit and urine. After being escorted out of the hospital in a wheelchair, Dolores drove him home in the Plymouth Valiant. Evan was still too impaired to take the wheel. Every footfall caused an explosion inside his head. Sunlight made him ache. Gloom consumed his spirit.

"How much is Mom drinking because of this?" he asked.

"She polished off three shots of booze right in front of the cops while they were taking her statement."

"Do the police have any leads on the burglars?"

Dolores looked askance at him, then focused on driving.

"What?"

"So you're sticking by this story about burglars in the house."

He glared at her with astonishment. "You don't believe me? Of all people…"

"Nothing was stolen."

"Two men were in the house!"

"You were tripping, Evan."

"Not before they sprayed me! I'm telling you, there were burglars!"

"Okay, okay, stay cool." She drove through the Mission District, past the tacquerias and pawnshops. "You left the bar and went to the top of Market Street."

"To look down at the city. That view I love."

"Were you tripping then?"

"A little drunk. That's all."

"Then what?"

"I drove to the house. Lights out. But I saw flashlights inside." A memory popped into his head. "The Martinos! I went next door to have them call the cops. Then I went into the garage, grabbed a baseball bat, and came in the back door. There were men inside, at least two, and I swung the bat at

them. I think I hit them a couple of times. Then they sprayed
something at me. Next thing I know, the world goes crazy."

"You went to the Martinos?"

"Yeah. I told Mr. Martino to call the cops."

"Hmm. Well, the cops aren't investigating."

"Why not?"

"They blamed the damage on you."

"For Christ's sake!"

"You admitted swinging the bat around! Mom came
downstairs and saw you – sure, she was completely in the bag
at the time – but there was nobody else in the house. Nobody,
Evan. No sign of a break-in."

Evan tried to tamp down his anger. "The cops must
figure I'm some hippie acid freak. That's just great!"

Dolores said, "I know you don't know this, but… Acid
doesn't come in a spray. It's in little tabs or blotters—"

"Don't patronize me, Dolo! It was a three-day trip. You
get that from BZ. Not LSD. And BZ *does* come in a spray.
Patrick used it."

"What are you talking about?"

"They used it in their experiments."

"They? What was Patrick doing with it? You aren't
making any sense."

Evan blinked. "How far into the diary did you get?"

She shook her head. "I didn't read any of it. Never got
a chance."

"Dolo!"

"I had an interview and then I had to go to work! When
I got home, you were freaking out! What the hell does the diary have to do with anything?"

"Godamnit, Dolo, it explains everything!"

"Calm down. You're still high. Take a breath. I don't
want you flying off the handle while I'm driving."

Evan wanted to cry. No wonder he seemed so irrational, even to his own sister. She hadn't read a word Patrick
had written. Explaining it all to her given his present condition
would only sound like gibberish or, at best, a lame excuse. He

wouldn't believe anything out of the mouth of a drug-addled man, either. Better to wait and show her the diary later when this storm had settled. Presuming his attackers hadn't found it and removed it from his hiding spot. If not, Patrick's own words would put her worries to bed. If they'd stolen the diary, though, he would only sound crazy. Evan's mind tumbled and dipped from the aftereffects of the powerful hallucinogen, and he couldn't yet fully sift out the sane from the bizarre. But he decided to remain mum about the diary until Dolores could read it for herself.

She turned the car off Eighteenth onto Eureka. When she pulled the Plymouth into the driveway, Alice appeared in the window with worried eyes and pale complexion. As they climbed out of the Plymouth, a car horn tooted down the street. A powder blue '57 Chevy rumbled toward the Dunne house, and Evan stood at the curb to greet it. The Kraut sat in the driver's seat. O'Hara had shotgun. The car slowed to a stop in the middle of the road.

"You back from Neverland?" Leiber asked as he blew cigarette smoke through the open window.

"I really owe you guys," Evan said with a flush face. He reached his hand in the window and shook with both friends. "Where's Vernor?"

"Icing his balls. You clocked him pretty good in the fruitbasket."

Evan hung his head. "Shit. I did?"

"His right nut is the size of a tennis ball," O'Hara said with a chuckle.

"How do you know?" the Kraut said with a wry grin. "Been massaging it for him?"

"Fuck you," O'Hara replied.

After an uncomfortable moment in which he tried to suppress tears, Evan spoke with a cracking voice, "Honestly, thanks. I mean it."

Leiber shook his hand again. "Don't let the war get to you. Okay, pal?"

Evan nodded as the Chevy drove away, even though he didn't catch the Kraut's gist. Did he blame the episode on Evan's fear of going to Vietnam? Had he said something while hallucinating? Or was he just acting paranoid? In time, he would clarify things so his friends understood. Or not. They were two-tone people in a world of living color. Keep it an unmentionable event, he thought, as with so many other things in the Dunne family's past.

Evan frowned with guilt at his sister's black eye and asked, "I hurt Vernor, too?"

"You accused him of... well, you got pretty rough with him. But mostly you were just out of it."

Instead of climbing the stairs to their front door, Evan staggered toward the garage. He had to check for the diary.

"Where are you going?" Dolores asked.

Evan didn't reply. He pulled out a key and unlocked the side door. Inside, he flipped a light switch and staggered to the rear of the garage. In his condition, he wasn't about to go burrowing into the crawlspace, and it wasn't necessary. He could tell at a glance that the diary was where he had left it. Later, when his mother was none the wiser, he would retrieve it for Dolores to read.

Inside the house, Evan and his mother hugged, but neither knew what to say. As he predicted, Alice avoided the truth, which had been routinely unkind to her. The dining room had been cleaned up from the damage caused three nights earlier. Aside from gouges in the wooden banister, no signs of the struggle remained. From all physical appearances, nothing had occurred.

"Corned beef and macaroni and cheese for dinner," Alice said.

"Thanks, Mom."

"Your Uncle Stuart would like you to call him."

So like her, he thought. Passing the buck. Alice avoided quarrel, at least when sober. Parenting had always been left up to their father. His mother never confronted or scolded him. Their father was the disciplinarian. From Alice,

Evan acquired passivity and obedience. Patrick didn't, which was why he and Neal Dunne butted heads.

Evan waited until his mother retired to the kitchen before dialing Uncle Stu's number. He held the mouthpiece close to avoid being overheard.

"Alice says you're doing drugs," Stu said in a berating tone.

"No, sir. Somebody doped me. I think it was the same people who came to the house posing as narcotics agents. I think they want the diary."

"Diary?"

Evan cursed himself. He'd told Stu that he had documents, not a diary. Now the truth was revealed, not that it really mattered.

"I told you to get rid of that stuff," Stu said. "For Christ's sake, don't mess around with those people."

"Who exactly are *those people*?"

"Cut the crap. You know…"

"Doesn't it strike you as odd how Patrick died? The biker confessed, but he had no memory of the killing. Said he'd been tripping for days when the cops arrested him. LSD doesn't last for days. BZ does. These men who messed me up, I think they might've had a hand in Patrick's death. I think it's all connected."

"That's crazy drug talk."

"I'm getting to the bottom of things."

"Christ almighty," Stu mumbled. "Drop it. Do you hear me? For Sandy's sake. If anything happens to her, Patrick will rise from the grave and rip your heart out."

"Sandy would want to know."

"Self-righteous bullshit," Stu muttered. "Goddamnit, you stupid kid."

Uncle Stu hung up. Evan felt a twinge of guilt over the curt conversation, but Stu was wrong about one thing. Self-righteousness didn't propel Evan. Justice did. Justice for Patrick.

As he climbed the stairs to his room, Dolores stood at the doorway and said, "I have to go to work."

He hurried back down the stairs and leaned forward to hug his sister, a sign of affection rarely employed in the Dunne house. "I'm sorry for hurting you."

"Yeah," she said.

Then he whispered so that Alice couldn't overhear. "I'll leave the diary in your room."

Dolores scowled at him with a combination of suspicion and pity, as if she couldn't believe anything he said. Then, without a word, she was out the door.

Evan worried how to interpret her reaction. Somehow, he'd hurt her, and not just physically. Patrick's murder and their mother's drinking had already taxed Dolores. He hated being another burden on her. Yet it wasn't his fault. Would she see it that way? She would if she only read the diary. But could he burden her with that, too? Even though she was nineteen, he still thought of her as the kid sister who needed his protection. With so much on her plate already, maybe keeping Dolores as a confidante was more than he should ask of her. In that instant, a snap decision was made. The drug hadn't worn off completely, and his thinking was muddied and weird. Yet his choice seemed clear.

Upstairs, he grabbed an old duffle bag from the closet and stuffed it with as many clothes as it would hold. Then he tossed in a toothbrush, toothpaste, and other essentials. He snuck down the stairs, careful to avoid his mother. But when she heard the front door creak, Alice waddled out of the kitchen to inspect. She spotted Evan with the duffle and stared with curiosity. He was hesitant to lie to his mother, and the worry in her eyes froze him.

"You shouldn't go out. You're not well."

"I have things to do."

Still no confrontation. Mother and son eyed one another for two brief seconds that stretched over a lifetime. Alice seemed to read his mind, and she did nothing to stop him. He walked out the front door, shutting it with a click instead of a slam.

Evan entered the garage, opened the Plymouth's trunk, and placed the duffle inside. Then he crept through the garage. The house had been erected on an incline, like so many houses in hilly San Francisco. As a result, a sloping crawlspace existed on the eastern side that ran underneath the kitchen and beneath the back porch. He climbed into the narrow space. Then his hand moved along a ledge, snatched a small canvas bag, and climbed out.

Inside the bag, the diary was covered in plastic wrap and intact. Good. The burglars hadn't discovered its hiding place. But they would return for it eventually, tearing the building apart if necessary. Uncle Stu was right about one thing: Patrick's diary brought danger to the Dunne house, and it had to be removed for his family's sake.

Evan climbed into his Plymouth with the canvas bag and drove away without looking back. He never saw his mother weeping as she watched him from the front window.

February 27, 1967

The newspaper reported that a nude girl fell from a third-story window. Died on impact. Not a stitch of clothing but a tube of toothpaste in her grip. Evidence of a bummer acid trip. They didn't show the girl's photo, but the article posted her name. I didn't recognize it. GH knew about the girl's death before I read it in the Chronicle, which made me suspicious. When I asked him, his face went flat, no emotion. Either he didn't care, or he was somehow involved. Or both. I asked if he sold to her. He couldn't recall. When I frowned, he got defensive. I never ask their names, he said. Besides, he can't be blamed. Again, he questioned my commitment to the operation. You've got to dissociate yourself from the targets, he said. That roiled me. Targets? He lashed out, questioned my military training, even attacked my manhood. Called me too soft. I mumbled that our goal was to quell riots, not to inflict harm on innocents. He brought up collateral damage again and how social experiments can result in unintended circumstances, but that doesn't mean you forsake the goals. He got so hot I had to shift the topic.

I asked if we're protected from prosecution in the event that our actions result in death. He mulled that over, saw the logic in the question, and turned analytical. GH's survival instinct is his paramount personality trait. Always looking out for number one. Always wondering how things impact him. Rarely concerned with how things affect others. Almost sociopathic. I guess that's what made him a prime candidate for this op. He said he'd run that by SG. There are a lot of legal issues we need to examine. The deeper we get into this operation, he said, the more legal indemnity we need. Some moral safeguards would ease my mind, too.

March 5, 1967

This bullshit about smoking banana peels is hilarious. Sounds like a rumor CIA planted. Kids all along the street are trying to get high off it. Just goes to show the herd mentality around here.

March 8, 1967

Took Sandy out to dinner for our anniversary. She didn't want to go to the Cliff House. Too fancy. But we'd eaten there plenty of times. Then she admitted she was embarrassed to be seen in public with me. People stare, she says. My long beard and scraggly hair. I insisted that anyone who was prejudiced against me because I look like a hippie can go to hell. Dinner was morose.

Afterward, we sat in the car at Ocean Beach and talked. She doesn't know what my assignment is exactly, but she hates it. Her friends have asked about changes in me. Not just my appearance, she says. I'm distant. I respect her concern. Told her it was a temporary assignment, and when it's over everything will be fine. Back to normal. She's being a real trooper.

But then I fucked things up. We were cuddling in the front seat at sunset, and kisses led to petting. I asked if she wanted to do it on the beach. I might as well have asked if she wanted to kill a puppy. She flew off the handle. That's just the kind of hippie crap I mean, she said. I've turned hippie on her, and she hates it. Needless to say, I won't be getting any loving from my wife for a while.

March 10, 1967
~~Got to admit that J is damn good in the sack.~~

March 11, 1967
A new batch of acid from TSS. Had J try it. The usual vivid colors, she said, but a much mellower sensation of peace. No edginess at all. She's getting too accustomed to the stuff. They also warned us not to smoke the new batch of grass. It's laced with something, they wouldn't say what. Non-lethal, they assured me.

March 13, 1967
When is this rain ever going to let up? Damned depressing.

March 16, 1967
Another Be-In is planned for Easter weekend, the equinox. Organizers are expecting an even larger crowd,

but I'm not so sure. The weather will keep a lot of people away. They're calling this a prelude to the summer when hundreds of thousands of hippies are expected to descend on the Haight. I doubt that figure. Maybe fifty thousand. The neighborhood can't hold much more. On the other hand, we see more and more kids on the street every week, it seems. New faces. Freshly scrubbed suburban teens in Edwardian costumes trying to figure out what the scene is all about. Too many of them turning on for the first time and completely unprepared.

March 20, 1967

I cannot believe the Navy has released information on our LSD experiments at Lemoore. Holy shit! Thankfully, the story is being buried in every newspaper and didn't air on Cronkite. But, damn, this is a powder keg. I wonder how this leaked to the press. Maybe a disgruntled shitbird objected to being used as a drug guinea pig. However word leaked, they better plug it fast. I mentioned this in a letter to SG and stated that if the story escalates I might be investigated, in which case I'll need to go to ground. Better yet, have the agency get me immunity. He told me not to worry about it.

March 24, 1967

Oddly enough, the Lemoore story seems to have evaporated. Good. I've got enough on my conscience with this operation.

March 25, 1967

I'm at home now with the family, but I could get called to the Haight at a moments notice. GH sensed tension on the street. He's still at his pad on Masonic, and he asked me to stay by the phone all weekend. If Matty and Sandy weren't so sick, I'd be out there now. GH is prepared to tackle any rioting on his own, or so he says. I told him to wait for the police. He has no faith in the cops. Thinks he can handle everything all by himself. Man, the guy is bonkers sometimes.

March 28, 1967

Department of Health is cracking down. Inspectors are swarming the neighborhood and citing health issues at hippie crash pads. The Diggers were especially hard hit, over a dozen citations. The Man is itching for a fight. If they keep harassing residents, rebellion isn't far off.

I sold a week's worth of tabs today. Practically gave the stuff away. Keep them all high, keep them all docile. Those are the orders.

I'm beginning to dread summer's arrival. If things get as hairy as SG predicts, my conscience might not lay dormant too long.

10
Crossroads

Gina's naked, tan body blended into the golden sand except for her giant brown areolas. They mesmerized him. She found them unsightly and ugly. To him, they were beautiful islands on which any seaman would gladly be shipwrecked. The bawdy wordplay was lost on her. She wanted to make 'mad Italian love.' That made him laugh. Sex isn't love, he said. Gina moped and wept and ran off into the sea. With stoic machismo, he stood firm and watched her glide into the blue water. The tide then took her under, and Evan dove into the spray to come to her rescue. He brought her body to the beach where a crowd had gathered. They snapped photos of her bronze skin. Before he could begin mouth-to-mouth resuscitation, her father, wearing Napoleonic garb, grabbed her by the hair and dragged her up the beach to the house. Evan tried to pursue, but his legs were buried in the sand. Waves crashed and submerged him until he was taken away on the current, adrift on the ocean on a wooden raft, unable to save her.

Faeries of light danced behind his eyelids. Then daylight seeped into his cortex and washed away the dream. Evan awoke with his mind as fogged as the morning sky. The world swam around him. Dizzy and giddy, a headache bombarded his skull. Paste filled his mouth and stuck to his gums. His entire body was a gelatinous mass, even the bones. Minutes passed before his muscles would obey. He then stumbled out of the car, unzipped, and urinated beside the back tire. Aside from sparrows and a squirrel, no one saw him publicly expose himself. Dew covered the Plymouth. Dampness, an unavoidable San Francisco trait, permeated his clothing.

The park's foliage camouflaged the green Plymouth. Evan had found a less-traveled road deep inside Golden Gate Park where traffic wouldn't wake him. He slept soundly on the front seat, even though he couldn't stretch out his legs. The Boy Scouts trained him to rough it, so sleeping inside a car was a step up from a pup tent. Combat circumstances would be far worse. But after months of balmy Italian summer, San Francisco's cool nights felt like Arctic winter, and he was ill prepared for the chill. Still he slept soundly. The drug probably accounted for that.

His first order of business for the day was breakfast. His stomach grumbled. The ignition turned over after two tries, and he drove the Plymouth through the park to the Inner Sunset neighborhood. Though diffused by fog, the sunlight stung his eyes and forced him to drive slowly.

Evan felt alone. Not lonely, just alone. Without support. Adrift. But tackling the matter solo was the best plan. Involving his sister or mother in his quest was now out of the question. He wouldn't involve Sandy if he could help it, and her usefulness seemed limited. Uncle Stu made plain his disapproval, so he'd be an unlikely ally. All family members were being kept in the dark for their own safety. The Kraut was generally unreliable, as were O'Hara and especially Vernor. Tracking down the truth of Patrick's death would have to be a solo mission. Bringing others into the matter might only endanger them. He was on his own.

At the corner of Ninth and Irving, he found a diner and a branch of his bank. After a meal of greasy eggs and hash browns, he stood on line outside the bank until it opened for business. Once inside, he withdrew four hundred dollars from the savings account he had established with inheritance from his father's death, and he left a shrunken balance. Over the years, he spent his money on the Plymouth and European travel, so the inheritance had dwindled. He wondered if Army pay amounted to anything worthwhile. Would he need access to cash once he was shipped overseas, or was money unnecessary in a combat zone? He had no clue. Next, Evan purchased cigarettes, as much a necessity as food and water.

At the street corner, he found a phone booth and slipped inside. A dirty, ripped Yellow Pages directory hung from a clumsy metallic folder. After thumbing through it, he found the street address for the San Francisco Chronicle. Then he flipped to L for Lawyers and ran his index finger through the many names listed. Once he found the information he sought, Evan tore the entire page from the directory. He plunked coins into the slot and spun the payphone's rotary dial. After a brief conversation, he hung up and slid out of the booth.

Moments later, he removed his brother's diary from the trunk of his Plymouth, rested it on the car seat beside him, and drove east toward downtown.

April 2, 1967

The cops played it cool today. The Diggers pulled another spontaneous stunt, this one a benign march down the middle of Haight Street. They got hundreds of hippies and Hare Krishnas to walk with them and chanted, Streets are for people. Police let them commandeer the entire street. Better to let them have their way than get violent. But then the hippies wanted to continue the march down Market Street. Clogging Haight Street is one thing, blocking the city's major thoroughfare is another. Somehow, that idea got shelved, and everyone stayed in the Haight. I don't know where GH was all day, but I bet he was prepared for mob violence.

April 4, 1967

Bailed GH out of jail this morning. An undercover cop caught him dealing in the park late last night. I asked, Why stew in jail all night? I'd have bailed you out earlier. He said he met two other dealers in jail, and he wanted to check them out, see if there were any other government ops in the mix. He met a guy who deals for Owsley, or buys from him and resells. Something like that. GH learned that Owsley lost his chemical connection. Can't make LSD without a raw materials provider. Word is he's scouring the nation for a replacement. That gives us an edge. We should now be able to control the flow of drugs on the street. SG will be pleased to hear that.

April 9, 1967

Andy's birthday. Cake and ice cream and schoolmates and presents. Sandy planned everything out just right. I showed up a bit late, but Andy was in his own world of joy. He's normally a shy kid, but his face was aglow tonight. J tells me that Andy is an Aries. I don't subscribe to that hippie astrology crap. But she says it's a good sign to be born under. On the positive side, he'll be adventuresome, courageous, and quick-witted. On the down side, he'll be impulsive and foolhardy. Well, then I guess he'll take after his old man.

Sandy is worried that Andy is too distant. What Sandy calls distant, I call deep in thought. He's a smart kid. Doesn't wear his emotions on his sleeve. I played catch with him in the back yard. All he could talk about was baseball – the season starting, Mays, McCovey, and Marichal, when could we go to Candlestick. Typical boy stuff. He seems okay to me. It might be he just misses his dad. I can appreciate that. I miss my dad, too. The difference is I'll never see mine again. Got to spend more time with the boys. Don't want them to grow up without me.

April 12, 1967

Sometimes J is a real drag. I go home to see my family for a couple of days and she gets all needy. She professes free love despite me being married and then gets weird when I don't show any jealousy when she's hanging all over another guy. Go ahead and fuck him. Don't expect me to fight over you. Be free. You're a runaway tramp who smokes too much dope. But no, she has to give me that puppy-love pout that says, I thought you love me. She's looking for a father figure, is all. Can't have her dulling my vibe with that baggage. When the real heavy shit comes down in another month or two, I might have to give J the kiss-off. It's a shame, because the girl needs a redeemer. Sorry, babe. I'm not him.

11
People Are Strange

The Chronicle building wasn't imposing, but the insti-
tution was. He'd never visited the newspaper offices before
and didn't know the procedures. Presumably, one didn't just
walk in off the street and ask for a reporter to print his story,
but that's what he intended to do. Surely, they had protocols.
The wise choice, he realized, would have been to call in advance and make an appointment, but his mental equilibrium
was still askew from the drug and that colored his judgments.
Besides, his days of freedom were few, and appearing in person might expedite matters. Maybe he would be required to
speak with a specific journalist. If so, he didn't know whom to
request. Evan never paid attention to newspaper bylines. He
wracked his brain to remember the name of the reporter who
wrote about him after saving Carmen Rodriquez's life. Sam-
son? Samuelson? Stinson? Something that began with the letter S. No matter. He would ask for Herb Caen. Everyone read
the long-time columnist. Maybe he would hear Evan's tale.

In his altered state of mind, absurd thinking seemed logical and he barely noticed the way he staggered as if tipsy or his glazed eyes or his ripe odor from not having bathed since before entering the hospital.

To his surprise, the wood-paneled reception lobby was no larger than his family's living room. One large desk dominated the room behind which sat a middle-aged matron who wore thick glasses and a sour puss. Flags on flagpoles were the only ornamentation in the brown room; one for the nation and one for the state. Plush leather chairs were located behind the reception desk. Closed doors hid the newspaper's internal business. He stood before the reception desk with the plastic-wrapped diary in his hand.

"How may I help you, sir?" the receptionist asked.

"I'd like to see Herb Caen."

"Your name, please?" the receptionist asked.

"Evan Dunne."

She lifted her phone, dialed a three-digit extension, and tapped her pen while awaiting a response. Then she said into the phone, "Hi, Jean, I've got Mr. Evan Dunne here... No, here in reception..." She held the receiver away from her mouth and asked Evan, "Do you have an appointment?"

"No," Evan replied.

The receptionist clucked her tongue in disgust.

Evan blushed. "I realize I should have called first, but..."

"Sorry, Jean, I'll handle it." The receptionist hung up the phone and eyed Evan with disdain. "What's this regarding?"

"It's about my brother. The newspaper reported his murder in August. But there's more to the story. I need to explain it to a reporter."

She sighed. "Mr. Caen?"

"Actually, any reporter will do. There was a man who wrote about me a few years ago. I rescued a little girl from a car accident. The mayor gave me a commendation. The name is Evan Dunne. I was an Eagle Scout at the time." He realized he was babbling and incoherent. "Any reporter will do. Anyone interested in what I have to say."

That seemed to appease her. "I'll see what I can do. Please take a seat."

Evan walked past her desk to the leather chairs and sat. People in business attire strode past him in and out of the building. Reportage occurred behind those closed doors. The receptionist spoke softly into her telephone, but Evan couldn't help eavesdropping.

"… says he wants to report a murder. Any reporter will do."

Evan wanted to rise from his seat and correct the receptionist, but that was pointless. Instead, he sat and waited for whatever attention he might receive.

The practiced words meandered through his mind again. During most of the previous evening, as he sat alone in the darkness in Golden Gate Park, he prepared what he would say. The explanation had to sound more plausible than what he'd told the Associated Press editor. Addressing people wasn't Evan's forte, and storytelling didn't come naturally. So he conceived a series of concise points in his head. However, the aftereffects of BZ lingered. His mind detoured to tangential thoughts. As strangers passed through the lobby, paranoia set in. His eyes darted from person to person. He fretted, but he couldn't fathom why. No one made any attempt to engage him in conversation – not even a hello. No eye contact. Why was he being ignored? Then Evan calmed himself and wondered why his thinking ran so irrationally. The drug, he told himself, had remained in his body like cockroaches living behind tenement walls.

Increments of time slithered by. The longer he sat inactive, the greater became his urge to bolt. Nothing would come from waiting. Action was needed. His ire surged. The brown wood-paneled walls undulated before his eyes. A passing truck outside growled for him to do something. He rose from the scat, marched to the front of the desk, and stood before the receptionist. "Ma'am, if no one is going to hear my story, I'd like to be informed."

With mild distress toward his curt tone, she said, "Someone will speak to you momentarily. Please take a seat."

Surprised and satisfied, he turned and marched back to the leather seats. His nerves still jangled, though he couldn't pinpoint why. On sitting, calm washed over him so that his backside melted into the soft leather chair. Tranquility rippled through his muscles. All residual effects of the drug, he assumed. His eyelids grew heavy. The clomping of shoe soles on the lobby floor faded. In a matter of seconds, Evan dozed off.

April 13, 1967

Watched the Diggers stop a tour bus this afternoon. The Gray Line has added Haight Street to its tourist package so out-of-towners can gawk at hippies. I don't know how the Digger got the driver to let him take the wheel, but he drove the blue hairs up Ashbury and told the old folks he was setting them free. Most didn't dare get off the bus for fear of being accosted by dirty hippies. Pretty hilarious, but it made me wary of the Diggers. They're getting bolder by the week.

April 15, 1967

An organized war protest march along Market Street today. GH insisted we attend. I didn't see any need but followed anyway. Pretty orderly. Everyone wound up at Kezar where some uptight Mobe organizers gave boring speeches about peace. Nobody really cared. The Mobe doesn't carry much weight in the Haight. The hippies I've come across are more interested in hedonism – drugs, sex, rock music, and making the scene. The anti-war crowd are a whole different subculture and pretty foreign on Haight Street.

April 17, 1967

In our weekly report to TSS, GH recommended taking preemptive action against the Diggers before they can foment rebellion in the Haight Ashbury. They conceive and perform all the street theater, with the exception of the Mime Troupe. (Only hippies would have talking mimes. How dumb.) If anyone is bound to instigate political unrest, he says, it's the Diggers. If we disrupt them, we can prevent any cataclysm this coming summer. I think GH has flipped his wig. What the hell can he and I hope to accomplish? We can't even identify all the Diggers. It's not like they have a roster. They don't even have meetings or organizational structure. I wanted to ask GH what sort of preemptive action he had in mind, but the whole idea is so fubar that I don't even want to know. I sure hope SG sees how nutty this idea is and passes on it.

A nudge awakened him. A young man in bow tie stared at him through round-rimmed glasses. He appeared to be Evan's age. His unblinking gaze and the way he sat on the very edge of the adjoining seat suggested his discomfort and desire to leave.

"Mr. Dunne?"

Evan sat upright. "Yes. Hello. Evan Dunne."

"I'm Darryl Van Derner."

He rose to his feet; in his mind, the young man had come to escort him to meet with a seasoned reporter, possibly Herb Caen. When he didn't rise in unison and instead remained seated, Evan sensed a misjudgment. Then he reclaimed the leather seat.

"I understand you wish to report a murder...?"

"Well, no. But yes. My brother, Patrick Dunne, you might have read about him. He was the drug dealer who was killed in the Haight Ashbury district in August." When he showed no recognition, Evan continued. "His arm was cut off. The suspect, I mean, the man convicted rode around with the arm in the backseat. Do you remember this?"

"No, I'm sorry." Although he carried a pen and notepad in the breast pocket of his white shirt, the young man had yet to write down a word.

"Oh. Well, it was reported in your newspaper."

"We already reported this man's murder?"

"Yes, but that's not why I'm here." He felt that explaining to the young man was a waste of his time, so he said, "Um, are you escorting me to… to see a reporter?"

When he pursed his lips with irritation, Evan realized his error.

"I write for the city desk. What is it you want, Mr. Dunne?"

Evan's spirit flagged. Barely a minute had passed and already he'd blundered. As a woman in a flaming red dress and high heels marched with purpose across the lobby, Evan caught a glimpse of a burly security guard who stood to the side of the reception desk. His face glowed with suspicion. Evan's hackles rose.

"Is there somewhere private we can talk?" he asked.

Van Derner glanced at his wristwatch. "My workload is piling up, so if you can get to the point…"

Evan inhaled deeply to gather himself and then began as rehearsed. "My brother was recruited by the CIA out of the naval base at Lemoore to work undercover in the Haight. He posed as a drug dealer in a clandestine experiment on unwitting civilians. But my brother didn't like what he was doing, knew it was wrong, and tried to expose his top-secret operation to the press when he wound up dead. A Hell's Angels biker was convicted of the killing, but it looks like he was set up. I suspect the CIA had my brother killed to hide their illegal activities, which he was about to reveal to the public."

Van Derner showed a blank face and then slowly ran a hand through his brunette hair as he stared at his lap. The reporter wrote nothing in his notebook. After a long pause, he said, "Well, that's a fascinating story."

Evan held out the diary covered in transparent plastic wrap. "This details everything."

Van Derner refused to touch it. "What's that?"

"A diary." He began unwrapping the book. "Some men, I think they're CIA, they're trying to get it."

The reporter accepted the diary as if it were moldy bread. Then he skimmed through the handwritten pages without reading, scowled with disdain, and said, "I would have no way of knowing the authenticity of this."

Evan blinked. "The diary is written entirely in my brother's handwriting."

Van Derner tried to suppress a grin. "I'd still need verification. Some other source." He glanced at his watch again but didn't seem to register the time. "Like I said, I have a mountain of work to get to. It was nice to meet you." He handed back the diary, rose, and extended a hand.

Evan shook. He knew it was a brush off, but he wasn't about to give in. "Suppose I bring you someone who can confirm the story? Will you print it?"

The reporter grinned and stammered and wouldn't meet his gaze. "Um, well, I can't guarantee that but... we'll see. I have to go. Goodbye."

He then scurried to one of the brown doors and disappeared behind it.

Evan strode out of the lobby onto Mission Street, rewrapping the diary as he walked. Sunshine made his eyes sting, and he wished for sunglasses. Although the brief interview hadn't concluded as he'd hoped, and although the cub reporter showed the same pessimism as the AP editor, Evan was undeterred. Strangers weren't likely to take his word on the matter at face value. They didn't know Patrick or the situation. In that instant, as he marched along Mission Street, Evan realized he had to take it upon himself to pull the story together for the reporter. Now his mission was clear. He needed to find someone to back up the claims Patrick wrote about in his diary. No one would believe any of it otherwise.

For now, though, the diary needed to be secured somewhere safe. But where?

Panic washed over him. Bile rose up to his esophagus. He clutched the diary close to his chest to prevent anyone from snatching it from his white-knuckled grip. Then he marched double-time down Mission Street toward his Plymouth, fearful of every stranger he passed. Every set of eyes on the street seemed to bore into him. Anyone could step up and spray him in the face. Perhaps there were more insidious ways to dope a man. Maybe radio waves could control minds. If so, any van or delivery truck could contain the apparatus to mess with his head. A postman turned a street corner and nearly bumped into him. Evan leaped back with a shriek. The mail carrier excused himself and moved on. Evan's heart triple jumped with fright. Then he rushed to his Plymouth, climbed in behind the wheel, and lit a cigarette to control his frazzled nerves.

Stick to logic, he told himself. The sudden rush of anxiety was irrational. What tripwire had activated such paranoia? The drug, he thought. It was still wreaking havoc with his mind and body. Flashbacks, the doctor called them. How was he to fight such demons? Identifying strange thoughts and dousing them with logic, he decided, would be the only way to cope.

✧

The second Evan exited the building Van Derner came back through the wooden door and approached the receptionist's desk.

"Sorry," the receptionist said. "I should have warned you about the smell."

"God, why don't those hippies bathe?" Van Derner said. Then he sidled up to the burly security guard, shrugged, and said, "Probably harmless, but..."

"Don't worry. If he returns, I'll show him the door."

✧

The plastic-wrapped diary sat on the car seat beside Evan. If he were nabbed while driving, the diary could be easily confiscated. Any apartment or motel room would be similarly unsafe. Patrick had mailed it to their mother's address under Evan's name for safekeeping. Evan needed to keep it hidden, too; somewhere he trusted yet where no one was likely to look. His mother's home was now out of the question. Then where?

The secret hiding place. Yes, that felt as safe a spot as any. He drove west toward the outer avenues.

Memories flashed through his mind. The dark round room. The staircase and landing. The wind whipping against the structure. The fear that someone might find him in such a public place. The possibility of vermin. The cold.

He'd learned of the secret spot because of its proximity to the San Francisco Public Golf Course. At age ten, Dad made him caddy to earn cash. He stumbled upon the place after a full, boring Sunday at the links. His curiosity led him to investigate the odd structure and, against his better judgment, he slipped inside. A trespasser.

Then he recalled what drove him to run away from home and encamp there. Age eleven. Another in a series of shouting matches between his brother and father. Their arguments had always been monumental, but on that rainy winter day Dad was bone drunk and beat teenage Patrick. Mom turned mute and wouldn't intervene. Dad pounded Patrick bloody because he posted poor grades. Evan cowered. His grades were no better. Was he next to be pummeled? Evan saw no point in waiting around to find out. Off he ran. Into the park. To the secret spot.

He stayed there for ten days. After a week, his caddy money dwindled. He froze in the fog and wind but survived on donuts and milk from the local shop. Then he was spotted.

Thanks to Uncle Stu, police had been on the lookout for him. Evan was welcomed back home but immediately grounded. He feared a pasting from his father, but none occurred. Quite the opposite.

Instead, his father, perhaps to save face, gave the episode a positive spin. Look at what my boy did, he told fellow firefighters. Surviving in the woods on his own for a whole week. Golden Gate Park was no wild forest; Neal Dunne's blarney was at work. But his father's constructive attitude spurred Evan to go further with the Boy Scouts, to get merit badges, to push for Eagle Scout status, to keep improving himself. That one curious event, and his father's surprising reaction to it, sprung a change in him.

Whereas their dad had been a hard-ass on Patrick, who he seemed to regard as a lost cause, he never beat Evan. The old man could be stern and demanding but not physically abusive, at least not to his younger son. Nor did he ever harm Dolores, to whom he rarely showed any favor at all. He seemed to have a different parenting tactic on each child. His mother, in typical fashion, left the discipline to her husband. She even refused to discuss what caused Evan to run away or what he did while gone. All she cared about was that life was back to normal. The matter was dismissed, and Evan's young life carried on as if the runaway incident was a character-building ordeal instead of a misadventure.

He had never told anyone about his secret hiding place. Would the diary be safe there now? If it could hide a young boy...

Evan drove out to the westernmost end of Golden Gate Park and did reconnaissance. The location and structure hadn't changed much in years – still ignored and in disrepair. He parked his car and stepped through the tall grass and rough brush that engulfed the building. The three short cement steps at the base didn't jibe with his memory; the slight descent below ground level seemed so much deeper when he was a lad. The heavy iron doors, as rusty as he recalled, still had no lock. The hinges creaked, but the doors opened with ease.

When no one noticed, he slipped into the darkness.

April 19, 1967

Dickie Trussdale boxed me into a corner. Hope I didn't blunder. Can't tell GH about this. Definitely not telling SG.

My first mistake was hitting the street while stoned. Gotta stay clean when dealing. But because I was higher than Sputnik, I was off my game. There was Dickie with his ignorant porkpie hat and badge. His partner busted my buyers while Dickie took me aside. Offered me some silly deal if I rolled over on my suppliers. When I refused, he started pummeling me. I told him he was assaulting a federal operative. Dumb, dumb, dumb. Should've let him wail away. But he stopped. Believed me without question. Claimed he knew, he just knew I was a fed. He asked what agency but I told him, Don't ask. He said, CIA, right? When I didn't answer, he assumed he was correct. Then he let me skate. I made him promise to keep my cover. Gotta hope the idiot keeps his word. But if the guy is so stupid to believe a drug pusher's ludicrous, unverified claim of being a government op, then how can I count on him to stay mum? He's a fucking moron. Should I throw some cash his way? No, that would backfire. Gonna have to ride it out and see if Dickie stays cool.

12
Strange Days

The lettering on the opaque door read: Richard Friedman, Attorney at Law. No partners were listed. When Evan entered the office and saw the shabby interior, he realized it wasn't a law firm, just a single attorney office, probably an ambulance chaser. A buxom redhead sat at a reception desk. Three file cabinets lined one wall. Opposite that was a bookshelf filled with legal volumes. Unfashionable chairs circled a coffee table on which rested the latest issues of Life and Time and Harper's Bazaar. The room needed painting or dusting or something to keep it from looking so drab. The receptionist turned away from her typewriter to greet him.

"I called earlier. The name is Dunne."

She excused herself, opened the door to an adjoining room, and spoke to her employer inside. Then she offered Evan a seat across from her desk.

"Mr. Friedman will be with you in a moment. Please have a seat."

A window looked onto the neighboring skyscraper and a sliver of gloomy sky. His reflection stared back at him, and Evan saw how grubby he appeared. Stubble covered his jaw. Bags showed under his eyes. His hair was beginning to grow out from its normal brush cut. His white dress shirt looked rumpled. He smelled bad, he realized, and he needed to use the bathroom.

After three minutes of waiting, the receptionist ushered Evan inside the main office. He shook hands with the man seated behind an oak desk, and the young lady excused herself.

Richard Friedman looked like an adult Charlie Brown in a cheap, checkered business suit. A thin crown of salt-and-pepper hair ringed his otherwise bald pate. A bulbous, pock-marked nose overwhelmed his face and looked like a moonscape. Prying his egg-shaped body out of his chair took effort. After a limp handshake, he motioned for Evan to sit.

"My sympathies to you and your family," Friedman said in a deep voice. "I didn't see you during the hearings."

"I was in Europe."

"Oh, I see… So… What can I do for you?"

"I'd like to speak to your client."

"Pulasko?" The lawyer narrowed his eyes in an expression of dismay and pity. "You don't want to do that."

"I know this is unusual, but I have questions."

Friedman sat forward and clasped his hands together. "I realize what a traumatic experience you and your family have suffered. Emotions are strong. But justice has been served. Pulasko is going to serve his time, which, by the way, we never contested with the court. There's to be no appeal. So if you feel his sentence was somehow too lenient or—"

"Pardon me," Evan interrupted. "This is no vendetta. I don't intend to chew the guy a new one or anything like that. Honestly, I just need to know what happened. That's all. I have no intention of contesting the sentence. I promise. Can you arrange a meeting?"

"Not a good idea, Mr. Dunne. I can't stop you from going up to San Quentin to request a visit, but I highly doubt he'll see you. And, to tell you the truth, I'd tell him it's not in his best interests. Or yours, quite frankly."

That response made sense, and Evan chastised himself for being so naïve. What convict would welcome his murder victim's brother? He wondered what he had hoped to accomplish by visiting the attorney. Again, the drug clouded his judgment.

"Maybe you can answer my questions, Mr. Friedman. Your client's explanation of what happened... Would you explain it to me, please? How did the murder occur?"

Friedman cocked his head to one side and narrowed his eyes. "If you're asking me to divulge what my client said to me in private...."

"No, sir. I just need to know what Pulasko told the judge. The allocution, I think it's called."

"There's a court transcript, you realize."

"Oh, okay. I'd like to have a look at that. What's the procedure?"

Friedman rested his chin on his fist, trying to figure out Evan's angle. "Why do you need to know this information, Mr. Dunne?"

"Since I wasn't able to attend the court proceedings, I've had to rely on other people's interpretations of what happened. I'd like to hear Pulasko's version."

The lawyer digested Evan's words. "You need to put your mind at ease. Am I reading you right?"

"Yes."

Friedman clasped his hands again. "Well, I don't see any violation of attorney-client privilege, so... Here's what he told the court. I'm paraphrasing, of course, but here it is. He had been on a bad LSD trip, he said. Drugged out of his mind. Nearly three days straight. When the CHP pulled him over, he was still high."

"Where was that?"

"Route One down near Pacifica."

"Where was he going?"

"He didn't know."

"Did he live nearby?"

"Would you like to hear the allocution or not?"

Evan sat back and clammed up.

"He said he honestly could not recall the crime," the lawyer said. "The judge asked him about the last thing he remembered. He said he was drinking with acquaintances in Golden Gate Park. No one could account for his whereabouts after eleven p.m. He doesn't know who gave him LSD or when it happened, but it was a bad trip and he remained 'out of it' – his words – for days afterward. Given the fact that all the evidence pointed to him, he said, 'I must have done something bad.' Spoken without emotion, I might add."

"He couldn't remember the murder, yet he confessed."

"Well, the preponderance of evidence.... Driving the deceased's vehicle, the dismembered arm in the backseat. Pulasko could do the math. And it's not as if he was a model citizen. The man was wanted."

"But he couldn't actually recall committing the crime?"

"Remember his state of mind."

"There were no witnesses?"

"The prosecution didn't produce any, but they didn't need to."

"Did he even know my brother?"

"He claimed they'd met once briefly. Your brother had a reputation in the neighborhood."

"Meaning…?"

"Let's not be coy, Mr. Dunne. Your brother was pushing drugs in the Haight. The prosecutor mentioned a drug rivalry as motive." Friedman then added, "I'm not saying he's correct on that point, by the way. Those are the DA's words, not mine."

"Yet Pulasko couldn't recall the murder. Does he at least remember stealing my brother's car?"

Friedman cocked his head to one side. "You're an odd one, Mr. Dunne. If I didn't know better, I'd say you question my client's guilt."

Evan gave him a measured stare. "I just need to know the truth."

Friedman tapped his fingertips together. "Jack Pulasko was already wanted in three states in connection with two rapes, violation of the Mann act, possession of stolen property, and drug peddling. Plus, he was a member of a motorcycle gang that the Feds have been trying to disrupt for years. The man was destined for prison one way or another. Now, I should think you and your family would be satisfied with a thirty-five-year sentence. Pulasko won't be eligible for parole until he's sixty-four, and even then his release will be unlikely."

"Did he make any statements to the district attorney?"

"About what?"

"Details about the crime scene."

"He couldn't remember a thing."

Evan nodded. He had heard enough, and his questions were getting on the lawyer's nerves. "So even he can't tell me exactly how the murder went down. Correct?"

Friedman huffed with exasperation. "I understand your need for closure. I truly do. Pulasko's confession was sufficient for the judge, so there's no way for us to know—"

"I was told my brother died in his apartment. How did Pulasko get in?"

"I don't know." Friedman pursed his lips with agitation.

"Why did he cut off my brother's arm?"

"I don't know. But the cops claimed he did it to get the briefcase."

That was news to Evan. "Why? What was in the briefcase?"

"You weren't told? The police said that the victim – beg your pardon, your brother had a briefcase that he handcuffed to his wrist. It was believed that the arm was cut off – sorry, this is rough, but the arm was cut off to acquire the briefcase."

"Why?"

"It contained drugs and cash."

"What about the handcuffs?"

"Handcuffs?"

"You said Patrick handcuffed the case to his arm."

"Oh. Hmm. You'd have to check the arrest report."

"And Pulasko doesn't remember."

"Jack was high on LSD. It's an insidious drug, I'm told." Friedman reclined in his chair. "You know, Mr. Dunne, you're making an interesting case for my client's appeal. Not that there will be one, but... Is there something you know that I don't?"

"You've got it all wrong. I'm in the dark here. I'm looking for daylight."

"Peace of mind. I understand."

"Were you aware my brother was connected to Naval Intelligence?"

"Yes. And he was discharged, as I recall. Is that somehow relevant?"

Evan was on the verge of revealing the diary to Friedman when doubt flared in his mind. The lawyer knew suspicious details yet showed little concern for his client. He wondered if the hack attorney could be trusted. Even if he could be, Evan doubted the man's ability or desire to help.

"In my experience," Friedman said, "ninety-nine percent of crimes don't add up neatly. Confessions like what Pulasko gave only happen on Perry Mason. But that's what happened in this case. Be thankful for it, Mr. Dunne. You've already got more answers than most grieving families ever get." He rose from his chair. "Now if you'll excuse me…"

Evan shook the man's hand and saw himself out, nodding to the receptionist as he departed. He pondered what the lawyer said. Maybe Pulasko was the true killer. Maybe Evan was seeing a conspiracy where none existed. Perhaps Patrick was a victim of random street violence. On the other hand, the CIA didn't acknowledge his association and carried on in secret. Evan felt no closer to the answers. Maybe he would find some at the scene of the crime.

April 22, 1967

Saw Dickie today. He completely ignored me. Can't tell if that's good or bad. Have to assume he's keeping his word and avoiding me so he doesn't blow my cover. The less I see of him, the better.

April 24, 1967

SG asked me to explain who the Diggers are. Unbelievable! Doesn't he read the reports I file? Jesus Christ! I've mentioned the group in at least six filings! What the hell's the point of this operation?

April 25, 1967

GH says those guys at TSS are only interested in their scientific experiments. The subjects don't matter. All they want to know is the results.

Then he explained that TSS actually <u>wants</u> us to face unrest. Our objective is not to prevent rioting. It's to quell it with drugs. We need a test. The big summer onslaught of hippies to the Haight is going to be our laboratory. Damn, I am <u>not</u> looking forward to that.

13
Dear Mr. Fantasy

Evan pressed all the doorbells. Someone was bound to answer. The afternoon sun warmed him and helped clear his muddled mind. Seconds later, a faint buzz emanated from the doorframe, followed by a click. He pulled the glass door and entered the unfamiliar apartment building. His shoes clacked against the tile floor, and the sound echoed through the barren hall and staircase. He climbed the steps but didn't know where to go.

"Who is it?" a male voice called out from an upper floor. Jimi Hendrix played loud guitar riffs on a stereo and the tune spilled into the stairway.

Evan climbed to the second floor. A barefoot man with long, scraggly hair stood in the doorway to his apartment. He wore dirty bellbottoms and a button-down striped shirt. A cigarette dangled from his lips that were buried somewhere beneath his unkempt beard and mustache. His blue eyes were glazed like baked hams.

"Sorry to bother you, but I have some questions, please," Evan said.

"About what?"

"The murder in this building back in August."

"Aw, shit. You the fuzz?" The tenant slid back into his apartment.

"No, I'm not. I'm the deceased man's brother."

The longhaired tenant slipped back into the hallway. His dilated eyes played over Evan. "Hmm. Yeah, I can see it. You kinda look like Tom-Tom. Except straight."

Evan stopped at the top of the stairs alongside the tenant's door. He could tell the guy was already high at ten a.m.

"Why was he called Tom-Tom?"

The tenant frowned as he smoked his cigarette. "You don't know?"

Evan shook his head. "I've been overseas."

"Like, in the Peace Corps?"

"Um, no."

"The Nam? You don't look Army."

"Which apartment did he live in?"

The tenant pointed across the hall to the only other doorway on the floor.

"Is it rented out now?"

"Nope. Who'd wanna live there? Know what I mean?"

Evan crooked his thumb at Patrick's old apartment. "I don't suppose you have a key."

The tenant shook his head and exhaled a plume of smoke. Evan walked to the door and tried the handle. Locked.

"Nothin' worth seeing inside," the tenant said. "They came and cleaned everything out."

"Who?"

He shrugged. "You know. The Man."

"The landlord?"

"Before that."

"Cops?"

"Not uniforms, if that's what you mean. Plain clothes guys. They worked quick."

"My name's Evan." He extended a hand.

"Bill." The tenant shook with a limp hand.

"Did you know my brother well?"

"Nope. Real quiet guy. Hardly ever saw him. Sold me some good shit, though. Damn shame what happened, man."

"Were you around when the murder happened?"

"Look, I told my story to the cops. Okay?"

"Between you and me," Evan said, dropping his voice, "I don't have much faith in the police."

The tenant's glare softened. Evan had said something agreeable; a statement calculated to curry favor. "I heard they busted the guy who did it."

"Yeah. A biker. Ever see any bikers in this building?"

"Never." Bill stared into the middle distance. Wheels turned in his head. "Hey, man, are you saying there was some kind of conspiracy here?"

"You tell me."

Evan had the young man's attention. He smoked his cigarette and contemplated the possibilities. "I think the guys who cleaned his shit out were Narcs."

"Men in black trench coats?"

"No, man. Narcs. You can spot 'em on the street. Dressed like hippies, trying to fit in. Older, though, a little too clean."

"Did you ever see a girl around here?" Evan asked.

"Sure, his girlfriend. She split sometime before he was killed."

"Do you know her name?"

"No."

"Starts with a J."

"Beats me, man. Do you think she had anything to do with it?"

"I don't know. Why?"

"She was always high, man. A trippy chick. I kinda thought he… Um, I dunno…"

Embarrassment washed across Bill's face. Evan pressed him.

"What is it?"

Bill shrugged. "I shouldn't say."

"Go ahead. It's cool."

"Well... seemed to me he kept her strung out. Like he used her. Know what I mean?"

Evan nodded. "Yeah."

"I mean, man, she was a foxy chick when she was clean. But she was most always fucked up, so... Takes a toll, y'know."

Music boomed from Bill's stereo. Jimi Hendrix's guitar played over slow motion lyrics, and Evan wondered if that was intentional or if the drug had kicked in again. After a moment's hesitation, he decided he was fine and the tune was distorted on purpose.

"You okay, man?"

"Yeah. Can you describe the girlfriend?"

"Tall, thin, pretty. About twenty, if that. Big hair. Not a great complexion but you couldn't really tell 'cause of her skin color. Hey, come to think of it, I got a picture somewhere."

Bill motioned him to enter the apartment. The place was a pigsty: dirty clothes strewn about, mismatched used furniture, ashtrays full of cigarettes, empty glasses lying here and there. Plus, the flat reeked of patchouli.

"I got in the habit of taking snapshots of people sleeping in the doorway outside," Bill said. "I was making a collection to send to the landlord in return for, like, reduced rent or something. You know, like, look at all these freaks I gotta put up with, man. Maybe I could get a discount on rent, seeing as how so many people were living on the property for free. That kinda ended, though, when most of the hippies went home. That whole Summer of Love thing? Nothin' but hype, if you ask me. Some crap the local merchants cooked up to draw in tourists. We had a groovy scene here before all that."

A Polaroid camera lay on the ersatz coffee table. A random pile of newspapers and album covers and rolling papers and leaflets and photographs rested beside it. Bill combed through the stack until he produced a black and white photo.

"Here she is." He handed over the picture, and Evan flinched with surprise.

She was black. The photo showed a black girl with a large Afro. She wore a cowgirl-style leather jacket with fringes up each arm, hip-hugger bellbottoms, and black boots. She lay passed out in the hallway just inside the building's front door, curled into a fetal position. Evan hadn't figured the girl would be black. At no point in Patrick's diary, to his recollection, had he ever written about her race. The revelation stunned him.

"Mind if I keep this?"

"It's all yours, man."

"Do you think any of the other tenants in the building would know her name?"

"I doubt it. Kyle and Martha just moved out. I guess the murder happening right above their bedroom freaked them out pretty bad. And the hombre upstairs no habla English."

"What about neighbors?"

"In other buildings? You could try. She was a sister, and this is a real mixed neighborhood, so… Neither of them seemed too social with the neighbors. Maybe some of his… what's the word? Clients? Ask on the street. Somebody might know her."

"How would I find his, uh, clients?"

"I dunno. Beat the tom-tom, I guess. That's how he worked, man. He'd stand out on the corner of Haight and Belvedere, right beside the bank, and beat his tom-tom. That was, like, his signal that he was open for business."

Evan thanked the tenant, pocketed the photograph, and left the apartment building.

J was black! Images of his brother with a black girl swam through his mind. Did Sandy know? How would she have reacted? Evan was no bigot, but sexual relations with a black girl… That seemed out of character for Patrick. He wondered what other surprises he would learn about his secretive brother.

May 6, 1967

J freaked out on speed, booze, and LSD all at once. Had to talk her down from the window ledge. This chick is driving me batshit! An obvious cry for help or attention or both, but I can't be dragged into whatever trip she's on. I give her shelter, food, drugs, and the occasional roll in the sack. She should be grateful I give her that much and equally grateful I don't send her home to her vicious father. She needs to shape up or ship out. This crap must stop!

May 8, 1967

As if coping with J's freak out wasn't enough torture, now I've got Sandy giving me the third degree about working the weekend when I was supposed to be home with family. Couldn't tell my wife that I had to rescue a crazy broad from suicide. She suspects I'm sleeping around. What the hell am I supposed to tell her? Yes, I'm fucking a teenage runaway, but it's part of my job. Hey, don't worry. She's over eighteen and I had her tested for the clap. I'd come home and screw you, honey, but I've got to work overtime.

GH was no help. Went to him for advice, and the bastard couldn't stop chuckling. Probably stoned.

What a goddamn mess.

14
The Golden Road (To Unlimited Devotion)

Since Haight Street was just three blocks away, Evan left his Plymouth parked near Carl and Cole. Searching for the girl meant stopping people on the street, showing the photo, and asking questions. That exposed him. He had planned to lay low. The shadowy men who drugged him might be any-where in the city. But the only way to find the mysterious J was to go out in public and flash the picture.

Two teenage girls approached him. Neither looked like hippies, more like prim suburbanites. Evan smiled, stood in their path, and held out the photo. They avoided eye contact.

"Hi, I'm looking for this girl…?"

The teenagers brushed past him and maintained their private conversation as if he were a streetlight pole. He marched on toward Haight Street.

One block later, he entered a different world. People of every variation strolled the street: men and women, mostly under age thirty, black and white, with free flowing hair and bell bottom jeans and peasant skirts and peace symbols and madras tops and sandals. The sweet smell of marijuana wafted by; young men smoked it openly to taunt authority. An elderly couple teetered down the sidewalk arm in arm; long-time residents who belied no emotions toward the youths who had seized their neighborhood. French-speaking tourists with maps and backpacks wandered as if on safari. But the majority of pedestrians were hippies, or those who fit the stereotype. Uniformity ruled Evan's world. His pals all dressed and acted alike. The Beatles' mop tops were alien enough, but Haight Street was alive with freaks. The kaleidoscopic disparity in appearance made him dizzy: Edwardian costumes, vertical striped white-and-blue jeans, corduroy jackets, a tie-dyed dress, vertical striped button down shirts, glittered black leotards, flowery shirts with puffed sleeves at the wrist, bright orange gossamer tops that barely covered bare breasts, black turtlenecks, paisley fabrics, banlon shirts, striped mod suit jackets, vests over T-shirts, clown hats, cowboys hats, floppy brimmed sun hats, sailor caps, painted faces and fully painted bodies, ankh symbols, bobbed hairdos, black hipster sunglasses, garlands of flowers as headbands, beads, peace symbols on chains, and sash headbands. Girls wore bikinis beneath corduroy jackets. Men wore ankle-length serapes of oddly patterned fabrics that looked like tablecloths with holes cut in the middle for heads to stick through. Despite four days worth of stubble, Evan had the least facial hair of any man on the street. Flowers, usually wilted, hung over men's and women's ears. Hippies blew bubbles as they strolled down the boulevard. People sat in circles on sidewalks, blocking the way. A woman played flute. Men strummed guitars and beat bongos. Others chanted. Palms were pressed together in Buddhist prayer. The atmosphere was a carnival without rides or cotton candy or children, although a few tykes among the throng made the scene all that much more bizarre. Absorbing all the colors and faces and sounds and smells overloaded Evan's senses. He couldn't take it all in fast enough, yet he stared with fascination and forgot his purpose.

As he strolled eastbound, some of the seedier aspects came to light. A mangy stray dog wandered through with a bloody hindquarter. No one gave the mutt any notice. Neither did anyone offer assistance to the figures slumped in doorways, either asleep or zonked out on drugs or dead. A long-haired man in Navy pea coat passed something into the hand of a pimple-faced teenage girl. Evan saw the man counting money, and his mind flashed to Patrick's diary. Was this Tom-Tom's milieu?

Evan held out the photograph to passersby and asked if anyone had seen the girl pictured. Half of the pedestrians paid him no attention. Some just offered stoner grins and held up the two-finger peace sign. Others glanced at the photo but didn't know her.

"Ask at the I/Thou," a portly hippie said.

"What's that?"

"A coffee shop."

Evan walked east to the first coffee shop he found. Inside, young people sprawled on pillows, couches, and chairs. Incense and scented candles burned. Few actually drank coffee. Instead, the shop seemed to be a place to loiter. A woman with severe cheekbones stood behind the counter. A crown of baby's breath wrapped around her long frizzy hair. She was the only employee, if she could be called that.

Evan showed her the photograph. "Do you know this person?"

"Looks like she's tripping," the counter clerk said. "What's her name?"

"I don't know. I'm asking."

"Why?"

"She's my brother's girlfriend."

"And…?"

"And she's missing."

The woman handed back the photo. "Maybe she wants to be missing."

Evan was dumbfounded. "Do you know her?"

"No, I'm just saying... Lots of people come to San Francisco to be free. To drop out, do their own thing. Maybe she doesn't want you bringing her down."

The illogic left Evan speechless. He stared at the woman.

"I think she's in danger."

"From what?"

Evan ad-libbed. "Bad drugs. BZ. Heard of it?"

"No. Why did you take a picture of her when she was tripping?"

"I didn't take the photo and I never said she was tripping." The woman's attitude was getting on his nerves.

"Looks like she's lying on a tile floor. Either she's tripping or injured."

"That's not the point. I'm trying to find her."

"Then ask whoever took the picture. They must know."

Exasperated, Evan marched toward the door. He had to exit before he lost his temper. When he reached the doorway, a tiny woman in tie-dyed T-shirt with no bra and tattered jeans held the door for him. She glanced at the photograph but shook her head.

"Try Hippie Hill," she said. "Always a crowd there."

"Where is it?"

"It's in the park, just off Stanyan. Follow the music. You can't miss it."

Patrick's diary mentioned Hippie Hill, and it made Evan wary. Even so, he marched down Haight to Stanyan Street where Golden Gate Park began. The pounding of bongos and the strumming of guitars and the high pitch of harmonicas emanated from behind trees and brush. Evan walked down a slope toward a small pond. Up the side of an incline lounged dozens of groovy people. Patrick wrote of his fear for the motorcycle gangs and what they'd done on Hippie Hill. Evan eyed the crowd for bikers but spotted none, not that they would have been obvious to him. Satisfied that it seemed safe to join, he skirted the edge of the throng.

Guitarists flailed away. Two harmonica players dueled. Drummers beat on anything; bongos, cowbells, buckets, woodblocks, tambourines. Strange bending notes were plinked on a sitar. One whirling dervish girl played wooden flute. The resulting cacophony sounded purely improvised, never ending, but somehow united in purpose. Dancers swayed and bounced to the rhythm; some found their own beat. Smoke rose from nearly every mouth, tobacco and otherwise. Despite the racket, sleepers dozed on the grass.

Wherever he walked, he worried suspicious eyes would squint at him. With his white shirt, slacks, and buzzcut, Evan knew he looked miscast for the sideshow. Nothing in his appearance could make him fit in, but he tried to look nonchalant. In fact, no one seemed to notice him. On a whim, he found a patch of grass, sat cross-legged, and pretended to enjoy the music.

On second hearing, the cacophony rang and swirled in communion that somehow made sense to his nonmusical ears, and his body melded into the hard ground with relief. Sunshine warmed his back, and the light breeze danced across his unwashed face. The sweet smells of marijuana and patchouli filled his nostrils. Altogether, the pleasant sensations buoyed him. Calm replaced his nervous jitters. In that instant, he was awakened to the simple pleasures of life; the sun's comfort, the wind's vibration, the earth to which he was anchored. Nature was made manifest to him, and the musicians added a soundtrack to his minor epiphany. Was this was the hippie ideal? Or was he still high from the drug? Moreover, was there any difference?

Two lovers lay on the ground before him. The girl ran her fingers over her man's beard and long hair, barely touching him. He lay on his shirtless back with his arms behind his head and his eyes closed to the sun. Dirt caked his nude torso. He looked like he hadn't bathed in a week.

In the middle of the pack, Evan spotted another couple openly engaged in sex without shame or concern. That mesmerized him. Even more surprising were the blasé reactions of those hippies surrounding the amorous pair. No one seemed to care.

Someone nudged him and broke his red-faced stare. To his right, a heavy Chicano with a red bandana and wild mustache presented a joint between two fingers. Without a word, he shoved it at Evan.

"No, thanks," he said.

The Chicano blew out a stream of bluish smoke. "Take a hit. Pass it on."

Evan took the joint but didn't know how to react. He'd seen guys smoke dope but never joined the party. Beer was his high of choice. He'd never even tried pot before. After his horrid hallucinations, he wasn't about to try it now.

The girl who lay with her lover reached up for the joint. Evan handed it down to her. She inhaled deeply and perched herself on her man's naked chest. Then she blew her exhale into his mouth as he sucked in. Evan found it oddly erotic.

The Chicano glared at him. "Cops ain't welcome."

Evan took in the intimidating stare and said, "I'm not a cop."

"Of course not," the half-naked boyfriend said. He didn't move from his supine position. "Undercover cops try to blend in with the scene. They wouldn't be so obviously square. This dude just wants to explore. Right?"

That the shirtless man even noticed his presence surprised Evan. The Chicano grunted, smirked, and turned his attention back to the musical hodgepodge.

"Actually," Evan said as he pulled the photograph out of his pocket, "I'm searching for somebody."

"Aren't we all?" the shirtless man said.

Evan handed the picture to his girlfriend, and she stared at it with pot-tinted eyes. "Tom-Tom's main squeeze."

Evan sat upright. "You know her?"

"Not really."

"You knew Tom-Tom?"

"Sure. He sells on the corner of Haight and Belvedere."

"Used to," the shirtless man beside her said.

"Busted?" she asked.

"He OD'd."

"He was murdered," Evan corrected. "I'm tracking anyone who might know what happened."

"You *are* a cop," the Chicano said.

"I'm Tom-Tom's brother. Anybody know the name of the girl in the picture?"

The hippie girlfriend wracked her brain, even pounded her palm against her temple to dislodge any information trapped in her head.

"Starts with a J," Evan said.

"Jenny? Jenna? Something like that."

"Do you know anybody who knows her?"

"Maybe."

The girl then handed the photograph from person to person, like a joint passed around for communal enjoyment. As the picture moved around the large group, Evan feared it wouldn't be returned to him. Paranoia struck him in the gut. He tried to follow its path, but the hippies passed the photo along quickly. Most didn't even glance at it. Evan wanted to dive into the crowd and snatch the photo before it was discarded or rolled into a joint. But then his fear was allayed. The hippie girlfriend retrieved the Polaroid print, which was now smudged with fingerprints. No one showed any hint of recognition of the girl pictured. The fruitless effort disappointed Evan, so he decided to move on. He rose and wiped grass from his pants.

"Try the Drogstore," the shirtless hippie suggested. "Everyone in the Haight flows through there."

"Which drugstore?"

"No, man, the Drogstore Café. Corner of Haight and Masonic."

May 3, 1967

Other dealers have gotten really bold. One guy, dressed in my standard uniform of pea coat and jeans, stands on Haight at Clayton and barks out his drug list like a carnival barker. When the cops arrive he flows on with the crowd. Another dealer wears a makeshift billboard. One side is a peace symbol. When he flips it over, it's a drug menu complete with prices.

I keep it low key, aside from banging my drum. Regular customers constantly bring me new meat because I keep prices low and don't care if someone stiffs me. We feign being competitors, but GH and I set the price on the street, and with Owsley out of the picture our supply is definitely flooding the neighborhood.

TSS gave me something new. The street name is STP. Not going to test this stuff, not even on J, because it's supposed to give a three-day trip. Too potent. But it's selling. Hippies will try any old drug.

What are we supposed to do with all this cash? Up until now, no problem. I used to dump it all into a private account at a bank out in the Sunset. But now I've got stacks too cumbersome to transport to the bank. Dollar bills are stuffed into pillowcases. I'm worried. GH laughed at me. He said, Do you think TSS cares how much money we pull down? Nobody asks questions. Makes me uneasy. Seems like another potential bombshell in the event we're ever exposed.

May 11, 1967

I bought a second-hand valise to carry around drugs and cash. Can't carry it all in my pockets anymore. Makes me look like a hippie businessman. All I need now is a pipe and some Borkum Riff.

More kids on the street than ever. Some are hippies, many aren't. Lots of curiosity seekers making the scene, trying drugs for the first time. Big mistake.

Evan marched six blocks east. Traffic crawled. Motorists and their passengers stared out of car windows as if ogling animals in a nature preserve. Irate hippies on the sidewalks flipped them the bird. Sweating, bug-eyed teens huddled in the doorway of a recently vacated storefront and begged for spare change. A record shop blasted Jefferson Airplane's *Somebody To Love* so loud that Evan's chest thumped from the bass line. A skinny woman in a body-length leotard and a shorter man in ripped corduroys and T-shirt skipped hand in hand down the sidewalk as joyous and buoyant as toddlers, their eyes wide with mania. Outside another shop, the scent of patchouli overwhelmed. All along the street, mom-and-pop businesses looked vacant while stores that catered to the hippie culture bustled. One exception was a small storefront called the Psychedelic Shop. A sign in the window said it was closed for good. At the corner of Haight and Ashbury, Evan passed the Unique Men's Shop, a starched collar clothier with an ironic name given the locale and the traditional merchandise. Two beat cops stood across the street in front of a jeweler's store, keeping their distance from hippies to avoid antagonism but showing a police presence on the street.

Two thin young black men stood outside a headshop shaking hands and laughing to expose gap-toothed smiles. Before they parted ways, Evan approached with the photograph in hand.

"Excuse me. I'm looking for this girl."

The shorter black man accepted the picture and glanced at it. Then his smile drooped into a sneer. He looked askance at Evan and handed the photo to his friend. Both men scowled as if their manhood were impugned. The Polaroid was shoved back at Evan, and he wondered what he'd done to offend.

"Uh-huh. Since we're Negroes we'll know where some junkie sister is hanging out. That's some kinda shit, man."

The men shook their heads, nodded goodbyes to one another, and strode off in opposite directions. Evan's face flushed. They'd misunderstood, but he felt no need to apologize. Then he marched on.

One block further east, the Drogstore brimmed with humanity. Popularity made the café a crammed fishbowl even at mid-afternoon. Entering required a greased body and no fear of claustrophobia. The scene spilled onto the street where dozens of hippies made the sidewalk their sun parlor. Two girls drew scores of chalk daisies on the pavement to form a mock garden. A communal pack of Lucky Strikes drifted through the huddle. People rapped and laughed and smoked. For those left out of the café, lounging on the street corner was the height of enterprise and showed the cachet of cool.

A peach-fuzz faced hustler in a navy pea coat and blue jeans leaned against the building and looked aloof. An entry from Patrick's diary flashed through Evan's mind: the coat designated the man as a dealer. Evan approached and pressed his back against the building. The young dealer eyed him with suspicion.

"Ever hear of a guy named Tom-Tom?" Evan asked.

The dealer scowled. "Fuck off."

Evan showed him the photograph. "I'm looking for his girlfriend. Seen her?"

Instead of looking at the picture, he crooked his thumb at the hippie horde on the sidewalk. "Ask Genevieve."

Eight people sat cross-legged in a circle along the Drogstore's exterior wall, blocking pedestrians without concern. Two men and a woman assumed the lotus position and repeatedly chanted 'Ommm.' A teenage boy, just past puberty, fidgeted and jabbered to himself with agitation. The long-haired man beside him made a harmonica whine.

"Genevieve?" Evan said, not knowing who might answer.

A pixie girl with short brunette hair stared up at him. Acne scarred her round face. She wore a knee-length jeans jacket and a pink silk sash as a headband. Her doe eyes showed no fear. Evan froze. An involuntary gasp escaped his mouth. On her cheeks he saw windmills. How could she have known? He blinked, stared again, and realized that what he thought were depictions of windmills were actually daisies. Someone had painted flowers on her face. It's the drug again, he told himself. Pull down logic and get a grip.

"Hello," she said.

Evan held out the photo. "Um, do you know her?"

Genevieve barely needed a glance. "Who're you?"

"I'm Tom-Tom's brother."

Genevieve's mouth formed an O, and her brow wrinkled with pity. Then she rose to her feet. "Sorry. I didn't really know him, but... I'm real sorry."

"Thank you." He pointed to the photograph. "What's her name?"

"Janey. We hung out together once in a while. She's real cool."

"Do you know where I can find her?"

The pixie girl shrugged. "She kinda fell of the face of the earth after Tom died."

"Do you know her last name?"

"Corcoran. Jane Corcoran."

Evan felt a rush of excitement. Here was an answer at last. "Any chance she went back home?"

"To her parents? I doubt it, but... You never know."

Evan thanked her and walked away. At last, progress was made. At least he had a name. After walking twenty feet, Genevieve scurried up to his side.

"Why do you want to know about Jane?"

"I need to ask her questions about my brother's murder."

"Tom kicked her out a few days before he was killed. I heard she crashed at a free pad on Waller."

The lingo confounded him. "A free pad?"

"An open flat. Free of charge for anyone who needs a place to sleep. There used to be a whole bunch in the neighborhood before the pigs shut them down. Now only one or two."

"Do you think she's there now?"

"I doubt it. But somebody there might know where to find her."

"Where's this free pad?"

The pixie girl gave him an address four blocks away. "Ask for Robby. Are you leaving the country soon?"

"Well, I just came back, but..." He flashed on his Army induction and said, "Maybe soon."

"The war?"

Evan stared with astonishment. "How did you know?"

Neither anger nor pity showed on her face. Instead, large doe eyes peered into his psyche, which made his skin prickle. "My horoscope said I'd meet someone today who was going off on a long journey." Then she handed him a wilted daisy tucked behind her ear and said, "Peace."

With that, she turned away. He held the withered daisy in his palm like an injured bird.

From deep in the crevices of his mind came a voice telling him to save her. Take her away from here before harm comes her way. Genevieve didn't appear to need a savior, but he couldn't shake the feeling that impending trouble would befall her. She was no distressed damsel, however. Besides, he was already on a quest. And so, with renewed purpose, off he marched into the dusk in search of Jane Corcoran.

May 16, 1967

No sign of J since Friday. Jesus, I hope she hasn't offed herself. She's a pain in my ass, but I worry anyway. Such a messed up kid. They all are, every pair of eyes you see on the street. I try to bury my guilt when I pass off lids or tabs to these bereft teenagers. Try to convince myself that I'm obeying orders and pursuing socio-scientific goals, all that horseshit GH spews. But I can't help feeling I'm only fueling delinquencies. I wish J would turn up. I hope she's not out on the street ruining herself. My conscience aches bad enough from this mission. At the very least, I hope somebody's taking care of her.

May 17, 1967

GH ranted about the Chronicle story. They're running an expose all week about an undercover reporter who lived as a hippie in the Haight for a few weeks. GH thinks the guy's a pinko because he empathizes with the hippie lifestyle. He thought about writing an anonymous screed to the Chronicle in opposition.

I asked GH if he'd seen J anywhere. He told me to let her go. Stay detached. He's probably right on.

May 19, 1967

Acid sales are falling off. The kids all need to make the scene, but you can't do that when you're tripping. It keeps them out of commission. So they pop pills. Now speed freaks bounce all over the neighborhood. It ain't right. It's making for a bad vibe on the street.

May 20, 1967

Found out who's supplying methadrine. It's the Hell's Angels. Great. We're trying to keep everybody mellow and the bikers are getting everyone wired. GH says we should incapacitate the violence-prone Angels. He's nuts. How are we supposed to do that? Spike their beer with STP or BZ, he says. And then what? They'll come out of their stupors in a couple of days, remember that they got dosed by hippies, declare us the guilty parties, and promise to chop off our balls. GH says they won't remember a thing. Forget it. I don't want to wind up worm food for messing with those psychopaths.

15
Are You Experienced?

The door was open, and on closer inspection Evan realized the hinges had been removed so that it remained permanently open. People talked inside. Even from the stone steps outside, pungent marijuana smoke assaulted his nose. Peeled paint hung off the siding on the dilapidated house. A dented mailbox clung by a single nail. The windows hadn't been cleaned since the building's erection. The chatter didn't cease, so he knocked. After a full day of marching about the neighborhood and with BZ lingering in his system, Evan felt weary. Jet lag still affected him, too. His mind and body sagged. He rapped on the unhinged door a third time.

"Unless you have a warrant, enter!" came a male voice.

Evan stepped onto a dirty, stained hardwood floor in a narrow foyer. To his left was a large central room with sparse, mismatched furnishings: two ancient sofas and three folding chairs. Three hippie men lounged there; all bearded with shoulder length hair and wrinkled shirts and blue jeans. Body language showed their thorough relaxation. A man with round-rimmed glasses held a lit match to a small square pipe and puffed. The other two loungers looked at Evan with glazed orbs. Thick drapes provided privacy and hid the dirty windows. The room contained enough smoke for an instant contact high.

"Welcome," said one of the hippies.

"I'm looking for Robby," Evan said.

The smoker passed the pipe to the beret-wearing man beside him, nudged his glasses up his nose, and said, "Guilty, your honor."

Evan approached and reached for the photograph. Before he could get it out of his pocket, Robby threw up his hands in protest.

"Whoa, man. If you're serving papers, spare me. They're clogging up my toilet."

Evan held out the picture, which the stoned man struggled to focus his eyes on.

"I'm looking for Jane Corcoran."

Robby squinted at him with suspicion. "You a cop?"

"No. Where can I find her?"

"Janey comes and goes."

"Came and went," said the man in the beret. He passed the pipe to the third hippie.

"Over and out," Robby said with a stoned salute. He offered the pipe to Evan. "Join the experience, brother."

Evan waved off the pipe and stood in the middle of the room. Distant voices came from down the hall and upstairs. "I was told somebody here might know how I can contact Jane."

"Who did you say you are?" Robby asked.

"I'm Tom-Tom's brother."

A momentary daze followed. All three wracked their addled memories for the reference. Then the third hippie nodded in recognition.

"Oh yeah. The dude with the bongo. He sold me some excellent dope. You selling?"

"No."

"You buying?"

"No."

"So, why are you looking for Janey?" Robby asked.

"I want to ask her about my brother's death."

The third hippie said, "Tom-Tom's dead?"

"Murdered."

"Holy shit, I heard about it," Robby said. "Lost his arm or something. Curious Jack went down for it."

Two lanky boys dragged an unconscious teenage girl through the front door, one boy under each shoulder. The girl's skin was pale, and her dirty bare feet slid along the floor as they pulled her in.

"Hey, Robby," one of the boys said, "got room for this one?"

"OD or tripping?" Robby asked. None of the hippies rose from the sofa with concern. "If she took an overdose, forget it. Don't need the hassle, man."

"I think she's coming down off speed."

Robby sighed with disgust. "Fucking bikers. Okay, upstairs. Leave her in the first bedroom."

"We'll stay with her," one of the boys said as they began carrying the girl upstairs.

"Bullshit!" Robby said. "You're not pulling that crap here, man."

One of the boys grumbled, "We aren't gonna do her."

"Leave her on the mattress and come straight down." Robby grimaced at his fellow stoners. "Can you believe these horny assholes? What happened to peace and love?"

"Tell the Diggers to come back home, Robby. Appeal to their sense of duty. The Haight needs 'em."

"Maybe after the fallout. Fucking Time magazine, man. This scene was real groovy until they blew their horns and all the flotsam settled in."

The third hippie aimed his glazed stare at Evan. "Sit down, man. Statues freak me out."

Evan feared that if he sat down fatigue would claim his body and mind. He'd been on his feet all day. Still, the temptation overwhelmed him, so he sunk into the smelly sofa with a tired exhale. Dust kicked up from the cushion. He wondered what filth had accumulated.

"Why is your door off the hinges?" Evan asked.

"Ginsberg, man," Robby said. "Read Ginsberg."

The answer bewildered Evan, so he let it go. "Tell me about the Diggers."

The beret-wearer took another hit on the pipe and pointed at Robby. "An original right there."

Robby took the pipe and refilled the bowl with fresh stash taken from a plastic bag in his shirt pocket. "Groovy people. Street theater. It just sort of evolved. Ever been to the Trip Without a Ticket? That's all because of the Diggers. All those free meals on the Panhandle? Diggers. Of course, that faded out back in, like, March or April. Peter saw the writing on the wall about the Summer of Love. He knew the Haight would be swamped with kids, and all the good, all the Digger ideals, would get co-opted for profit or tourism and chaos would bring the whole scene down with a thud." Robby lit a match to the pipe, sucked in the pot smoke, and spoke while attempting to keep from exhaling. "Peter is a seer, man, but I didn't listen. Keep the dream alive, I said." He finally released the smoke from his lungs. "Still trying, I guess. But even the Thelin Brothers closed up the Psychedelic Shop, and a lot of the Diggers left the city to live in communes up in Mendocino or Marin or wherever. More power to 'em. But the spirit of the Haight is flaming out without them."

The beret wearer turned to Evan and asked, "So how's Tom-Tom?"

Evan cocked an eyebrow at him. "Dead."

The hippie shook his head in self-disgust. "Sorry, don't mind me. I'm fucked up."

"When I heard it was Curious Jack," Robby said, "I was like, Whoa. I partied with that dude. Real quiet, kinda in his own head most of the time."

"You think he did it?" Evan asked.

"Didn't he? I mean, he seemed capable. All those bikers have this air of evil, y'know. Jack was no different. That marked the beginning of the end. That and the murder of Superspade."

"Who?" Evan asked.

"The cat's name was Superspade. A black drug dealer. His body was found thrown off a cliff. In the Marin Headlands, I think. They killed Shob, too. Gruesome shit. Drug dealers are battling over this turf, man. And nobody wants to cross the Hell's Angels. That's a death sentence. Kesey brought 'em in here. Told us they were cool. I think Ken was tripping too much."

"Tom-Tom had a partner," Evan said. "A fellow dealer. His first name would've started with the letter G." He waited for a response, but the marijuana slowed thoughts processes.

"Billy Batson," the third hippie said.

"Yeah," Robby said with a nod. "They joined forces. Couple of months ago, they gave away free dope out of a van that Billy stole from some freaks down the street."

"The guy I'm looking for would've had the initials GH," Evan said.

"No, it was Billy," Robby insisted. "He used to live a block from here."

"You sure his name didn't start with G?" Evan asked.

"None of the dealers use their real names," the beret wearer said. "Is your brother's real name Tom-Tom?"

Evan ignored the use of the present tense and shook his head.

"Billy Batson?" the third hippie said. "I read enough comic books to know he made that up." When Evan scowled with confusion, he said, "Billy Batson was the alter ego of Captain Marvel."

Evan sat up. "He lives down the street?"

"Gone," Robby said. "I think he got busted or he bugged out or something."

Still worth investigating, Evan thought. Someone there might know where to find the mysterious GH aka Billy Batson. Or they might know where to find Jane Corcoran. Anything was better than sitting and rapping with a trio of stoners.

And Evan had to keep moving before he fell asleep on the dirty sofa.

"What's the address?" he asked.

"Hell, I don't remember," Robby said. "One block down. Or was it near Stanyan?"

"Maybe going down there will jog your memory."

"My memory went out for a jog a long time ago, man. Can't say when it's coming back." The beret wearer sniggered. Robby rose from his seat. "I'm going upstairs to see what's taking those horny fuckwads so long."

The beret wearer relit the pipe and sucked smoke. Robby trudged up the staircase and called out the names of the boys who carried in the unconscious girl.

"Ever heard the name Owsley?" Evan asked.

"Who hasn't?" the beret wearer said.

"The acid king," said the third hippie as he accepted the pot pipe. "Best high in the Haight." He then filled his lungs.

"Wanna drop acid?" the beret wearer asked.

Evan shook his head. "So, this Owsley…"

"Worth millions, they say. All from selling acid."

"Really? I don't get that."

"What don't you get, man? Hippies want acid. He supplies."

"For a price."

"Sure."

"The hippies want everything to be free," Evan said. "No possessions. Burn money. Right? Yet the drug dealers are rolling in dough. How does that jibe?"

After a blank silence, the third hippie said, "Owsley gives back to the community,"

"How?"

"He finances some of the bands."

Evan grinned expecting a punchline. But the stoners showed straight faces, albeit with glazed stares. Like anywhere, the Haight had its share of contradictions, but the denizens either ignored them or, like the men in the room, were too high to care.

Seconds later, Robby hustled the two young men down the staircase. They wore guilty faces. The girl wasn't with them. "…in the morning when I get around to it," Robby said. "I've gotta check in at Park Precinct, and if her face turns up in Missing Persons… Whadda you care anyway, Ellis?"

The taller of the two young men scowled and kept walking to the front door. "Fuck you, man. I'm just playing the Good Samaritan."

"Yeah, right," Robby said with a smirk. He spotted Evan and a notion struck him. Then he called out to the young men who were already descending the front steps. "Hey, Ellis, didn't you have a thing with Jane Corcoran?"

Evan rose from the sofa and sidled up to Robby in the hallway. Ellis and his pal stopped at the bottom of the stairs and looked up. "No."

"But you know her, right?"

Evan walked halfway down the steps into the fading twilight. "Do you know where I can find Jane Corcoran?"

Ellis, with hands in pockets, looked askance at his pal. He hesitated and then replied, "Maybe."

"I need to ask her some questions."

"Twenty bucks gets you the straight dope."

Evan's eyes narrowed. Such an amateurish shake down, but he let it play out. Evan grabbed his wallet and handed over a twenty-dollar bill.

"I grew up in San Leandro," Ellis said, "just around the corner from the Corcorans. Janey's parents live on Gilmore Drive at the corner of Johnson."

"So?"

"She's there. According to my mom."

Evan scowled with disbelief. "According to your mom?"

"Hey, man, my mother is, like, the neighborhood busybody, okay? I called her yesterday for money and she talked my damn ear off. If she says Janey's back at her parents' house, then Janey's there."

"I'm not coughing up twenty bucks for that bullshit story." Evan snatched the bill from the young man's hand.

"That's no bullshit, man! Check it out for yourself!"

"How do I get there?"

"Easy. Take 880 to the Davis exit. Go left off the ramp onto Davis. First right is Gilmore. Go one block to Johnson. Their house is on the corner."

Evan made him repeat the instructions. Then he held out the twenty. "If this is a con, I'll be back for my money."

"It's cool. Scout's honor." Ellis pocketed the cash.

Evan brushed past him and his silent pal. "Somehow, I doubt you were ever a Boy Scout."

Once Evan was thirty feet away, he heard Ellis grumble beneath his breath, "Fuck you, man."

Evan ignored the complaint. He marched down tree-lined Waller Street to Cole and then trudged uphill to where he had parked his car near Carl. Streetlights were now at full illumination. Passing cars shone headlights. He contemplated climbing into the Plymouth and driving to San Leandro to test out the kid's story. If it turned out to be a bust, he'd rush right back and reclaim his twenty bucks. But Evan held out hope that the tale was true and that he would find Jane Corcoran before too long.

May 25, 1967

Poor J. Had I known she was at SF General, I'd have visited. She keeps insisting she sprained her wrist from falling, but I'm not convinced. Those bruises on her upper arms didn't come from slipping on a wet floor. She's pretty withdrawn, doesn't want to get high, just stays indoors and sleeps. Someday, when she's ready, she'll tell me what happened. Or maybe not. Doesn't really matter now.

GH was right. Stay detached. I can't save this girl. All I can do is encourage her to save herself. I feel the same way about the hundreds of other poor souls on the street. Save yourselves, you pathetic fucks.

May 29, 1967

I miss home. GH insisted that with so many hippies carousing on weekends we need to stay vigilant. Overzealous, if you ask me. Come to think of it, his attitude might not have all that much to do with the mission. I think GH digs dealing. Who knows what he's doing with all the cash he's accumulating. Yeah, that's it. He digs the money. Goddamn it, this operation is getting perverted.

May 31, 1967

Had to get and stay high all day. Been jittery for days. Worried about the impending summer hippie invasion. Within the week, we predict.

Yesterday, GH and I went over our battle plan, as he calls it. TSS stocked us with a shitload of BZ, acid, and STP. When things get wiggy, we're supposed to dose as many people as we can. Predetermining when to dose potential rioters is the hard part. We'd need to be everywhere all the time, just the two of us. Not possible. And if this is such a grand socio-scientific experiment, as SG keeps stating, then why aren't any TSS scientists recording the results? SG expects me and GH to report our findings after the fact, as if we're going to have time to jot down observations while we're in the middle of a giant mob freak-out. GH insists TSS ops are on the streets recording our actions, but I don't see them. Why keep them secret from us? Why make us record our observations? Nothing feels right. More and more, this operation feels like a major snafu.

16
Stone Free

He needed coffee. Sleep was preferable, but time wouldn't stop for that. Evan's remaining days before boot camp grew scant, and memories of his Italian summer faded like a distant radio signal. Unearthing the full truth might require weeks or months, he realized, or maybe come to naught. But if Jane Corcoran could corroborate the diary or provide clues about how the murder really occurred, then someone – a journalist or the police – could reinvestigate Patrick's death while he was off to war. Evan contemplated what action to take next. Should he visit San Leandro? The one-way drive would take less than an hour. But he was beat.

He trudged up Cole Street and across the trolley tracks toward his Plymouth, which was parallel-parked at curbside. At the corner of Carl and Cole he spotted a peculiar storefront. A colorful, hand-painted sign filled the glass door. It read, *Free Store*. The incongruity of that title made him blink. A sight inside brought him to a dead stop. Then he backed up and took another look.

Inside stood a Green Beret in full uniform. Evan stared with curiosity and wondered about his own impending induction. The soldier reminded him of his neighbor Harry Perryman but with hardened features. His face was chiseled out of quartz and covered in a four-day stubble. His eyes seemed vacant and aged. A bundle of civilian clothes were draped over his left arm; jeans, plaid shirts, and a windbreaker. He could have walked on, but Evan felt compelled to enter the odd store and talk to the man.

The interior was Spartan; a dirty bare floor, no shelves, and little in the way of furniture. Stray clothes littered the place; no store he'd ever seen was so haphazard with its merchandise. In the center or the room, a child's playpen acted as a clothes bin. It contained old shoes, dresses, boots, men's button down shirts, dirty jackets, skirts, ripped jeans, women's blouses, aged corduroys, and even pairs of dark dress socks. Ornate charcoal and color sketches on fine paper decorated the walls with nothing more than pushpins holding them in place. Also peculiar was the absence of a cash register.

Three young hippies – two girls and a bearded young man – squatted on the floor with a deck of tarot cards. A joint passed between them. The trio on the floor didn't acknowledge Evan except for one of the girls who smiled and waved hello. They made no effort to sell him anything.

The Green Beret wouldn't meet Evan's gaze as he crossed toward him.

"Excuse me," Evan said. "I'm about to go off to basic training, and I was wondering—"

"Back off!" The soldier faced Evan with blazing eyes and clenched jaw. He was a cobra ready to strike.

Evan jumped back and threw up his hands in surprise. "Whoa, sorry."

"What do you want?" the soldier asked. His gaze bore laser beams into Evan.

"I was just wondering what it's like over there," Evan said in a sheepish voice.

A moment passed. The soldier stared a mile into the distance.

One of the hippie girls leapt to her feet and wedged herself between the men. She offered Evan a stoned smile and two fingers splayed into a V sign. "Peace to you, my friend." Then she motioned with a sweeping arm to the clothes on the tables. "Help yourself. It's all yours anyway."

A tall bearded hippie walked out from behind a canvas curtain. He wore a long multi-colored dashiki and sandals and kept his shoulder-length hair in a ponytail. In his hand he held identification papers small enough to fit in a wallet. He motioned for the Green Beret to follow him. The soldier marched across the store and disappeared behind the canvas curtain into a back room.

Evan turned his attention to the attractive hippie girl. She wore no bra, which was apparent from the gossamer white blouse that covered yet exposed her breasts. Daisy petals had been painted onto her skin around her exposed navel. Her skirt hung low and loose over her hips. With a stoned grin, she repeated, "Go ahead. It's free."

His eyebrow arched. "What sort of place is this?"

"Like the sign says."

"A free store?"

"People give, people take. We eliminate the money."

"How do you stay in business?"

"Ooo, you just said a dirty word."

"Business?"

The two hippies getting stoned on the floor booed and hissed in mock fashion. Evan took no offense. He grinned.

"Join us," the girl said.

They made room for him on the dirty floor and Evan sat. "Who owns this place?" he asked.

"No one. And everyone."

"Who's in charge?"

"You are."

One of the hippie girls took a long toke on the communal joint. She then handed it up to Evan, but after the BZ attack he was still wary of drugs and waved it off.

The bearded hippie guy replied. "Tell me you're not a Narc, man. That would be a bummer if you were."

"I'm not. What's with the soldier? Seems kinda touchy."

"They come here to drop out," the sexy girl said. "We can help you do it, too."

"Do what?"

"Be free."

Evan arched an eyebrow. "You help men go AWOL?"

"We point the way."

"Did you say you're going into the Army?" the bearded hippie asked. "You don't have to, you know. We've helped a lot of guys."

"But the law..."

"Be free, brother."

Evan chuckled. "But the reality is..."

"If you don't like reality, change it."

These people are serious, he thought. He'd stumbled upon a sort of underground railroad for draft dodgers and deserters. Such subversion in his United States of America made Evan's head swim.

"How about a reading?" the shorter hippie girl said. She shuffled the tarot deck. "Nothing elaborate. Just a three-card spread. Here we go." She cut the deck and placed three cards face up before Evan. Then the girl took a hit on the joint and nodded with perceived wisdom. "First card is the Fool. This is your past. It means that you used to be simple. Your self-image was unclear. Maybe a virgin. Your spirit was basic, unrefined."

"In other words, you were a typical kid," the sexy girl added.

"Could be more than that," the tarot girl said. Then she pointed to the second card. "This is your present state. It's the Hanged Man. This might mean you're persecuted or shunned by society. Do you see how he's upside down? That suggests you now have a different view of the world." She pointed to the third card. "Finally, here's the Chariot. This is your future. There's a great struggle ahead. You can overcome it if you have the conviction."

"Or it could just mean you're going to get in your chariot and ride," the sexy girl said.

Evan paid little attention to the tarot reading. His eyes were glued to the sexy girl's breasts, which reminded him of Gina's perfect dark orbs. The stoned hippie guy caught him staring, so Evan looked away with embarrassment.

The Green Beret and the dashiki-wearing hippie emerged from behind the canvas curtain. But now the soldier wore civilian threads that ill fit him. When he saw that Evan was still in the store, he recoiled and pulled the dashiki hippie aside. They exchanged hushed words, after which the hippie sidled up to Evan.

"Hey, friend," the hippie said. "Everything cool?"

Evan shrugged. "I just wanted to rap, ask about the war. That's all."

The dashiki hippie guided Evan to the transformed Green Beret and said, "This guy means no harm."

Evan extended a hand, which the soldier shook. "Evan Dunne. I'm due at Fort Ord in a few days and—"

"You wanna know what it's like?" the Green Beret said. His face and body were taut with intensity. The edgy aura he gave off made Evan recoil. Then he spoke without emotion.

"I killed two little baby girls."

Evan froze. Blood drained from his face, and bile roiled in his gut. The man's intensity set Evan's nerves on edge, a cold tingle that ran up his spine and across his shoulders to culminate in an involuntary shiver. Up to that moment, the war was an unknown abstract concept that he wouldn't comprehend until he was in the midst of it. In that one moment, he knew all he wanted to know about the war, and his fear multiplied.

With nothing more to say, the Green Beret marched out the door onto the street, leaving silent shock in his wake. At that moment, an inbound Muni train stopped at the corner. He boarded, the train door closed, and off the soldier disappeared into the night, a free man.

The dashiki hippie placed a hand on Evan's shoulder. "Looking for a way out, brother?"

It couldn't be that simple, Evan thought. All the soldier did was change out of his uniform and into civvies. But then he recalled the identification card that the dashiki hippie held in his hand. Maybe they arranged fake IDs. He couldn't believe that such revolt took place in his city. And yet, having seen the Green Beret's feral stare, he understood why. And he couldn't decide whether or not he approved.

Without a word, Evan strode out of the store. He walked half a block to his parked Plymouth and sat on the front seat in stunned contemplation. The Green Beret's decision to chuck it all and go AWOL mesmerized him. Running away seemed such a chickenshit action. Yet he, too, had run away from violence - as a boy, hiding out for days to avoid being beaten by his father. That was different, of course, the action of a child. Desertion was serious. The soldier had a duty to uphold. He'd given his oath and allegiance to his country. On the other hand, he'd admitted to killing innocents. Evan wondered if he, too, would have to face such a galling conundrum. Was that typical for Americans in Vietnam? How would he cope with it?

A Muni train barreled out of the Carl Street tunnel, stopped at the intersection, and passengers poured out. Trains ran along the surface from Ocean Beach to the corner of Carl and Cole, but then entered and exited the tunnel that burrowed beneath the Haight. On the other end lay his neighborhood, Eureka Valley. Only one mile separated the two districts, but they seemed like different countries. He imagined driving his car through that tunnel to move through time and return to his past. On the other end of that rabbit hole, the year was 1962. His father was still alive, as was JFK, and life was in black and white. Evan was still a boy, and peace ruled. Better days lay through that tunnel. But the notion was meaningless. There was no reversing the calendar.

He wiped away the thought and focused on his task: finding Jane Corcoran. What plan of action to take next? Should he drive to San Leandro? Maybe he could call first. He spotted a phone booth on the corner outside a laundromat, dug change out of his car, and strode toward the payphone. An operator found him the number for Corcoran on Gilmore Street in San Leandro, California. In case Ellis had conned him, he asked for a person-to-person call. The phone rang four times before a lady answered.

"I have a person-to-person call for Jane Corcoran," the operator said.

"Who's calling?" the lady asked.

"Mr. Evan Dunne is calling from San Francisco."

"Janey isn't here."

"When do you expect her?" Evan asked.

"If you wish to complete the call, sir, please pay an additional forty-five cents."

Since he heard no response from the lady on the other end of the line in San Leandro, Evan opted to drop the call. As much as he wanted to talk to Jane Corcoran in person and ask her all she knew about Patrick, he had no desire to travel across the bay for what might turn out to be a dead end. So he dialed the operator, asked for the number again, got the connection, and dumped coins into the slot. No person-to-person this time. The same woman answered after three rings.

"Ma'am, my name is Evan Dunne. I'm looking for Jane."

"She's not here."

"When do you expect her?"

The lady hesitated. A voice spoke in the background but a passing Muni trolley roared and made Evan temporarily deaf. He jammed his finger in his free ear and listened, but the rumble from the two-car train canceled her soft voice.

"… and that's all we know."

"I'm sorry, ma'am, could you repeat that?"

A man came on the line. Evan could hear him loud and clear. "Don't you people got enough information? Decent folk live in this house! Just leave us be!" With that, he hung up.

Evan wanted to call again, but he had no more spare change. The man clearly said "you people." What did he mean by that? What information? Had someone harassed the Corcorans? Who? The police? Could the same shadowy men who drugged him be searching for Janey, too? If so, was she cooperating with them? Maybe not, if her parents' agitation was any indicator. Was it worthwhile to trek over to the East Bay to hunt her down, knowing that she might not even be there? There was only one way to know for sure.

Evan returned to his car, turned over the ignition, shifted into gear, and drove through the Haight to Oak Street and toward the Bay Bridge.

June 5, 1967

As per our directive, GH and I unleashed thousands of tabs of STP for free onto the street. Well, at least I was giving it away. Somebody told me a dude matching GH's description sold his for a buck a tab. That's why everyone flocked to me. I used intermediaries to distribute however they wanted. Presumably, most of them turned a profit. When they asked why I was giving the drug away, I said it was all in the spirit of Diggerdom. The drugs are free because they're yours. Most assholes bought my rap.

June 6, 1967

Heard a rumor about the Diggers. They're breaking into splinter groups. City hall sent health inspectors to shut down their free food giveaways and even boarded up their crash pads. The Diggers aren't getting the same charitable offerings they're used to, so the more militant members are leaving. Good sign.

You can hear the new Beatles album everywhere you go in the neighborhood. It's blasting from speakers aimed out windows so passersby can't avoid the music. Not sure I like it. Why'd they let Ringo lead off the album? The guy can't sing. And what's with all the horns? I don't know about this Pepper album.

June 10, 1967
The fog freaks out most newcomers. They think it's a temporary cold spell. Wait until mid-July. Most of them will freeze their bare-naked asses off.

June 11, 1967
Sandy asked about the wad of cash in my pea coat. About five hundred bucks in small bills. Forgot I left money there. Must've been stoned. My mind raced, but I couldn't concoct a believable lie, so I just stood there looking dumb. Then she gave me the silent treatment for the rest of the day. I took the boys to Candlestick for the afternoon, and she still wouldn't say a word. Can't tell if she's mad or afraid or what. So I left. I'm back in the Haight now. What the hell am I going to tell Sandy?

June 16, 1967
To my surprise, the street is emptying. Everyone's headed south to Monterey for a huge concert. GH said I might as well go home for the weekend since business is drying up for a few days, but I chose to stay. Haven't seen Sandy since Sunday, and I still haven't come up with an excuse for the bundle of cash she found.

June 17, 1967

A chick assaulted me on the street today. Out of the blue. Never seen her before. Kicked and slapped and punched me. Said her boyfriend was in the hospital after taking STP that I gave him. Can't remember who he is, but I won't forget her. The anger in those eyes. I offered to pay for his medical bills, but she flipped me the bird and stormed off. I got off the street in case she informed the cops.

No more STP. Too many kids freaking out. J heard that the emergency rooms are treating it like a bummer acid trip with thorazine, but it has the opposite effect. The trip gets even worse. STP is only for worst-case scenarios from now on.

This is the problem. TSS is supplying us with drugs that are inefficient or ineffectual for crowd control. There's no easy way to administer STP or acid to a rioting mob. Even BZ can't suppress hundreds of people, not if administered by just two of us. GH argued that we need to keep the neighborhood continuously high in order to prevent unruly mobs. Yet he told me just a few weeks ago that TSS wants us to face a riot just to see how the drugs will affect rioters. Which is it? What the fuck are we really doing here? Most of the hippies preach peace and even tell people to run to Golden Gate Park in the event riots break out. Everyone predicts unrest in the black neighborhoods. I don't sense any impending riots in the Haight at all.

I'm beginning to think GH and I are the real guinea pigs here, and TSS is experimenting on us.

17
She's Leaving Home

At a gas station just off Route 880, a vending machine poured hot black java. Since the Plymouth was running on fumes, Evan had an attendant fill the tank while he purchased a styrofoam cup of coffee to go. Caffeine was necessary to stave off drowsiness. Whereas he'd never acquired the taste as a teenager, Gina had introduced him to the irresistible kick of Italian espresso. The vending machine swill tasted worse than instant coffee, especially when he caught a whiff of gasoline fumes from the pump. Still, he guzzled the acrid brew, paid the attendant, climbed behind the wheel, and was right back on the highway.

San Leandro was foreign territory he had never visited before, and his recollection of Ellis' directions was hazy. He should have written them down. Because he hadn't, a half hour trip turned into seventy-five minutes of frustrated wandering. The caffeine kicked in, which only amplified his irritation. Rather than turning left off the Davis Street exit ramp, he took a right and found himself lost. When he doubled back, the name of the street didn't pop into his head as he hoped it would. On a fourth try along Davis, his Plymouth turned up Gilmore Drive into a residential area. One block later, he discovered Johnson Street, just as Ellis had said. But in which house would he find the Corcorans?

Evan parked his Plymouth, walked up to a random house, and rang the doorbell. A pregnant woman with a beehive hairdo answered. A three-year-old clung to her pant leg.

"Excuse me. I'm looking for the Corcorans."

"Over there." She pointed to the exact address.

He crossed the street to a white house with green trim. The neighborhood was filled with pillbox homes no more than one story tall. Yards barely contained the buildings, leaving little room for grass or flora. Needed home repairs were obvious even in the dark. The uninspired house designs suggested blue-collar residents. Up the short walkway he climbed to the front door and pressed the chime.

A tall, grey-haired white man answered. Even at nine pm, he wore a three-piece suit with the tie pulled tight. Round-rimmed glasses adorned his gaunt face. One glance at the stern-faced white man and Evan knew Ellis had flimflammed him.

"Is this the Corcoran residence?"

The man stared at Evan. "Yes."

"Sorry, wrong address." Before the man could close the door, Evan said, "Excuse me but I'm looking for a girl."

Flames of hatred shot from the man's eyes. "I'm tellin' you people for the last time, quit comin' around."

Evan realized he was in the right place after all. Maybe Jane was an adopted child. The man stepped closer with balled fists at his side. Blood rushed to his cheeks.

"Sir, I'm not with any group. My name is Evan Dunne. I'm here on my own to speak to Jane."

"About what? That hippie that got himself killed?"

"Yes, sir. He was my brother."

As Evan anticipated, the man's anger froze. He blinked. His fists unclenched.

"Well, Janey ain't here."

"When do you expect her back?"

"A year ago," the father said with bitterness. "We ain't seen her since last autumn. She turned eighteen and pffft! Off she went. And, far as I'm concerned, she can stay gone. So if you find her, tell her... Hell, we don't even know if she's alive."

Heartbreak came out in his last sentence, and Evan took pity.

In the hallway behind him, a middle-aged woman in a housedress and black-rimmed glasses appeared. Her equine face was drawn, and her eyes were hollow. She stood with folded arms and peeked at Evan with strange detachment.

"If you don't mind me asking," Evan said, "how did you learn about my brother's death?"

"The cops told us."

"Police were here?"

"Yeah, from San Francisco."

"Oh, in August, you mean."

"Just a few days ago." The father looked over his shoulder to his wife.

She stepped forward and said without emotion, "The first time was Thursday. They came again yesterday."

"They said they was investigatin' the murder and they had questions for Janey," the father added. "Well, we don't know what she's gone and gotten herself into, but we're Christian folks, and we don't wanna get hooked into any murder trial."

Something didn't add up. The murder occurred in August, and the killer was already behind bars. What were SFPD officers doing in the East Bay? Had detectives reopened the case? Evan followed a hunch.

"These policemen. Did they show you badges?"

"Can't recall."

"Did they leave a card or a number where they could be reached?"

"No, which I thought was odd," the wife said. "That's why I wrote down their names." She grabbed a sheet of notepaper from a table and read from it. "King and Menard."

Evan blinked. "One wore glasses like yours, ma'am, and the other had a thin mustache. Is that them?"

"Yes."

That explained it. Evan realized the shadowy men – who he suspected were the burglars, his assailants – were also searching for Jane Corcoran.

"Did you tell them your daughter's whereabouts?"

"We don't know. So don't bother askin' us."

"Alright, sir, but what did they tell you about my brother's death?"

"That they were investigating. Janey knew him somehow. Maybe lived with him." The tall man leaned his face forward and jabbed a finger into Evan's chest. "Let me be real honest here, son. If your brother was the no-good bastard who got our little girl hooked on drugs—"

"Don't, Sam!" The wife grabbed his arm.

"Maybe he got what he deserved."

Evan bowed his head. The man's anger was understandable and not without justification. Evan recalled what Patrick had written in his diary. Janey was a lost girl, and he'd taken advantage of her.

"I want to help your daughter, sir."

"Christ, you sound just like them cops. But you guys don't give a shit about Janey. To you bastards, she's just another Negro on drugs. Well, that ain't how we raised her. We took her off the streets of Oakland at the age of five and-"

"He doesn't need to hear our family history, Sam," the wife said.

The father scowled, waved his hand, and marched back into the house. The housewife sidled up to the doorframe but showed no intention of letting Evan inside. Hers were the sunken eyes of a sufferer of great sadness. Evan recalled an entry from Patrick's diary; something about J's deplorable home life that made her run away. The sorrow in the woman's eyes suggested she, too, lived under oppression.

"Sorry to be a bother, ma'am," Evan said. "You say the men came twice. Did they search the house?"

"First time, no. I wouldn't let them. Not without Sam home. But the second time…"

"What were they looking for?"

"Clues, they said."

"Like what?"

"I have no idea. I explained that Jane had been gone for months, but…"

"Did they find anything?"

"No. But I think they weren't really searching for clues to your brother's death. I think they were trying to track down Jane. I'm afraid she's mixed up in something awful." The woman belied no emotion, not even a tear for her missing child.

"Ma'am, do you think she's still in San Francisco?"

"She could be anywhere."

"What about Oakland?"

"Why Oakland?"

"Well, your husband just said…"

She shook her head. "She has no relatives there. Her birth mother is in prison. We're her only family."

"If I find Jane, do you want me to pass along a message?"

The woman gazed off into the middle distance and sighed. She craned her neck to see if her husband was within earshot. Satisfied that he wasn't, she faced Evan with an eerily blank expression, folded her arms tightly around her midsection, and said, "She won't come back here and… don't encourage it."

That dark statement chilled Evan. The woman nodded a glum goodbye and slowly closed the door on him. He walked back to his car. Whatever cruelties occurred behind the walls of that suburban home were stories Evan didn't care to learn. And he had no intention of telling the Corcorans what he knew about their daughter from reading Patrick's diary.

Within minutes, his Plymouth charged the highway with San Leandro in the rear view mirror. He tried to suppress his pity to no avail. For the entire drive back to San Francisco, past downtown Oakland and across the Bay Bridge, his heart ached with sympathy for a perfect stranger, and he day-dreamed of rescuing the black girl from mysterious circum-stances.

June 18, 1967

J has puked on consecutive mornings, which has me worried. I know morning sickness when I see it. So I confronted her. Is the baby mine? She said she's not preg-nant. I insisted that she is, and she needs to see a doctor. She broke down in tears, not like her at all. The shock of being pregnant hit her like a missile. Then she told me why she wound up in the hospital. She was raped. I had a feeling. Poor kid. What am I going to do with you, babe?

18
Don't Let Me Be Misunderstood

After scouting the vicinity for ten minutes, Evan felt certain there was no stake out and crept toward the house. Although it seemed safe to approach, the hour was late. The boys must have been asleep by half past ten. Sandy probably was in bed, too. But a flickering light shone behind a curtain, which gave the impression that someone was watching television. Rather than ringing the doorbell and awakening the sleepers, he tapped on the front door. Then a second time. Just as he was about to give up and walk away, the door opened, if only a crack. Sandy peeked through and then swung the door open wide.

"God, you scared me." She held a switchblade knife and was prepared to use it.

"Sorry," Evan said. "What's that for?"

"Protection," she said as she folded the blade. "Come on in."

She wore pajamas beneath a checkered bathrobe and slippers on her feet. Her long hair was mussed. Without make-up, her eyes seemed bluer. Evan preferred her natural appearance.

Inside, he smelled popcorn. The TV volume was low, and the black-and-white set got snowy reception. The picture flipped every three seconds. Two empty beer bottles sat on the coffee table. A bowl of popcorn rested on the sofa. The boys were nowhere in sight. After she stashed the switchblade in a drawer, he followed her into the living room.

"Your mom is worried sick, Evan."

"I imagine."

She wobbled when she walked and plopped herself onto the sofa, a consequence of drinking beer, he assumed.

"Where have you disappeared to?"

Knowing she would ask that question, he had prepared an answer. "I'm about to go into the Army, my girlfriend dumps me, Mom is acting like a drunken crazy woman, and on top of all that I get assaulted in my own home. I haven't even had an opportunity to properly grieve my brother yet. I just needed to get away."

Sandy frowned. "You could've told someone."

"Yeah, well…"

"You'll show up when we spread the ashes, won't you?"

"Friday, yes, of course."

"Secretive, like your brother. You worry me."

"Spare the worry. I'm fine."

"Sit. I'm having another beer. Want one?"

"Just a soda, please."

While she walked off to the kitchen, Evan glanced around the living room. Sandy maintained a clean house, which must have been a chore with two young boys. She preferred photographs on bookshelves to books or knickknacks. Framed photos of Matt and Andy dominated a side table. One large picture showed Sandy and her gangly brother Mel in their early teens. A bookcase was filled with pictures of Patrick holding his infant sons. One showed him in his Navy uniform. A much more recent snapshot, not yet framed, showed tall, hulking Mel as a Marine. Such an ugly fellow. Another photo showed Patrick, Sandy, and Evan – all as teenagers – at a beach party, laughing and posing for the camera. Both shirtless brothers had an arm around the swimsuit-clad beauty, her bouffant ruined by the wind.

"I remember that," Evan said when Sandy returned with two bottles: one cola and one beer. He pointed to the photo on the bookcase. "You were so mad about your hair."

"Half Moon Bay, just after graduation," she said as she turned down the television volume and then handed him the bottle of soda. "Hungry? There's popcorn."

Evan drank the cola and dug into the bowl for a handful of corn. She sat beside him and swigged her beer.

"At least call Dolo. She's flipping out, y'know."

"I will." He stared at the television without really registering the images. The picture flipped, and he wanted to adjust the horizontal hold. How could she watch TV like that?

"She told me about your… your episode. Dolo's afraid you're having… what's it called? Flashbacks?"

"I'm fine." The flipping picture mesmerized him until he grew paranoid that the TV was messing with his head. "Mind if I fix that?"

He rose from the sofa, swiveled the television set so that he could access the back, and found the tiny knob. After an almost imperceptible twist, the TV picture stabilized. As he sat back down, Sandy reached behind the sofa to an end table. She grabbed a princess telephone and set it on the seat beside him.

"Not yet," he said.

"Why not?"

"Mom's in bed by now, and Dolo's at work, no doubt."

Sandy raised a scolding eyebrow.

"Relax. I'll call tomorrow."

"What's going on, Evan?" she asked with furrowed brow.

As was so often the case when confronted with matters he didn't want to face, Evan changed the subject. "What ever became of Patrick's Impala?"

"I sold it."

"Don't you need a car?"

"Do you think I'm going to drive my kids around in the car that their father's killer...?" Her voice fell to a trembling whisper, and she choked on her words. "I was afraid of always seeing his arm in the backseat."

Evan nodded with sympathy. The image of his brother's severed arm haunted him, too, and he'd never even witnessed it. Sandy sniffled, withheld tears, and slugged back the bottle of beer. She showed quiet stoicism in the face of his questions.

"Did Patrick ever talk about a partner?"

She shrugged. "A friend. I don't know if he was a partner."

"Who?"

"Gil Harkess."

Evan sat upright. The initials GH were a perfect fit. "You've met him?"

"Twice. First, this dirty hippie showed up at our home and asked for Patrick. We went at it tooth and nail later. I never wanted any hippies at our house. Not around the kids. Patrick swore it would never happen again."

"Did it?"

"No, thank God."

"The second time?"

"A week after Patrick's death, he showed up in the supermarket. Just appeared out of the blue in the cereal aisle. Handed me a slip of paper with his name and address. Told me to write to him if I need anything."

"Like what?"

"Beats me. Gave me the creeps."

"Do you still have the piece of paper?"

"Maybe." She rose from the sofa. Her purse rested across the room on the table beside the front door. She rifled through it. Then, before finding the slip of paper, she took an unframed photo from a drawer and handed it to Evan. "Here."

The photograph showed shirtless Patrick in blue jeans. His brunette hair was shoulder length, and his beard was as full as a bird's nest. Sunshine made him squint as he posed for the camera. Behind him was a sea of people, mostly hippies, standing and sitting on an open field. This was Patrick under-cover, Evan realized. He barely recognized his brother. Sandy pointed to one of two men in conversation standing behind Patrick.

"That's Gil," Sandy said.

Evan pulled the photo closer to examine the man. The picture showed him in profile. He wore a Navy pea coat, and his frizzed hair grew out from his head like a willow tree. A hooked nose was his most prominent facial feature.

"Where'd you get this photo?" Evan asked.

"Patrick's belongings were brought to me from his den of iniquity."

"Who brought you his things?"

"The cops."

"Just police officers?"

"What do you mean?"

"Older men? Not in uniform? Do you recall the names King and Menard?"

She kept searching through her purse. "No. But one of them was in plain clothes. Wore a funny hat."

"A pork pie hat?"

"What's that?"

Evan struggled to come up with an explanation. "Flat on the top. The brim is sort of curled upward."

"Yeah, I guess. Here it is." Sandy produced the slip of paper and handed it over.

Poor penmanship displayed the name Gil Harkess and a P.O. box in Fairfield, California. Evan knew that the town, just forty miles northeast of the city, was home to a military base.

"Can I keep this?"

"Why?"

"I want to talk to this guy."

"About what? What are you up to, Evan?"

"Tell me what you thought Patrick was doing for the past year."

She scowled and chewed popcorn. "What I thought? Well, I thought he was working for Naval intelligence. But after his death, the Navy said he was honorably discharged a year ago."

"Did they say why?"

"He'd served his time, that's all."

"So who do you suppose he was working for during the past year?"

She scowled with confusion and shook her head. "He was dealing drugs, Evan. Didn't anyone tell you?"

"Yet he kept receiving paychecks. Didn't that strike you as odd?"

"He said he did, but I never dealt with our finances, so I never knew. I found all this cash on him, in his pockets. Patrick kept money secrets from me."

"But you know now, don't you? About checks he received. You've been to the bank…?"

Her head bowed. "I'm not that savvy with… I mean, I try, but… Math was never my best subject. I only just learned how a checking account works."

"Next time you're at the bank, ask for monthly statements for the last year. See if he deposited checks from the Maskelyne Group."

Sandy stared at him as if he'd just performed a levitation trick. "How do you know about that?"

"You've heard the name?"

She nodded.

"Now ask yourself: How does a Naval officer leave the service without anyone knowing and then lead a double life as a drug dealer?"

Worry lines creased her brow.

"Suppose he was with Naval intelligence," Evan said, "or some other agency, right up to the end. If he had been involved in, let's say, questionable projects, the government might not admit his association with them."

Her scowl deepened and she shook her head. "No, no, no."

"Don't be naïve, Sandy. Maybe his murder wasn't as simple as it seems."

She gave him a sideways glance. "You're under a lot of stress, Evan."

The urge to divulge the diary's contents was tough to repress. Granted, Patrick's widow had a right to know his involvement in strange misadventures, especially if they caused his death. But telling all he knew might only bring her harm. So he sat in silence, stared at the television, and said nothing.

Frustrated, she rose from the sofa. "You Dunnes. Always so secretive. Patrick and you and your mother with her drinking. And Dolo. God, what a weird family you are."

He took offense. "Leave Dolo out of it."

She spun around and thrust her hands on her hips. "Oh, really? Do you know she's done LSD? She was doing hard drugs before we suspected anything about Patrick. And she begged me not to tell you."

The news stunned Evan. His sister wasn't a nun, but he never suspected she'd delved into acid. On the other hand, her knowledge of how to treat him after the BZ attack should have been a sign. Dolo had grown up while he was away at college, but he never realized how much.

"Enough secrets!" Sandy said. Drunkenness took control, and she spoke loudly enough to awaken her sons. "You, too, Evan! Whatever secrets you have, spill them! Tell me what you know about Patrick!"

"I don't know anything for sure. I just have suspicions. But this guy Harkess… He'll tell me."

She shook her head and looked down on him with pity. "Don't take this the wrong way, but I think your drug episode might have..." She cupped a hand to her mouth to suppress her words.

The corners of Evan's mouth twisted in shame. He bowed his head and stared at his lap.

Sandy slid onto the sofa beside him, slipped her arms around his bicep, and sighed. "Stay here tonight. You shouldn't be alone so soon after your... your incident. I realize your mom isn't exactly the best company. Not in her condition. But you shouldn't be off by yourself."

"I don't want to be a burden."

"Not at all. The couch isn't much to sleep on, but... Hey, I'll make breakfast and you can see the kids before I take Andy to his kindergarten class, and... Just stay here, okay? You'll make me feel better. Besides, it wouldn't hurt to have a little extra protection around here."

"Protection from what?"

"Oh, you know. A woman alone. There are a lot of creeps out there."

"Have you seen anyone skulking about?"

She waved off his question. "Nothing like that. So, you'll stay?"

"Sure."

With that settled, she dug out a clean blanket, pillow, and pillowcase for him to sleep on. He watched her rush about the house with purpose. Then he washed up in the bathroom. A full shower would have been appropriate, but then he would have climbed back into the same filthy clothes, so he opted instead to rub away the grease and dirt and germs with a soapy washcloth. A dose of mouthwash cleaned his breath. Then, once his sister-in-law went off to bed, he stripped down to his underwear and spread out his frame on the sofa. As soon as he laid his head on the throw pillow, sleep devoured him as swiftly as turning off a television set.

Evan never heard Sandy on the phone in her bedroom telling Alice Dunne that her son was accounted for and fast asleep on the couch.

June 25, 1967

God, I need a toke. Mel is an upstanding guy, a good brother-in-law. I respect him, but he has no right butting into marital affairs. Granted, he was cool. He could've cleaned my clock, hollered at me to show more respect for his sister, and left it at that. But he talked to me man to man. Sandy told him I'm working for naval intelligence, so he's treating me with respect, but he says Sandy's stories worry him. The mysterious cash. Gone for days without communication. Coming home dirty and high and all hippie, as he put it. I told him there's no problem. That's a lie, but the truth would sound absurd. It IS absurd. I promised Mel I would never do wrong by Sandy or my sons. When I told him I unequivocally could not discuss my job with him, he nodded and accepted it. But then he warned me, with a cold stare, that if I brought any harm to Sandy or the boys he'd make sure I could never have any more children. Judging by his massive butcher hands, he could do that with a single punch. I get the message.

Then Sandy fobbed the boys on me and disappeared for most of Saturday and today. She left me to feed them, clean up after them, keep them occupied, put them to bed, read them stories, the works. Andy and Matty are fun, but I'm exhausted. Sandy came home late last night with a buzz on, probably too much wine at Denise's house. I didn't ask. Then she slept in late, made me fix pancakes for the kids, and went shopping until 4:00. After dinner, which I had to clean, she barely said a word to me. When I put the boys to bed, Sandy was already under the covers. Right now, the sun is still peeking over the horizon, if only a thin red line, and I'm writing in the kitchen all alone. And I'm pooped.

Maybe I deserve the cold treatment. Maybe I don't. But if she knew what I'm going through in order to advance my career, she'd back off. For now, I'll play it cool. She can owe me later.

Flower petals spun like windmills on Gina's terrified face. Evan pulled her from the wreckage, rolled with her on the hot sand, and inserted himself in her. Her screams turned to moans of pleasure. The sand blended into her skin, turning it darker and darker until she had deep brown African pigmentation. He thrust his manhood into her glistening black body. To his surprise, his brother and father stood above his nakedness with disapproving glares and arms folded across their chests. Then he glanced back down at the woman beneath him and instead saw little Carmen Rodriquez.

Evan jolted off the sofa and fell to the hardwood floor. When he realized he was in Sandy's house, he climbed back onto the sofa and rolled onto his back. After tossing and turning and grinding his teeth for several minutes, he rose, turned on a lamp, and checked his watch. Four-thirty a.m. At least ninety minutes before daybreak.

Sleep eluded him. He sat upright. Evan donned his clothes, grabbed the slip of paper with the Fairfield address, stole the photo of Patrick with Gil Harkess, and crept out the front door.

19
Time Has Come Today

Morning sunlight shone on the Fairfield post office. Evan's Plymouth was parked curbside in front of the only doorway. Anyone who entered or exited would pass by his car. Whenever the door swiveled open, he could see the exact postal box – number 2321 – that Harkess gave as his address. If anyone opened that box to retrieve mail, Evan could witness it. He slouched in the car seat to avoid being detected. The photo of Patrick and Harkess rested on the passenger seat to make a quick identification. Also on the seat beside him were the early edition of the Chronicle, the Examiner, a bag of white bread, a package of cold cuts, and a warming six pack of cola. Coins for the parking meter were stacked on the dash-board. It would be a long day, but he was prepared.

The drive to Fairfield took an hour. Once he found the city's only post office, he parked his Plymouth out front and waited for businesses to open for the day. Finding Harkess by this method would be long, dull, and potentially fruitless. But the man had no listed phone number in the area. Also, the postal employees weren't permitted to give out personal information about one of their box renters. So a stakeout of the post office seemed the only alternative.

In two and a half days he needed to report to Fort Ord. As each minute crept by, he worried he might be on a fool's errand. How had he even conceived the notion that he could expose his brother's mysteries, especially in such a narrow window of time? Had the drug kidnapped his logic? He should have been spending time with his family. But to what end? All he had left was Dolores, his drunken mother, his nephews, and Sandy. No, he also had the memory of Patrick and a brotherly obligation to avenge him. The truth of his demise lie buried just beneath the shifting sands, and he was the only archeologist to dig it up. Of this Evan convinced himself.

He wished he had showered and changed clothes before leaving Sandy's house, but he didn't want to wake her or take advantage or stun his nephews when he popped out of the bathroom. On the other hand, he needed a shower and shave. And proper sleep.

Harkess might not show up for days or weeks, he realized. The box might not contain any mail for him to retrieve. The address could have been thoroughly fake, in which case the stakeout would be a waste of time. Evan was willing to spend one full day but no longer than that. As he sat in the Plymouth and repeatedly yawned, he wondered if he'd even last until noon before tedium and the warm sun lulled him to sleep. But napping behind the wheel of his Plymouth might mean missing Harkess. He had only one chance to find the man, so Evan forced himself to remain awake and vigilant. His bladder ached, and he wondered how much longer he could go without a bathroom break.

He glanced up over the top of the newspaper every few minutes as people entered the post office. None of them looked like the frizzy-haired, hook-nosed man in the photograph standing in profile behind Patrick. Evan kept glancing out of habit anyway.

Hours passed. Evan read every article in both newspapers; different reporters but the same basic stories. How Vice President Humphrey flew to Saigon for the inauguration of new South Vietnamese President Nguyen Van Thieu. How the whacky San Francisco mayoral race was coming down to the wire, and how a multi-millionaire named Alioto was the only standout in a horde of incompetents who wanted the office. How war protests played out across the country. How tens of thousands of protesters wrote graffiti on the Pentagon building. The news irritated Evan. Nothing but politics. The world could spin lighter without so much of it, he decided.

Shortly after eleven thirty, a slender girl with long blonde hair entered the post office. She looked twenty-five and was all legs. She wore odd attire for midday: knee-high go-go boots, a skin-tight blouse, and a striped mini-skirt. Every man in the vicinity turned his head at her. A sight right out of Hugh Hefner's magazine.

To Evan's surprise, she fit a key into Harkess's post office box.

He sat upright in the driver's seat and stared to be sure he wasn't mistaken. A short elderly man entered the post office and held the door open for his tiny wife. That gave Evan an unhindered view. Even from twenty-five feet away, he could read the box's number: 2321. The young lady pulled a single envelope from the mailbox slot, locked the door, removed the key, and sauntered out of the post office.

Evan's initial reaction was that the address was a fake. He'd wasted half his day waiting for a ghost to appear. Dejected, he turned over the key in the Plymouth's ignition and revved the engine. Time to go back to San Francisco. What a disappointment.

Then a notion struck him. What if Harkess employed the girl to fetch his mail? Patrick wrote how he used Janey to test drugs. Using others to do their manual labor seemed to be standard operating procedure. Maybe the go-go girl was Harkess's girlfriend.

She crossed Union Avenue to a parking lot and climbed into a shiny blue Chevy Camaro, a sporty number for a young lady. She pulled the car out of the lot and drove away. Evan followed in his Plymouth. She drove west and then turned north without showing signs she knew or cared that he was on her tail. Within minutes, her sports car headed east on Interstate 80 with Evan's car not far behind. The gamble was sure to prove foolhardy, but he played the hunch anyway and followed the go-go girl in the blue Camaro to points unknown.

June 21, 1967

So this is the Summer of Love. That's what all the hippies keep calling it. Everywhere we went today, J and I overheard tourists mentioning the Summer of Love like a hippie mantra. More like an advertising slogan. Seems like expectations are awfully high, no pun intended.

It officially began at daybreak since today is the summer solstice. We joined the slow caravan of lovesters into the park. Organizers had set up stages at that open space out near the Polo Fields. Kind of cramped. Too many people. Everyone was still buzzing about the Monterey shows with the Who smashing instruments and Jimmy somebody or other who lit his guitar on fire. The usual SF bands performed in the park for the solstice, the Dead and Quicksilver, but people seemed disinterested. Maybe too much fun and sun in Monterey.

We also heard that Owsley was back in business at Monterey. A brand new batch of acid cleaner than anything in the Haight.

Found GH on the periphery of the crowd by himself. We spotted him from a distance. Because of his body language and darting eyes, the guy beside me swore GH was a Narc. I waved him over, told him to be cool. He asked if I was prepared. Prepared for what? The scene was as mellow as a church service. An absolute zero chance of rioting. He gave me that narrow-eyed drill instructor gaze, as if I'd disobeyed a direct order. Then he marched off. He seemed almost pissed off that there was no mayhem, not even any bad vibes. I think he's really aching for action.

June 22, 1967

Cops all over the Haight. So is the media. Can't sell under their watchful eyes. SFPD seems to have things under control. A few drunk and disorderly busts, but no violence. Some of the arrests were suburban hippie-haters. Mostly, the cops are letting the scene flow. They can't incite violence with all the cameras and newsmen around.

Met an AP reporter today - Carl Burnblad. Funky name. He learned that I was a Haight Street regular and wanted to ask questions about the scene, how it had evolved, what people were expecting. I declined to answer, even though he seemed genuine and promised anonymity. I still refused but took his calling card.

GH said he can't even give away his STP anymore. Too many bummer trips, and word has spread to stay away from the drug. I told him I'd already given away my entire supply for free. Then I went back to my pad and flushed about 1,500 tabs down the toilet. No more of that nasty shit.

June 28, 1967

Tired of all the runaway losers on the streets. Most of the flower power types have vanished. Few signs of the Diggers. The Haight is now overrun with slacker kids, mostly boys, looking to get high or get laid. They sleep in my doorway. Different kids each night. Got to walk over them every morning. This isn't the scene that the Diggers had in mind. This is more like the violent scenario SG warned about. And it has me on edge.

June 29, 1967

Goddamn bikers. I wandered into the park at sundown and passed Hippie Hill. The place is usually filled with groovy people getting stoned and mellow. Tonight, a phalanx of Hell's Angels stood guard. When I approached, one biker stopped me. Five bucks for the show, he said. What show? Pay up and find out. Curious, I forked over a nickel bag instead, which he readily accepted. Hidden from sight behind a tree stood a group of men in a semicircle. They stared at an activity at the base of the tree. I poked my head in. It was a gangbang.

The girl couldn't have been a day over sixteen, though it was hard to see her face clearly in the twilight. Totally zonked out on booze or drugs or both. Guys took turns doing her. It made me sick.

I walked away without a word and marched straight toward Park Station. How that could be happening in broad daylight only a few hundred yards from a cop precinct blew my mind. I'm still seething from it.

But I never made it to the station door. The police must know I'm a local dealer. I've seen them eyeing me before. Couldn't blow my cover. So I stopped two girls, both customers of mine, and told them to inform the cops. They rushed right over to the station.

Don't know what happened after that, but I hope I don't have to cross paths with the Hell's Angels again. If they ever learn or even suspect that I blew the whistle on their private party, they'll rip my head off, put it on a skewer, and parade it up Haight Street.

20
Hurdy Gurdy Man

The Camaro took the freeway exit at Vacaville and drove past a mile of new tract homes built at the base of rolling hills. Evan hung back to avoid detection. Then the girl ran a red light, and he had to speed up to find her. Maybe she knew she'd been tailed. That didn't matter as long as she was headed toward Harkess and so long as he didn't lose her trail. The Camaro sped along a rural road and turned into a dirt drive at a trailer park. Forty double-wides filled the lot, which was surrounded by a grove of fruit and nut trees. Migrant laborers' homes, Evan guessed. Fruit pickers lived and worked there. Where was the girl going? Was this where Harkess lived? Her car disappeared in the maze of trailers. Evan rolled the Plymouth over rutted dirt paths and searched for the blue Camaro. The midday sun hid behind a cloud. He saw no one in the trailer park. Then he spotted the car parked beside a double-wide at a far corner of the large lot. Evan brought the Plymouth to a stop three trailers away and cut the engine. The cloud passed and sunshine heated up his car, so he rolled down his window. He saw no sign of anyone inside the trailer. The girl had parked her Camaro at an angle as if in a hurry. Maybe she knew she'd been followed and rushed out of the car in a panic.

Evan pondered how to approach the situation. Directness seemed the logical choice. If Harkess didn't live there, then his hunch was a failure and he'd move on. But his gut feeling was that his brother's ex-partner was inside that trailer. He reached for the car door to exit.

Someone pressed a handgun against his temple. He froze with fright.

"What do you want?" a man said in a gravelly voice. Evan couldn't see him. The man stood behind and to his left with his arm and gun thrust into the open car window. Evan raised his hands to show he had no weapons.

"Don't shoot! My name is Evan Dunne."

"That wasn't the question."

"I'm looking for Gil Harkess."

"Why?"

"To talk to him about my brother's murder."

The gun was lowered and the man brandishing it moved into Evan's peripheral vision. Although his hair was cut short, the hooked nose was unmistakable. Chest hairs flared out of the top of his plain white T-shirt like wild brush. Either the stubble on his face was permanent or he had a five o'clock shadow at mid-afternoon. Dark eyes glared at Evan with suspicion. He lowered his piece but kept a finger on the trigger.

"Talk."

"Sandy told me about you," Evan said with a nervous tremolo in his voice. "She gave me a photo and the address you left her. I followed your girl from Fairfield. I just have a few questions."

Harkess's squinty eyes never left Evan's face, as if he were waiting for a blink or a flinch that would signal a lie.

"The facts of Patrick's murder don't add up. The biker, for instance. Awfully convenient. I thought you might have another opinion of what happened. Can we go inside and talk?"

Harkess hesitated, never averting his gaze. Then he pressed the safety on his revolver, stashed it in the waistband of his blue jeans, and motioned for Evan to follow him. He didn't enter the double-wide where the Camaro was parked, however. Instead, he walked to the trailer directly across from the Plymouth. Evan climbed out of his car and followed. Harkess turned and whistled. The go-go girl appeared at the doorway to her trailer down the way. He gave her the OK sign, and she disappeared back into her home. No other tenants appeared in the park. Then Evan climbed two creaky metal steps and entered behind Harkess.

Once inside, Evan was patted down. Harkess wasn't bashful about reaching underneath Evan's shirt, inside his pockets, and even up both thighs. Shades were drawn over every window to vanquish a spectacularly sunny day, so Evan's eyes had to adjust to the dimness. Despite reeking of cigarettes, the place was neat, clean, and bereft of furniture. Satisfied that Evan wasn't hiding anything on his body, Harkess motioned for him to enter. The trailer wobbled as they walked. A refrigerator hummed. Harkess reached inside it and pulled out two bottles of cheap beer. He pried the caps off with an opener and placed one on the ersatz dining table. Then he motioned for Evan to sit at the table beside him. Both men slid into booths and sat. Harkess placed his revolver on the table within easy reach, grabbed a cigarette from a pack, and lit up. Then he offered one to his guest. Evan passed on the Lucky Strike – he couldn't handle non-filtered cigarettes – but he accepted the beer.

"Sandy says hi," Evan began. "She told me how you showed up at the supermarket and gave her your address."

Harkess inhaled deeply, blew out a plume of smoke, and stared without emotion.

"I was in Italy," Evan said. "I don't know if Patrick told you…"

Harkess took another pull on his non-filtered cigarette. The man's silence intimidated Evan. He would have to instigate conversation since his host's defenses were as thick as a bank vault.

"When was the last time you saw Patrick?"

No response. The hook-nosed man inhaled so deeply that one third of his cigarette turned to ash. He reached across the table for an ashtray.

"Did you ever suspect his life was in danger?"

Harkess exhaled another cloud of smoke and flicked his butt into the ashtray. He never took his suspicious eyes off Evan. Patrick had written about the man's caution and wiliness. Whatever knowledge he held would be kept close to the vest. Harkess wasn't likely to tell Evan everything, but he would be invaluable in getting to the bottom of things. There was no sense in lying or withholding what he knew.

"Operation Shunpiker," Evan said.

Up to that moment, the man's granite face expressed nothing more than distrust. But, for a microsecond, Harkess flinched. Those two code words cracked his armored exterior just as Evan suspected they would.

"You and Patrick were under deep cover."

Harkess stubbed out his cigarette and sipped his beer. Then his steely eyes met Evan's gaze. "Supposing I say I don't know what you're talking about...?"

"My brother left behind documents. Operational details... Billy Batson."

The man sat statue still, unwilling to give an inch. His eyes bore right through Evan. Cigarette smoke wafted up through the silent tension. Evan deferred conversation to the hook-nosed man.

"Here's how this is gonna work," Harkess said. "Cast your line first, and then maybe I'll swap fishing stories with you."

"I want to find out who really killed Patrick."

"His murderer is in San Quentin," Harkess said.

"Pulasko never knew Patrick. Or Tom, or Tom-Tom, or whatever the hell name he went by."

"He knew him alright."

"Sure, they had a brief encounter, but—"

"You met this biker?"

"No."

"Then what the fuck are you talkin' about?" Harkess took another swig of beer and then pulled a second cigarette from the pack.

Evan shifted in his seat. "Were you aware Patrick talked to the press? A reporter named Burnblad. Patrick intended to expose the operation."

Harkess lit up his second cigarette and never belied any emotion. He sipped his beer with calculated calm. Evan waited for a reaction, which was slow in coming.

"Intentions and actions are two different things, Boy Scout."

Evan blinked. Clearly, Patrick had discussed Evan's past with Harkess at some point. Harkess knew more than he was letting on. Evan continued.

"Patrick left a diary."

Harkess turned back into stone as if Medusa caught his gaze.

"He was about to turn it over to the reporter, but he died before that occurred. He mailed the diary to me at my mom's home. Patrick knew I was overseas. So he must have mailed the diary to me for safekeeping knowing he could retrieve it at a later date. But that never happened. A strange plan, but maybe he was too stoned to think clearly or too paranoid or both. Whatever the case, the diary awaited me when I returned to San Francisco." He paused to sip his beer. "Pretty fascinating reading. He wrote about you and Janey and TSS and the Diggers and his various exploits in the Haight. He spelled it out as clear as a bell. You two worked for the CIA."

Another long pause followed. After exhaling a noxious cloud, Harkess said, "You'll never get me to admit that."

"I need you to authenticate the diary."

"To who?"

"The press."

Harkess twisted up his face. "Are you nuts?"

"If I take the diary to the press, that means little. But if you back it up…"

"Why would I wanna do that?"

"To reopen the investigation into Patrick's death. To expose the truth."

"What? No, no, your brother's killer is behind bars, man."

"Come on. You can't believe the biker did it. Nothing about it makes sense."

"Of course not. The guy was tripping his brains out and butchered your brother's arm for a briefcase full of pot. There's no sense to it at all."

"Patrick was your partner. Don't you want to know what really happened?"

"I *know* what really happened!"

"Then come forward and corroborate what's in the diary."

Harkess screwed up his face in disbelief. "What do you expect me to do? Appear on *To Tell the Truth*? You and me and Kitty Carlisle. 'Will the real undercover spook please stand up?' Gimme a fuckin' break."

"Patrick deserves better than—"

"He was involved in dangerous business. A biker killed him. Case closed."

"Not for me."

"I can't help that."

The argument was exhausted. Patrick's diary alluded to Harkess's eccentric personality and his odd dichotomy of loyalty and self-preservation. Asking him to turn on his superiors, and his nation by proxy, appeared to be a fool's errand. Asking him to jeopardize his personal safety was equally pointless. Evan's eyes roamed around the trailer in search of a new tactic. Then a notion struck him.

"Why are you hiding out in a trailer park?"

Harkess twitched.

"Shades over the windows. Sending a girl to get your mail. Pulling a gun on strangers. Seems like hiding to me."

He took a long pull on his beer and then said, "Call me a misanthrope."

"You're not with the agency anymore, are you?"

The man stared off into the middle distance but said nothing.

"Patrick tried to get out of the game, and he got killed for it. Am I right? You know they're not going to let you wander around free and easy with the sensitive information you've got stored in your head. That's why you're hiding. Isn't it? Well, how long do you think you can live like this? You've got to bring the truth to bear before you wind up like my brother."

Harkess stared with disbelief. "Man, you have got one overactive imagination."

Up to that moment, Evan was convinced of his position, but Harkess's intimidating glare sent blood rushing to Evan's cheeks. His supposition sounded preposterous, he realized, and he'd done nothing more than made an ass of himself. He was in over his head. Embarrassment spurred him to bolt. He rose from the chair and muttered, "Thanks for the beer."

As he reached for the door handle, Harkess said, "Show me the diary."

"Didn't bring it with me. It's in a safe place, though."

"Bring it here," Harkess said, "and I'll consider throwing you a bone."

"It's in San Francisco. So is the press."

"Meaning?" Harkess stubbed out the last of his second cigarette.

"Come with me to the city." Evan leaned against the chair back. "Once you read what Patrick wrote, you can go with me to—"

"Jesus, slow down, Boy Scout. I'm not making any guarantees. You dig?"

"But you'll come?"

Harkess drank the remainder of his beer. Wheels turned in his head. Evan felt confident that his argument had reached him. "I don't have a car."

"Really?"

"Too easy to trace."

"No problem. I'll drive."

After a long silence, Harkess rose and grabbed the gun from the table. "Wait here."

He entered the small bedroom at the rear of the trailer. Evan heard drawers opening and closing. Evan felt relieved and excited. The gambit had been a longshot up to this point, but confidence swelled in him. Getting Harkess involved was only a first step but crucial. Despite his cynical nature, the man would do the right thing. Evan was sure of it. From the back bedroom, Harkess called out, "Where in San Francisco?"

"Golden Gate Park."

Harkess stepped out of the bedroom wearing a jeans jacket and carrying a small leather bag. A pair of Rayban sunglasses hung from a jacket pocket. No sign of the weapon. His eyes narrowed. "You hid the diary in the park?"

"It's safe. You'll see."

They exited the trailer and Harkess locked the door. Evan walked toward his Plymouth and climbed into the driver's seat. Harkess approached with his bag, but his attention was drawn to the go-go girl peering out her trailer window. He opened the passenger door and rested the bag on the seat.

"Hang on," Harkess said. "I forgot to pay her."

He strode down the dirt drive and climbed the steps. The young woman opened the door just a crack. They exchanged words; Evan was too distant to overhear. Harkess pulled cash from his wallet and handed it over. He spoke instructions to the girl. She listened, stared at the cash, nodded, and stole a glance at Evan in his car. Then she ducked into the trailer, and Harkess returned.

"Okay, Boy Scout. Let's go."

21
Tales of Brave Ulysses

Impatience made him punch the accelerator. The sooner they got to San Francisco, the sooner events could take shape. His passenger's unsettling silence made him edgy, too. Evan wished Harkess would initiate a conversation, just one, but the man was as airtight as a submarine. Chain-smoking gave away his discomfort. Body language suggested calm – his right elbow perched on the open window – but Harkess was surely putting on an act, Evan thought, just as he had on Haight Street under his guise as a hippie drug dealer. Suspecting that his passenger was equally nervous made Evan breathe easier, if only a little, but Harkess's aloofness made him clench his teeth. At least the scenery was pleasant. The Plymouth flew on Highway 80 past rolling hills covered in sun-baked grass. Clouds mingled overhead, occasionally blocking the sun that tilted to the south. The Plymouth's tires whirred over asphalt along multiple lanes full of cars and trucks. With windows rolled down, holding a conversation over the roar of other vehicles and the whooshing wind was a task Harkess showed little interest in taking on. But the lack of repartee made Evan's stomach gurgle.

"Are you sure you're okay with this?" Evan asked. He hollered to be heard over the noise of a passing semi-truck.

"Quit asking," Harkess said. His gruffness intimidated.

"So, what did you think of Patrick?" Evan asked. Even as the awkward sentence tripped out of his mouth, he wished he could retrieve it and produce a better question.

An acrid plume sailed out the window. "What did *you* think of him?"

"Well, he was my brother, so..."

"Don't mean much. I hate my brother."

Evan looked askance at his passenger yet kept his eyes on the highway. He couldn't imagine hating a sibling.

"Oh, yeah? Well, I don't... Didn't." Using the past tense made Evan feel blue. He would have to get accustomed to that.

"Bit of a loner," Harkess said.

Evan frowned. He would never have described Patrick that way. "He had a family."

"That he didn't see all that much."

The description roiled Evan, and he wondered if Harkess was being antagonistic on purpose. The man was difficult, but his opinion might have been valid under the circumstances. Patrick acquired an alternate personality as part of his cover. The man Harkess knew might have been unrecognizable from the brother with whom Evan grew up. But Patrick was no loner.

"Secretive," Evan corrected. Sandy's accusation echoed in his mind. "I suppose that's why they picked him. Right?"

Harkess inhaled his unfiltered cigarette and held the toxicity deep in his lungs before aiming the discharge out the window. He didn't take the bait about discussing the operation. Panning for gold would have been easier than prying information out of Harkess. Yet Evan needed the man to be forthcoming, not just for his need to know but for the press. The reticence raised Evan's ire.

"Did you and Patrick see eye to eye on things?"

"Like what?"

"I dunno. How about girls?"

Harkess grunted, the closest noise he made to a laugh. "He liked the dark meat."

"Not you?"

"Hey, I wish they all could be California girls."

"Janey helped keep Patrick's cover."

Harkess screwed up his face. "Come again?"

"That's what he wrote. By having her around, hippies weren't suspicious of him. They probably respected him for being with a black chick."

"Hmph."

"She seems to have disappeared," Evan said. "Any idea where she's gone?"

"Nope."

"What did you think of her?"

"Just another messed up hippie chick." Harkess took another cigarette from his seemingly inexhaustible pack. Without asking, he then pressed the Plymouth's cigarette lighter to ignite the filament.

"Patrick wrote about you," Evan blurted out.

He waited for Harkess to ask questions, but no response came. When the cigarette lighter was hot enough, he lit up another cigarette, as if oblivious to Evan's statement. Harkess leaned his elbow on the window and puffed away. Rayban sunglasses obscured his eyes as he peered straight ahead through the windshield.

"He grew disillusioned with Operation Shunpiker," Evan continued. "Did you?"

Again, Harkess said nothing. He picked a tiny tobacco leaf from his tongue and flicked an ash out the window. Then he inhaled the cigarette like his lungs subsisted on smoke instead of oxygen. Evan's anger boiled. If Harkess intended to be forthcoming with a reporter, Evan couldn't see how.

Brimming with frustration, he turned the wheel sharply to the right so that the Plymouth swerved over two lanes and onto the road shoulder. Then he slammed on the brakes, which caused the squeal of rubber on asphalt. The car's rear end fish-tailed toward a drainage ditch, but Evan spun the wheel to prevent going off the road. When the Plymouth came to a complete stop, Harkess had both arms outstretched, palms against the dashboard to keep from lurching forward. With the cigarette clutched between his lips, he glared at Evan.

"Get out!" Evan shouted.

Harkess didn't move.

"Get the hell out!"

"Calm down, Boy Scout."

"You have no intention of talking to the press! Do you? So screw you! Get out!"

Harkess whipped the cigarette out the open window, rubbed a hand through his hair, and stared at his lap. But he made no move to exit the car.

"Okay, you want answers," Harkess said. His tone was apologetic. "I can dig that. Drive on."

Evan didn't budge. He stared daggers at the man beside him.

"Go ahead," Harkess said. "You drive, I'll talk."

Evan put the car in gear and drove on. The Plymouth merged into westbound traffic. According to signs, the city of Vallejo lay just a few miles ahead. In another forty minutes, they would cross the Bay Bridge and enter San Francisco.

"We were both recruited from Naval Intelligence," Harkess said. "I'd only met Patrick once at Lemoore. Barely remember him then. But the agency wanted him because he was a local. Knew the city well. I didn't, but... well, I don't know what my qualifications were exactly. They singled me out, and I got a hard on. Never bothered to ask, Why me? I just leapt to attention, saluted, and off I went."

"What does TSS stands for?" Evan asked.

"Top secret shit."

Evan shot him a glance of bemused disbelief. "Are you kidding me?"

Harkess grinned. "That was my nickname. Technical Services Staff, it's called. You won't get me to talk to the newspapers about them."

"Come on," Evan said. "What *are* you going to talk about?"

"I'll verify what's in the diary. Period. I assume he wrote about our assignment."

"Experiments on unsuspecting hippies," Evan said.

"Any specifics?"

"LSD and STP and BZ, among other drugs. Spray canisters. You were testing for crowd control."

Harkess shook his head with scorn and started a new cigarette.

"But he never told anyone person to person," Evan said. "Not his wife, not me, not a soul as far as I know. He wrote stuff down to cover his ass. You know, in the event he was ever arrested or if the CIA disavowed his employment. As insurance against prosecution. Or if he was found dead. Was Patrick's life ever threatened?"

Harkess blew out another column of smoke. "Not by the agency."

"You're sure?"

"Look, the biker killed your brother. Get that through your head. We dealt with some very seamy assholes. You won't get me to overturn Pulasko's conviction."

Evan frowned with disappointment. Harkess sounded sincere. But he wondered whether or not the man was too blindly loyal. "Maybe Pulasko was hired by… someone."

"You're reaching, Boy Scout. There were a lot of dealers on the streets. Profits weren't that great. Most kids didn't have too much spare cash, so we sometimes gave our stash away. The bikers didn't like that. They wanted to kill the competition. Literally."

"Then why didn't they go after Owsley?"

Harkess shook his head with surprise. "Christ, he wrote about him, too?"

"Tell me why you're hiding."

Harkess said nothing and stared out the windshield.

"You know too much. Are you in danger?"

"Cut the shit," Harkess said.

"I'm not naïve," Evan said.

"Look, I'll verify what's in the diary, but that's it. And it has to be under deep, deep cover. Complete anonymity. You need to set that up in advance or no go. If your reporter doesn't dig it, tough fucking luck."

"You're doing the right thing."

"For who?" Harkess sneered.

"For you. The truth will buy you protection."

Harkess muttered, "And you're not naïve?"

The Plymouth wheeled around a bend past an oil refinery with giant cylindrical tanks. Sunshine glinted off bay waters. Far in the distance lay the Bay Bridge, the gateway into San Francisco. A white cottony blanket covered half the city with the massive antenna atop Twin Peaks poking through. Evan passed slower moving cars and rushed to get to the fog-shrouded city, even though he trembled at the thought of what might happen there.

22
Pictures of Matchstick Men

He drove along Fell Street. The one-way boulevard ran from the freeway exit, up and over a hill, and west toward the park. Eventually, Fell Street ran flat and parallel with the Panhandle, which stretched for eight blocks; a popsicle stick of lawns that preceded the larger expanse of Golden Gate Park. Aging Victorian homes lined the north side of the street. Three blocks to the south lay Haight Street. Evan stopped the Plymouth for a red light at Masonic, and Harkess peered at the Panhandle. A young woman in tie-dyed T-shirt and two long-haired, barefoot men sat cross-legged on the grass beneath an oak tree. They passed a joint between them. Few other people traversed the parkway.

"You lived nearby, didn't you?" Evan asked.

"Summertime was crowded, man. Nothing but wall-to-wall hippies." Harkess almost spat out the last word as if it were a curse.

A dark blue sedan pulled up beside the Plymouth on the passenger side. Harkess turned his head toward it. Out of the corner of his eye, Evan spotted the sedan. The driver was a middle-aged man in suit, tie, and fedora. A man of similar appearance sat in the passenger seat. The driver caught Evan's eye and then turned away his gaze. Harkess faced forward. The moment raised Evan's hackles. Did Harkess and the man in the next car just have an unspoken exchange? Or was Evan being paranoid? Both men wore sunglasses despite the fog, which made him doubly suspicious. The light turned green, and he drove on.

"So, where are we going?" Harkess asked. "It's a big park."

"Hang tight."

Evan drove across Stanyan Street and past McLaren Lodge. At the fork, he veered right onto North Drive, which had recently been renamed after fallen President Kennedy. He peered out the rear view mirror at the sedan that followed. The two dark-suited men in the vehicle reminded him of King and Menard. When Harkess leaned forward to adjust his seat, Evan suspected the move was a ruse to catch a view out the passenger mirror. Then Harkess draped his arm out the passenger window so that his hand was down and out of sight. Evan wondered why had he done that. Was it a signal to the sedan? His back stiffened. Something was amiss.

In that instant, the plan changed.

Evan drove past the Conservatory of Flowers. The road curved at the rear of the De Young Museum, and the Plymouth turned left onto a side road past a log cabin. The sedan followed at a distance. Evan's mind scrambled for an ad hoc ploy.

Within moments, the Plymouth rolled up beside Stowe Lake and Strawberry Hill – a mountain surrounded by a circular lagoon. Pine trees, brush, and tall grass rose up in all directions creating a buffer from city life just blocks away. Ducks floated on the green water. A father rowed his family in a canoe rented from the nearby boathouse. Two bicyclists rode the path that encircled the lake. Tourists sat on picnic blankets on the ground, which would have been perfectly in keeping with the lovely surroundings if not for the drifting fog that blotted out the sun. Westerly winds brought skin-tingling chills. Rushing waters sounded nearby.

Evan parked near a bridge that spanned a narrow part of the lake and cut the engine. "Wait here."

"You left the diary *here*?"

"Give me a few minutes."

"What did you do, bury it like pirate treasure?"

"I'll be right back."

Evan strode away from the car and across a footbridge to the base of the five-story hill. To his right was a dirt path that wound around the hill in a rising spiral to its peak. To his left was a dirt path that led to an Asian pagoda at the base of the manmade falls. Directly ahead was a flight of wooden stairs built into the side of the hill. Evan chose that path and climbed to the top.

From above, he was afforded a one hundred eighty degree view of the lagoon. He stood beside the waterfall that rushed over rocks to the lake below. The gush of cascading water drowned out surrounding noises. Looking eastward over the falls, he could see the largest expanse of Stowe Lake, and to the north was a partially obstructed view of his Plymouth parked near the footbridge. The waterfall's white noise calmed him, if only a little. He paced, peered down at the scenery below, and pondered his next move.

Since encountering the sedan on Fell Street, Evan's internal alarms blared, calling for immediate reaction. His faith in Harkess vanished, so he improvised the ruse. The diary wasn't anywhere near the hilltop - nowhere near Stowe Lake, in fact - and he now had no intention of retrieving it for Harkess.

Evan peeked through tall bushes to see his Plymouth below. Harkess stood outside the car, stomped out a cigarette, and craned his neck to peer down the circular roadway. Evan followed his gaze. The mysterious blue sedan was parked along a curve in the lakeside road one hundred yards beyond the Plymouth. Evan squinted through the fog and spotted one of the two suit-and-tie men standing behind a growth of ferns. The man held binoculars to his eyes. Evan stared at the stranger below.

The binoculars were trained on him.

In a split second, a jumble of thoughts flashed through his mind. Harkess had somehow alerted them. His allegiance was still with the CIA. He wanted the diary, probably to destroy it, and had no intention of speaking to the press. Were the men in the sedan out to get him? Logic said yes. He knew too much. Or was that drug-induced paranoia?

He then looked down at the Plymouth, and his heart jumped at the sight of Agents King and Menard inside their black sedan as it rolled up alongside his car.

His adrenaline spiked and his intuition said run. The only routes off the hilltop were the stairs he had just climbed or the dirt path that spiraled around the hill. Moving away from the edge of the falls to avoid being seen, Evan jogged down the spiral dirt path. His heart thumped and he sucked air. Which way out? Strawberry Hill was an island surrounded by a lake with only two bridges. Harkess and the mysterious agents waited at one. His only escape, unless he swam, was across the southern stone bridge.

From the hilltop, the stone bridge was directly below. At the edge of the dirt path was a severe forty-foot descent to the bottom. With a seventy-degree angle to base, the drop was like falling from a two-story home. The hillside was covered in brush, grass, and jutting stones. But there was no better direct route to the bridge; otherwise, he would need to circle the hill and then double back. He stood on the edge and, after taking a deep breath, began the descent down the sheer hillside. Momentum took him down feet first. His back and buttocks smacked against the rocks. His clothing caught on prickly brush. His palms scraped against the dirt. His shoes kicked up dust. But he reached the base with minimal damage.

A dog walker and his hound came upon him. "Hey, pal, you okay?"

Evan didn't answer. He ran up and over the stone bridge and jogged across the asphalt drive that encircled the lake. Then, after looking over his shoulder to be sure no one had tailed him, he slipped into the brush and down a narrow trail to the main roadway.

Still, he wasn't in the clear. Cars were parked all along the roadway. Tourists sauntered along the sidewalk toward the Arboretum and Japanese Tea Garden. Beside the sidewalk was a chain link fence that enclosed the Arboretum. If the sedans came upon him out in the open among the tourists, he'd be trapped. His only escape was over the fence. Despite stares from onlookers, he climbed up and over, slipped inside the arboretum grounds, and blended in with the manicured trees and bushes. The public park was large enough to hide in for hours, and dusk was descending. He could wait for the cover of darkness.

Evan worried what to do about his car. Returning to the Plymouth any time in the next twenty-four hours would leave him exposed. And he suspected that Harkess had arranged for the welcoming party. But how?

The go-go girl. Just before departing, he handed her something more than the money he owed. Maybe instructions or contact phone numbers. The arrival of the two sedans was no coincidence. Harkess had planned it. Evan had deduced the ambush just in time. Leading them to the diary might have resulted in him suffering the same strange consequence as Patrick. But now what?

He sat on a wooden bench hidden behind a cluster of rosebushes, sucked air, bemoaned the turn of events, and wondered what in the world to do next.

July 1, 1967
Last night was a total snafu. Couldn't sleep thinking about it. My conscience is taking a beating.

GH shows up with a new drug. The Technical Services boys whipped it up – tetrahydro-something or other. He says it's the active ingredient in marijuana in capsule form. THC for short. Don't know if they extract it from the plant or if they recreate it in the lab, but everybody knows what THC is. Our instructions from SG were to move it onto the street. So we did. Brazenly.

GH got a Volkswagen van. Actually, he nabbed it from some freaks who owed him for a month's worth of drugs on credit. They were living in the van and didn't expect him to kick them out.

We drove it to the corner of Haight and Clayton. People crammed shoulder to shoulder on the streets. GH got on the roof of the van and turned into a carnival barker, preaching the new drug to everyone in earshot. Check out the beauty of THC. All the high of grass without the smoke. I sat in the back of the van and dealt the stuff. Since the street was jam-packed on a Friday night, we had more customers than product. Within the hour, over 500 capsules sold.

Then a biker named Curious Jack climbed into the back of the van with me. He's an intimidating oaf with stringy, long hair. An ape with a beard. Pretty sure he knows I'm a dealer. We've seen each other around. He closes the van's back doors so there are no witnesses. I'm scanning around for a weapon. Then he asks me if I know what's in the capsules. Yeah, it's THC. Where'd you get it? Like a chickenshit, I said GH was the supplier, I'm just dealing. Then Curious Jack opened a capsule and let the crystalline powder spill out onto his palm. See that, he says. That's PCP. Angel dust. Animal tranquilizer.

I nearly shit my pants.

After I pounded on the roof of the van to get his attention, GH climbed down and joined us in the vehicle. He took a tough-guy attitude with Curious Jack. Who's this bozo? What's he doing in my van? The biker didn't blink. He warned us not to move any more PCP. This shit is our domain, he said. Then he blew the powder into my face and climbed out of the van.

I demanded the car keys, climbed into the driver's seat, and burned rubber. Didn't want to be around when the drugs kicked in and someone either died or went on a rampage. That shit is unpredictable. I'd seen men fly into uncontrollable rages, tear phone books in two, rip at their skin. After what happened with the broad who assaulted me because of her boyfriend's STP bummer, I didn't want to face any more revenge for bad trips, especially from a PCP freak.

When we got back to his flat, I asked GH if it was angel dust. He admitted it was and he knew it. I landed a right fist into his chest and a left hook onto his jaw before he pushed me off. He hollered, I was following orders! Well, why wasn't I informed? GH said he was protecting me. From what? He knew I'd disapprove. PCP was never part of our plan. But TSS wants to see results. They're pushing the agenda. The rioting can't come soon enough for them. So they're instigating with powerful drugs.

GH was right. I completely disapprove of dosing anyone with PCP. The very idea is sadistic and reckless. Even GH can't excuse that bullshit. But he felt compelled to follow orders. The only way to comply with those orders, he said, was to keep me in the dark. He promised never to withhold the truth from me again.

Then he tells me to prepare the BZ. Our instructions are to follow the PCP users, spray the most violent subjects, and record the results. I can't believe it. I called GH a motherfucking liar. He insists it's true. TSS actually wants us to double dose people. BZ on top of angel dust. No fucking way. Murder isn't part of the program.

He backed down. As gung-ho as he is, even GH realized that the order is crazy. Double dosing would result in someone's death – either a victim would croak or someone would take revenge on us. Even in the best-case scenario, we'd be looking at an attempted murder rap. The CIA will cover our asses, he said with a smirk. Translation: we can get away with a little death here and there.

No, I said, we're not officially on the payroll. They'll dis-avow any knowledge of Shunpiker and hang us out to dry. GH conceded my point. But he has a hang-up about dis-obeying orders.

So we agreed to lie and tell SG that the operation went south. Angry bikers disrupted our sales and threat-ened us, so we aborted the BZ phase. Otherwise we'd have risked our own lives. If TSS has spies on the street, which GH insists is true but I heartily doubt, then the ac-tions of Curious Jack will help support our tale.

We also agreed to lay low for a few days until the PCP thing blows over. Selling bad drugs makes us marked men. Then I told GH to get rid of the van first thing in the morning, just in case some prick spots him driving it and takes revenge for being suckered into an angel dust experience.

As I write these words on Saturday afternoon, I'm also drafting a formal complaint to SG regarding all that went down last night. In my opinion, Operation Shunpi-ker has plunged us into murky waters, and I don't like swimming in these black depths. Granted, I knew when I signed on that our experiments were directed at the drug culture, which takes substances willingly for recreational purposes. That's why they were chosen for the operation – small risk of reprisal from test subjects, few of whom would be aware of their involvement. But BZ and PCP and STP aren't recreational grade drugs. They're too po-tent and dangerous.

I was also told we'd be targeting radicals with these drugs. I always assumed that meant political radicals. Revolutionaries. The Mobe. Anti-war agitators. Well, al-most none of those types live in the Haight. They never really have. That crowd is in Berkeley or with the Black Panthers in Oakland. Yes, the Haight still has Timothy Leary turn-on dropouts and the Diggers, but they're in-creasingly a minority here. Most newcomers are runaways like J. Many are suburban teens who think the Monkees epitomize hippie culture. SG and the select few at TSS who are privy to Operation Shunpiker don't seem to comprehend what's happening on the ground here.

From what I've heard, soldiers have the same gripe in Vietnam. Makes you wonder who's running this damn country.

23
Can't Find My Way Home

Sleep beckoned like a siren song. Evan wanted to doze off in the Arboretum, but paranoia nudged him awake. He sat in zombie stupor and contemplated his plan of action, which taxed his tired mind. A park attendant strolled by and announced that the Arboretum was about to close for the night; staying meant being locked behind the gates inside the walled garden until morning. Time to move. Sunset provided cover, so he crossed the road, walked over the baseball fields, slipped through to Sharon Meadow, and found his way to Hippie Hill.

Darkness winnowed the number of hippies hanging out on the hillside to just a dozen. No one talked. One guitarist strummed out of rhythm with three bongo players. Others sat and listened, or not, in drug-induced somnambulism. Evan sat apart from the huddle and kept a wary eye on the surroundings. No cops that he could detect. No sign of Harkess.

Then an idea popped into his mind: Robby's free pad. No one would think to look for him there. Evan left the hippies to their tribal gathering and darted across Stanyan Street. Then he strode up Waller toward the dilapidated apartment house.

The unhinged door was open, just as it had been the previous day, so Evan entered the crash pad without knocking. Voices echoed from upstairs. In the main living room sat the beret-wearing hippie. A teenage girl lounged beside him on the sofa. She wore painter's pants and a denim jacket two-sizes too large for her medium frame. A painted peace symbol covered the pimples on her wan face like connect-the-dots art. Her stringy brunette hair hung flat and lifeless. She draped her legs over the sofa arm and smoked a cigarette. Her eyes flashed defiance.

Evan waved to the beret wearer. "I need a bed."

The hippie made no move to assist him. He appeared even more stoned than earlier. "Remove your face when you enter, masked man."

Evan hesitated, unsure what that meant, and then began climbing the stairs to the bedrooms on the second floor. He stopped when the teenage girl called out to him.

"The inn's full tonight."

Evan eyed the girl.

"Every bed taken," she said. "I got dibs on this." She then stretched out on the sofa to stake her claim to it and continued smoking.

Evan trudged back down the stairs and into the living room. His sluggish mind tried to concoct a new plan, but he couldn't think straight. If only he had his car, he'd be free to go wherever he pleased. But he dared not go into Golden Gate Park to retrieve it. Harkess and his shadowy partners probably awaited him there in ambush. Then an idea came to him. He sidled up to the beret-wearing hippie and reached for his wallet.

"Wanna earn twenty bucks?"

The stoner took in Evan. "Your aura is orange and blue. I see your soul. It's electric."

Evan blinked.

"His acid kicked in about an hour ago," the girl said.

"What about you then? Want twenty bucks?"

Without a hint of intimidation, she replied, "Nothing kinky."

"Can you drive?"

"Not a stick."

"Automatic?"

"Yeah. Why?"

"I need you to go get my car."

The girl sat up and took his request seriously. He removed the keys from his pocket and showed them to her.

"It's at Stow Lake. Drive it here to me. What's your name?"

"Mirabelle." The dainty name seemed incongruous with her appearance. "Robby wants me to stay with this one. Keep him mellow."

"I'll stay here. It shouldn't take you long."

"Why don't you go get it yourself?"

"If you want the cash, don't ask questions."

"Right. And then the pigs bust me for running drugs. No thanks."

"There aren't any drugs in the car. Search it once you get there. Nothing illegal at all. Just a duffle bag full of clothes in the trunk."

She eyed him with suspicion. "How am I supposed to get to Stow Lake?"

"On foot, I guess."

She slumped back into the sofa. "Shit, that must be, like, a mile. I'm not walking a mile for twenty bucks."

Evan reached in his wallet and pulled out an additional twenty-dollar bill. "Another twenty bucks when you return."

"Forty more," she said.

Evan hesitated and then nodded. "Okay."

She sat up, paused to consider the offer, and said, "What's the make and model?"

Evan had her retrieve a pencil and scrap paper, which Mirabelle had great difficulty finding in the sparsely furnished crash pad. When she finally returned with a pen and notepaper, Evan wrote down his make, model, and license plate number. He also drew a map of the Plymouth's location.

"If it isn't there, just bring me back the keys. Then you'll get the additional forty."

Mirabelle stuffed the keys and map into the pocket of her dungaree jacket, clambered to her feet, and sauntered to the front door. Then Evan rose and stopped her at the doorframe.

"Oh, and don't park the car in this driveway. Circle till you find a spot."

"Are you serious? That could take all night."

As was the case throughout San Francisco, street parking was at a premium. "Try anyway. Please. If you can't find a space, pull in here. And, hey, I really appreciate this."

She walked off into the night, and he returned to the living room. Evan pushed aside doubts about the girl. He was too tired to worry whether or not she would succeed. Chances are, the Plymouth had either been towed or was still being watched for his return. If the girl didn't come back, then three scenarios were possible. First, the car was gone and she chose not to come back. That seemed unlikely because he promised more money and Mirabelle claimed dibs on Robby's sofa for the night. Secondly, Harkess might try to nab her and force the girl to cough up Evan's whereabouts. In which case, if she didn't return within forty-five minutes, he needed to leave before she led Harkess to him. The third scenario he didn't want to think about.

The beret-wearer sat on the sofa and tripped in silence, oblivious to Evan's presence. That suited him fine. Voices drifted from elsewhere in the large house. He couldn't be sure if what he heard was laughter or crying, but Evan had no intention of investigating. The soft, dirty sofa claimed his body. He didn't fight the drowsiness. His eyelids fell and consciousness caved in.

The beret-wearer giggled like an infant and jolted Evan awake. His chin had fallen to his chest, and he suspected he might have been snoring. The grinning hippie on the sofa beside him waved his arms through the air as if conducting an orchestra underwater.

Then Robby and two bearded young men appeared. They stood in the doorframe and assessed the tripping hippie. Robby frowned. "Where's Mirabelle?"

"She's running an errand for me. Don't worry. I've kept my eye on him."

Robby's friends ignored Evan, sat cross-legged on the floor, and got busy with a plastic sandwich bag full of marijuana. Each carried a folding record album, which they used as a tool to separate the pot seeds from the stems and leaves. Robby slouched onto one of the sofas.

"What sort of errand?" The question carried a heavy dose of suspicion.

"I sent her to get my car. She should be back soon."

Robby raised an eyebrow. "To get your car? She ain't old enough to drive."

Evan blinked. "She said she was."

"Hmph. You'll never see your car again."

Evan shrugged. "The odds were already against it anyway. But if she shows up with it intact, that's golden. Hey, is there a back way out of here?"

Robby furrowed his brow. "Why? You need to make a getaway?"

"Let's hope not."

"Don't go bringin' trouble to my pad. We get hassled enough as it is."

Evan said nothing. The hippies paid little attention and kept sorting pot on the floor.

"There's a back yard," Robby said. "But this is San Francisco, man. All the houses..." He pressed his palms together.

"I know. I'm a native." As was the case all over the city, residences were built with no space whatsoever between them. That meant no alleys or other routes of escape. But he also knew that most garages were accessible through the back;

climb over a fence, into another yard, through a garage, and onto the next street. "Which way?"

Robby pointed. "Through the kitchen."

Evan marched down the hall past an open doorway where stragglers slept on two bare mattresses tossed on the hardwood floor. The kitchen's tile floor had never seen a scrub brush, and the stink of rotting garbage wafted as he passed through. A flimsy card table served as the sole dining area with three mismatched chairs around it. The back door creaked when opened and led onto a mudroom, similar to his mother's home. Then he walked out onto a yard of overgrown weeds to a five-foot-high wooden fence. He looked over the obstruction into the neighboring yard. As he suspected, a multi-car garage filled the ground level of the apartment building with a clear shot to the garage door. Satisfied, he doubled back into the hippie crash pad, through the kitchen, and down the hall to the living room.

"I can taste your heartbeat, Robby," the tripping beret wearer said. "It's cinnamon and salt."

Evan stood by the front windows and pulled back the grungy drapes just enough to peek outside. No traffic passed under the streetlamps.

"Did you find what's-her-name?" Robby asked.

"Not yet," Evan said.

"That kid Ellis steered you wrong, didn't he?"

"Yes and no."

Robby kibitzed with the pot-sifting hippies on the floor. They made small talk that Evan neither understood nor cared about. He stood sentry at the window. With each set of headlights that passed the apartment house, his breathing fell shallow. But his Plymouth didn't show. By his estimate, Harkess or the agents might arrive within another fifteen minutes, give or take. If he lingered, they might pounce before he could escape.

Minutes passed, and then there it was – his green Plymouth Valiant. Mirabelle could be seen at the wheel. The car rolled down the street without stopping. Good, he thought. She was following his instructions and searching for parking. Then the Plymouth drove out of view. Evan kept his eyes on the street before making a move.

Minutes later, Mirabelle appeared on foot, strode up the stairs, and entered the apartment house. When she entered the living room, Robby stared at her with a surprised smirk. Evan held out his hands for the keys, which she handed over.

"Parking was a bitch," she griped.

"Did anyone hassle you about the car?" Evan asked.

"Nope." She took two twenty-dollar bills from his hand.

"Nobody approached you?"

"Nope." She flopped onto the sofa and dangled the cash to the hippies sifting pot on the floor. "You guys selling?"

"Where's it parked?" Evan asked.

"On Cole, corner of Waller."

Evan peeked out the drapes one last time, and then his heart quickened. The black sedan was double parked in front of the apartment house. Agent Menard sat at the wheel and stared up at the building. Had he spotted Evan peeking out the window? Adrenaline flowed. Time for action.

Evan dashed down the hallway. "I was never here. Okay?"

Before Robby could respond, Evan ran into the kitchen and grabbed a wooden chair in stride as he bolted out the back door. Then he darted across the weed-filled yard to the fence, set the chair in place, climbed atop it, and hoisted himself over the fence onto the asphalt of the neighboring property. Pain stung his left ankle when he landed from the five-foot drop. Limping through the ground level garage, he found a doorway onto the street. Before passing through, he looked back at Robby's place but saw nothing.

Evan raced through the garage without being spotted, outside onto the sidewalk, and then among the shadows. He stopped at the street corner. Streetlights illuminated him more than he wanted. He peered around the corner but saw no sign of the black sedan or the shadowy men. Then he ran down Cole Street in search of his Plymouth, which was inexpertly parallel parked beside a fire hydrant. No matter. He hopped in, turned over the ignition, and drove off. The black sedan never appeared in the rear view mirror. Relief washed over Evan. But it was temporary. He was still tired and paranoid and at a loss for where to turn or who to trust.

July 3, 1967

GH called me at home, something we agreed he would never do. Fortunately, I answered instead of Sandy or the boys. He said SG ordered us back onto the streets. But we agreed to lay low for a week. GH claims we never discussed leaving the Haight. I recall that we did, that I would go home through the Fourth of July to let things cool off. GH told SG everything that occurred on Friday night, and he sounded pissed off. Wants us back out there for tomorrow night. Maybe he's afraid the fireworks will foment a rebellion. Christ, the people running this circus have their heads screwed on all wrong. I told GH that I'm staying put. I also told him my report will have addendum re: my misgivings about the operation. He advised against that. It's not a complaint, I said, just my opinions. He said, Keep your opinions to yourself. I can't get behind that. Not one damn bit. This is my ass on the line.

July 4, 1967

Fog draped over the city, as usual, so the fireworks were a joke. Andy complained. Matty cried. Sandy tolerates their behavior better than I do. I snapped. She snapped at me. Matty stopped crying, but only because my reaction frightened him. We drove to the Presidio with half of the other drivers in San Francisco, so it took us an hour to get home. A long, slow, silent ride.

Happy fucking birthday, USA.

July 5, 1967

Sent in my weekly report along with my typewritten personal opinions about the operation to date. I felt terrible reluctance given what GH said the other day. But my conscience needs clearing. Awaiting a response.

July 6, 1967

J is coming out of her doldrums. Cleaned up the flat for me while I was away. Didn't expect that. I wonder if she has an ulterior motive. She got high with me today, but she's not ready yet for sex. Don't know if she ever will be. Great. Now I've got two women in my life who won't sleep with me.

July 7, 1967

Still no reply from SG regarding my opinion letter. He's probably on vacation while I'm stuck here in acidville with PCP freaks and murderous bikers who might be on the warpath for me. Thanks for the back-up, Sid.

July 8, 1967

Hippies on the cover of Time magazine. The lead story. How crazy is that?

24
A Whiter Shade of Pale

A tap at the window made Sandy leap up from the sofa with fright. She grabbed little Matt in her arms to protect him. Andy peered over the sofa at his uncle peeking through the pane. Evan waved and pointed toward the back door. Sandy scowled, exhaled, and then nodded.

After a snick of the deadbolt unlocking, the door swung open. Sandy still held Matt in her arms and backed inside to permit Evan to enter. "Why are you sneaking up on me like that?"

"Sorry." He reached out and rubbed Matt's blonde hair. "Hiya, buddy."

"You're driving everybody crazy with worry, Evan." Sandy carried her son through the kitchen to the living room where Andy sat watching television. She pointed to the princess phone that rested on an end table. "Call home right now."

He hesitated. Phone lines were easy to tap. Coming to Sandy's house was risky enough. Making a phone call from her living room would prove his whereabouts to anyone listening in, and if his mother's telephone was bugged…

"Evan!" Sandy's voice carried bite that he couldn't refuse.

He spun the telephone dial, and then the phone rang at the Dunne house. After three rings, Dolores answered.

"Hey, it's me," Evan said.

"Where are you?"

"At Sandy's."

"Come home."

"Not yet."

"You're scaring the shit out of me, Evan! I've had Leiber and his guys out searching the whole city for you! What the hell are you up to? Sandy told me some crazy shit about Patrick and the CIA and, and goddamnit, you're just out of the hospital for a drug OD! Where the hell have you been? Mom is having a nervous breakdown!"

"I'm okay." Evan looked askance at his young nephews who sat quietly on the sofa and watched the Flintstones. Raising his voice in response to Dolores's anger would only alarm the boys. He remained cool. "When are we spreading the ashes?"

"Tomorrow. Two o'clock. Come home, Evan."

"Soon." Then he hung up.

Sandy had glared at him throughout the conversation with arms akimbo. Her harsh expression didn't change when he placed the phone on the cradle. She glanced at her sons, both engrossed in the cartoon, and motioned for Evan to follow her. They left the boys in the company of Fred and Barney and took seats in the kitchen at the round formica-topped table. She leaned close and whispered so the kids wouldn't overhear.

"You need help, Evan."

He ran his dirty hands across his short-cropped hair. "You can't imagine what I've been through today."

"What are we supposed to do when they come for you?"

That turned Evan's head. He flashed surprise. "Who? Has Harkess been here?"

"Harkess?" Sandy's face twisted in confusion. "I'm talking about the police. Dolo and I assume you're dodging the draft."

He chuckled, but the notion wasn't far-fetched. He could see why they might think it. "No, no, don't worry about that."

She looked at him sideways and cocked an eyebrow with skepticism.

"Swear to God, I'm going on Saturday," he said. "You need to know the facts, Sandy. I hid everything from you because I didn't know the truth myself. It's all a bit fantastical. But now that I've heard it from the source... Patrick worked for the CIA. Gil Harkess was his partner. They were assigned to flood the Haight with—"

She threw up her hands. "Stop it! Just stop this nonsense!"

"I've spent the afternoon with Harkess. He verified everything."

That made her freeze. She teetered between belief and doubt. Andy peeked his head around the kitchen doorway. His face was flushed with concern.

Evan spotted him and said, "It's okay, pal. We're just having grown-up talk."

Sandy rose to attend to her son. She poured a glass of tap water at his request and escorted him back to the sofa beside Matt. After a moment, she returned to the kitchen and spoke in whispers to avoid alarming the boys.

"You met that hippie? Where?"

"I tracked him to Fairfield. He confirmed the whole CIA thing. And he wants something from me. Patrick's diary."

Sandy stared into his eyes for any hint of lying or drunkenness or drug use. His gaze was steel. Although the story sounded preposterous, the mention of the diary gave her pause. Her head cocked to one side.

"He used to keep a diary, but..."

"I have it. Patrick sent it to me. He wrote down all the—"

"He sent it to you? How?"

"Long story. Here's the point; he wrote down daily events about his CIA drug operation. Completely off-the-charts illegal. Patrick didn't even like what he was doing and wanted to quit. He was afraid the government would leave him dangling in the wind if he was ever arrested. The diary was the only leverage he had against prosecution. A get-out-of-jail-free card. Patrick was trying to expose the operation to the press before they could make him a patsy. But then you spotted him on the street and things changed. Two days later he was found dead. Just before his murder, though, he mailed the diary to me, as if he anticipated something bad was about to happen to him."

Her creased brow and pained expression suggested he'd divulged information faster than she could digest it, like a two-minute crash course in astrophysics. Her lower lip trembled.

Evan said, "I think the CIA knew he was about to expose the truth and had him eliminated."

The corners of her mouth curled downward, and her eyes moistened. Her thin hands covered her face to wipe away erupting emotions. Then she leaned back in the chair and turned her head away. "How did I get reeled into this family? You people. You Dunnes. You're all goddamn crazy."

"Think about it, Sandy. Patrick told you he was working undercover for Naval Intelligence. Well, it wasn't the Navy. Those checks he got from the Maskelyne Group? It was the CIA. But everything else he told you - what little he said about it - was on the mark. He couldn't tell you details because then you'd be in trouble. Or in danger. And his orders were to not tell you anything. The fact that he discussed matters at all was a security breach."

With head in hands, she stared off into the recesses of her mind. Tears and her running nose dripped onto the kitchen table, but she didn't elicit a sound. Neither of them spoke.

Only dialogue from the Flintstones on the living room television filled the silence. Without lifting her head, she whispered, "You're not well, Evan."

Her reaction hurt his feelings. "If you don't believe me, ask my Uncle Stu."

Sandy's reddened eyes flared at him. "Your uncle told me not to trust anything you say."

Evan blinked. "What?"

"You had a drug overdose, Evan. You're not yourself."

"Uncle Stu said that?"

"He knows what drugs can do, and he knows people who can help you."

Evan scowled at his uncle's interference. The ex-cop wasn't helping at all. "Look, if you don't trust me, trust the diary," he said. "Written in Patrick's own hand."

"Fine, let's see it." Her reaction was curt and venomous.

"It's hidden."

She threw up her hands in disgust.

"I'll get it and bring it here," he said. "You need to see for yourself."

She couldn't look at him. Instead, Sandy wept without making a sound, a practice of having to hide her emotions from her young sons.

After thirty seconds of uncomfortable silence, Evan said, "Mind if I crash here tonight?"

She shot daggers at him. In hushed anger, she said, "Go home, Evan."

He rose from the seat just as the Flintstone's theme song played on television to signal the end of the program. "I'll go get the diary," he said. "You'll see, Sandy."

"Mom!" Matty called out from the living room. "Show's over!"

Sandy stood, wiped tears from her cheeks, and regained composure. Evan walked to the back door. Before he stepped out into the night, she whispered to him again.

"Please, go home. Your poor mother… and Dolo. For your own sake."

Evan proffered a slight, insincere nod and then slipped out the door into the darkness. Unlike most neighborhoods in San Francisco, the West Portal district homes weren't built abutting one another. With plenty of room separating houses, Evan darted through back yards and between buildings. Hunkering down to avoid detection, he jogged through the dark to Wawona Street where he'd parked his Plymouth at a vacant curbside spot. He scanned the avenue for signs that he was followed. Satisfied that all was clear, he dashed beneath a streetlight to the car, jumped in, revved the engine, and sped away into the night toward Golden Gate Park. It was time to retrieve the diary.

July 9, 1967

Too many runaways on the street. My conscience can't handle it. These kids have no cash and aren't buying from me, and even if they did I wouldn't sell to them. They're not the political/societal revolutionaries we're assigned to disrupt. They probably couldn't even tell you what the initials LBJ stand for. They're just looking to be part of something bigger than themselves. But this scene has become nothing more than a media invention. Oh, sure, the Diggers still maintain their thing, but they've gone sour on the Summer of Love. True hippie culture can still be found at places like the Psychedelic Shop or the I/Thou or the Trip Without a Ticket, but the Psych Shop just closed down from lack of sales. This Summer of Love idea is just commercialization, and most of the Haight residents know it. That's why the Diggers objected in the first place. When the summer began and the flood of kids washed in, whatever movement existed went astray.

In effect, the media did our job for us. Subversion through drugs wasn't the answer. Mass media manipulation – that's how you deconstruct a revolution. Somebody should tell that to psy-ops in Vietnam. Forget bombs and bullets. Destroy the enemy by co-opting their ideals. Manipulate their message. Overwhelm their infrastructure, and watch the center collapse.

I no longer see a point to this operation. Most of the kids on the street are runaways like J with no political persuasion at all. They're not revolutionaries. All they really care about is music, making the scene, and drugs. They're hedonists and escapists. The true radicals are off protesting elsewhere, trying to raise the Pentagon and other buffoonery. We're not needed here.

25
Get Off of My Cloud

Paranoia fought exhaustion to keep him alert, and Evan's darting eyes took in everything in sight. When he turned northbound from Wawona onto 19th Avenue, a busy six-lane thoroughfare with a median strip divider, a vehicle he hadn't noticed before appeared in his rear view mirror. It, too, turned onto 19th from Wawona. Although the car was one block behind, streetlamp illumination made it clear. The black sedan was on his tail. Evan's heart rate jumped. They must have staked out Sandy's house. The shadowy men had found him.

Nighttime traffic was heavy, so once he merged the Plymouth into the center lane he had little room to maneuver. By the same token, other northbound vehicles, including a large delivery truck, merged to block the black sedan's direct access to his Plymouth. It remained two cars behind. As for evasion, 19th Avenue didn't permit left turns – not legally, anyway – and a stoplight appeared on every other intersection.

Evan would have to roll with traffic until an opportunity arose to shift lanes.

The moment arrived. A Volkswagen in the right lane jerked along and couldn't keep pace with the cars before it. A full car length opened to Evan's right. He yanked the steering wheel and hit the accelerator with just enough room to avoid the VW bug. Then his Plymouth darted along the lane with traffic and, without signaling, turned right onto Taraval. He sped up the block, did a U-turn, and was back at the intersection just as the traffic light turned green. That provided an open drive westbound across 19th Avenue with all northbound traffic stopped. As his Plymouth crossed the broad boulevard, he turned his attention to the black sedan, which was still blocked in the center lane behind the delivery truck. He couldn't make out the driver, and the sedan made no effort to give chase. Still, he was convinced it was King and Menard. Evan then sped the Plymouth along Taraval toward the ocean, and he breathed with relief.

Rather than driving straight, which would have made him easier to follow, he zigzagged the car throughout the Sunset District, the vast residential neighborhood that filled the southwest quadrant of the city. Evening traffic along the residential avenues was light, and that made speeding less dangerous. But stop signs at every other intersection impeded Evan's escape. Still, he maneuvered the Plymouth north one block, then west one block, then north, then west, over and over, until he reached Sunset Avenue and Judah. He then sped north into Golden Gate Park. South Drive then took him all the way out toward Ocean Beach. Traffic at the extreme end of the park was sparse. One half block shy of the Great Highway that ran parallel to the beach, he slowed the Plymouth at a curbside. No other vehicles were in sight. Evan cut the engine and climbed out of the car. He approached the structure that rose up just above the treetops but was almost obscured at ground level by an overgrowth of bushes and pines.

His secret hiding place. The north windmill.

San Franciscans rarely visited the twin windmills that stood at the western end of Golden Gate Park. Some locals didn't even know they existed. Both structures had been in neglectful disrepair for as long as Evan could recall and neither functioned. The blades didn't even twirl despite strong winds that blew off the Pacific. As far as Evan could tell, the windmills were merely dilapidated, antiquated ornaments left to rot. One block to the north, just beyond the trees and bushes and overgrown grass, the carnival sounds of Playland at the Beach mingled with the crashing of waves on the beach and the whipping wind. Evan stepped through overgrowth to the base of the windmill. With dilated eyes, he stared into the darkness for anyone who might witness him; teenage lovers or perverts in the woods. Satisfied that no one was in sight, he stepped down three short steps to the iron doors at the base, pulled one open, and slipped into the windmill's pitch-black interior.

The chill and din of the ocean wind dropped drastically inside. He flicked his Zippo lighter, which offered only vague illumination of the twelve-foot-wide round room. Something scurried across the dirty cement floor. Maybe a rat. Evan didn't want to know. He walked into a spider web and wiped it away from his face. Evan kicked against something on the floor that made a tinny racket. His lighter shone on an empty beer can that rolled across the cement. That bothered him. There were no beer cans on his previous visit. Someone else had been inside the windmill in the past few days. Teenagers getting drunk, he guessed.

He climbed the wooden staircase that rose up through the windmill's interior. The steps creaked beneath his weight, and he wondered if they would hold. His lighter grew too hot to the touch so he extinguished the flame and climbed the stairs in darkness. Yet to his surprise, light emanated from the first landing. The flickering of candlelight danced on the wall. Evan's heart thumped. After hesitating to hear, he climbed to the landing.

Then came an effeminate voice. "Randy?"

A bespectacled middle-aged man in a gabardine suit and tie sat huddled on a cement block. Two candles illuminated his pockmarked face with trim moustache. A bottle of red wine was perched between the candles. The man trembled as Evan ascended the stairs and clutched his knees.

"Are you Randy?" he said.

Evan didn't respond. Instead, he searched the landing. Unnerved by the stranger, he wanted to snatch the diary and run. But where was it?

Wooden cross beams built into the structure acted as narrow shelves, and that was where he'd left the book. The bowel of an abandoned structure was as secure a spot as any he knew. It never occurred to Evan that other people would trespass in the windmill. He quixotically regarded it as his own private space where everything, including him as a boy, was safe from detection and harm. But apparently, things had changed. Strangers had invaded his childhood hiding place. And now his brother's diary was missing.

26
Don't Bring Me Down

The floor was bare except for dirt and chewing gum wrappers and three empty beer bottles and two spent condoms. He spun around the cramped space but saw no sign of it. Had he not left it right there on the ledge? The diary was nowhere in sight.

"Where's the book?" he snarled at the man in the gabardine suit.

The stranger pressed a trembling hand to his mouth and whimpered, "You're not Randy?"

"Stand up!" Evan ordered.

The man glared with fright and didn't move. Evan then pulled him up by the suit collar and forced him to one side. Then he grabbed a lit candle and inspected the space around the cement block. No sign of the diary.

"What did you do with the book?"

"I-I-I don't know w-what you mean."

Evan pressed his nose close to the man's face. "The book! What happened to the book?"

The stranger cowered. His eyes bulged with fear. "Don't hurt me!"

"I'm not going to—Did you see a book in here?"

"No! I swear! I never saw any book!"

Evan then took the candle down the wooden stairs and searched each step. He peered into every nook and crevice. Then he scoured the base at the iron door. Aside from the beer can, he saw nothing. His breathing labored. Then he rushed up the stairs, brushed past the stranger on the landing, and went to the ascending stairs that lead higher up into the windmill. But a thick, bolted door blocked the way and couldn't be budged. If the diary were any further up into the structure, he would need a crowbar to rip the rusty locks off that door. And if the second staircase could have been entered someone would have done so long ago.

Where was the diary?

With the candle dripping wax on his left hand, Evan rushed down the steps to the base, out the iron doors, and searched the exterior of the windmill. Wind whipped tree branches and leaves and blew out the candle. He tried flicking his Zippo to life, but the wind killed it each time. Down on his hands and knees, Evan scoured the bushes and overgrowth that surrounded the windmill. His heart pounded with worry. Involuntary whimpers escaped him. He wanted to holler and cry. The search proved futile in the darkness, but he kept feeling around, to no avail.

Then he heard voices nearby. He walked through the brush and almost fell down an embankment. From the top of the ridge, he saw the huge, open tunnel that ran underneath the roadway just beyond the windmill. He remembered it from his youthful runaway experience. Five men stood in the darkness. Tips of burning cigarettes glowed near their faces. The conversation was cheery. A bottle passed between them. Two men held hands. Homosexuals, he reckoned, like the effeminate man in the windmill.

Just as he was about to climb down the ridge and demand to know what had become of the diary, a siren blared.

Red lights flashed through the trees. Evan hit the ground and flattened out. The homosexuals in the tunnel scattered. A cop car screeched to a halt, and officers poured out. From his hidden vantage point, Evan saw three burly SFPD officers barrel toward the windmill's iron doors.

He froze in place. Getting up and walking away would only make him look suspicious. If it was a bust, he wanted no part of it. Instead, Evan lay motionless in the deep brush.

Seconds later, the man in the gabardine suit was escorted out of the windmill and toward the police car with hands cuffed behind his back. Two of the three cops put him into the backseat. Another cop inspected the tunnel with a flashlight and stooped to pick up a still smoldering cigarette and a bottle of cheap booze.

A flashlight beam ran up Evan's back and shone on his face. He squinted and flushed.

"C'mon, get up," a hefty male voice commanded.

Evan rose to his feet. The flashlight beam roamed all over his face and body, and for a moment Evan could make out the beefy officer before him. His mind raced. What excuse could he provide that would sound at all plausible? Certainly not the truth. He couldn't admit trespassing inside the windmill.

"What the hell are you doing in the bushes?" the cop asked.

Evan said nothing. His shoulders slumped. The situation deflated him, and he knew better than to complicate matters with excuses.

"Let's go," the cop said. He then took Evan by the arm and guided him out of the bushes, past the windmill, and to the police cruiser. The officer asked for identification, and Evan handed it over. Then he was placed in the backseat beside the stranger in the gabardine suit who sat weeping.

"Please take these cuffs off me," the stranger whimpered to the arresting officer. But the cop ignored him. From a squawk box on the dashboard, a flat-toned police dispatcher announced a vice squad bust in Golden Gate Park. When the officer spoke his name into the radio handset, Evan's muscles tensed with anxiety. He tried to defend himself, but the cop left the vehicle to round up homosexuals.

Evan sat back, closed his eyes, and wished the past fifteen minutes had never happened. For once, he prayed this was another drug hallucination. It just had to be. Not only had he lost his brother's diary, he had to face this humiliation. He couldn't decide which was worse. Evan's heart sagged in his chest. His life was a catastrophe. The BZ assault was bad enough. His friends and family probably considered him a druggie because of it. How would his family interpret an arrest in a homosexual raid? What a royal fuck up. This would be a stigma he'd never outlive.

"What happens now?" the effeminate man said in a trembling voice. Evan paid no attention. He could only gaze out the patrol car window into the darkness at the windmill. What a stupid place to hide the diary, he thought. But he had no idea this location had become a hideout for perverts. Still, he hated himself for it.

"What will become of us?" the handcuffed man said. The twirling red light from another squad car flashed across his face. His lower lip quivered. "I have to be to work in the morning. Do you think they'll let us go? I mean, I wasn't doing anything. Right? You saw me. I wasn't doing anything. Well, trespassing, I suppose, but nothing else."

"Shut up!" Evan barked. He laid his head back on the seat and sighed while the effeminate man whimpered.

A paddy wagon arrived. SFPD officers climbed out of the van, opened the rear doors, and began herding men inside. Despite the commotion, sleep tugged at Evan. If he dozed, maybe he'd awaken in his own bed at home. No, that was denial. This was sad reality. If you don't like reality, change it. So said the sexy hippie chick. Under these circumstances, that was a naïve, empty slogan. But if he could change reality, he wouldn't hesitate.

The car door opened beside him, and a police officer reached inside to guide him out of the backseat. Standing before him were three men in dark clothing: Agent King, Agent Menard, and Gil Harkess.

"He's all yours," the cop said.

July 10, 1967

Rough stuff on the street yesterday well into the night. My nerves are still jangled from it all. The day started out tense. Never saw so many tourists, all coming to watch the freak show. Wall-to-wall people spilled onto the street. Some came to taunt. Saw three separate altercations between straights and hippies in the afternoon.

Around four o'clock, a buzzcut teen knocked me to the ground. Someone apparently identified me as a dealer and he disapproved. J intervened, but the kid moved on before I could even retaliate. As I got up off the sidewalk, I heard a hippie say, 'Don't help him out, man. He deals for the syndicate.' That might explain why I could barely even give my drugs away this week. Word must've spread that I'm mob connected. Don't know how to combat that allegation. Not sure I want or need to.

By nightfall, GH and I suspected rioting was about to explode. Tensions had built all day. Tourist cars blocked the street, halting traffic. Car horns blared. People screamed and yelled. Hippies climbed onto the hoods of cars and bounced up and down. Straights punched out a longhair for no reason. Bikers guzzled beer and enjoyed the mayhem. J was frightened, so I sent her back to my pad.

SFPD arrived with 50 men with nightsticks ready. One dumb chick called for an assault on the pigs and got a faceful of billy club. She spat out teeth and blood. Then the melee really began. The suburban teens flailed away at any guy with long hair and assumed that the cops would back them up. But the officers attacked wherever fighting broke out and were just as likely to clobber a straight as a hippie.

GH removed two cans of BZ from his pockets and prepared to spray. I told him no. We couldn't dose SFPD. And wherever there was a fight, there was a cop.

Then GH found a battle around the corner on Clayton. Two punks in James Dean leather jackets kicked the shit out of one of my regular customers – I think his name is Tutley. GH sprayed all three. One of the punks pulled a switchblade, so we both backed off. Tutley's beating continued unabated. GH wanted to spray them again. I pulled his reins. Once should've been sufficient. If not, then we report that back to TSS. In seconds, the two punks and Tutley fell into a weird trance. Cops appeared and arrested all three. They were hauled off to an awaiting paddy wagon before we could fully assess the BZ effects, but the results seemed pretty clear. Fast and effective.

The commotion kept building, and all rioting centered around SFPD. Someone chanted, 'Off the pigs!' So GH sprayed the dude in the face. That shut him up. But GH didn't follow the guy to record the drug's effect. I did. No doubt about it, the dude was incapacitated, thoroughly out of sorts. Then he passed out in front of an empty storefront. I checked his pulse and his pupils. Really gone. A tearful girlfriend came to his aid screaming and cursing at me, so I split.

Couldn't find GH in the madness. Ten minutes later, he appeared and asked where my aerosol can was. I showed him all I had was acid tabs. He thought I was kidding. He handed me a can of BZ and told me to stick with him. We needed to get into the midst of the fracas. But the combatants weren't centralized, and where they did converge SFPD beat them off.

Before I knew what hit me, a cop clubbed my arm, sending my can of BZ to the ground. When I bent to snatch the can, he kicked me in the ribs and knocked me away from it. GH dosed him in the face. The cop growled with rage but then staggered away to a cruiser.

My arm felt broken. My left rib ached from the cop's boot. Worst of all, GH drugged a police officer! Everything was out of control. I hollered at GH that we had to split. Seeing how I'd been injured, he told me to go. No! I shouted in his face. We both needed to get the hell out! He called me a pussy, reminded me of our battle plan, and told me to leave if I was wounded.

Then a nightstick dropped GH to the ground. It hit his right shoulder, and I could've sworn I heard a bone snap. He clung to his BZ canister, and the cop who'd hit him reached for it. I kicked the can away, and GH managed to trip the officer. I then snatched the aerosol can before the police could discover what it was, and I ran like hell down Haight Street, never looking back to see if GH was safe.

At my pad, J treated my bruises with ice. Nothing broken, thank God. But I'm now sporting some deep contusions on my arm and chest.

GH called me shortly before midnight and asked if I had the BZ. Yes. I asked if he'd gone to a hospital. No need to, he said. What about his collarbone? I heard it snap. He ached, but there was no break. GH said we'd done good work and deserved credit for what we accomplished. I flipped out. Are you high? What the fuck did we accomplish? What salient information could we take to TSS? It was a fuck up! The whole damn operation is a snafu! What does TSS expect to learn from this experiment? Why the hell are we putting our asses on the line for this lost cause?

GH didn't respond to my tirade. Instead, he hung up. I haven't heard from him yet today – as I write these words, it's eleven a.m.

I've already completed a report on what transpired yesterday. Tried to remain objective and disengaged. Not easy. My frustration probably shows in the report, but fuck it. I'm not going to give those lab monkeys any bananas. They get my honest assessment, and if they don't like the results of their ill-conceived experiments, they can go to hell.

27
Strange Brew

If Evan didn't get a cigarette soon, he'd leap out of the sedan, rush across the highway, race onto the sandy beach, and hurl himself into the Pacific. Harkess read his mind and produced a pack of Lucky Strikes. Evan couldn't handle non-filtered cigarettes, so he refused. Agent King then produced a pack of filtered menthols and offered a light. Harkess sat with Evan in the backseat of the black sedan, and they smoked in silence. King, who sat behind the wheel, lit up as well. Within seconds, the sedan was cloudy with smoke, and they cranked down the windows. Evan filled his lungs with relief.

Menard approached the sedan through the yellowy headlight beams, climbed into the front passenger seat, and slammed the door with assistance from the wind. He turned to King and said, "His car is clean."

King shifted and leaned his right arm onto the seat to stare back at Evan. He presented an Army drill instructor's bulldog glare but with half the bark and little bite. Evan was too tired to be intimidated. "Where's the diary, son?"

Evan exhaled a plume of smoke out the slit at the top of the window. The wind howling off the ocean carried it away on a jet stream of nighttime fog that sailed past the car like ghosts rushing off to war. He remained silent.

"You're lucky we were monitoring police reports," King said. He pointed to a police scanner attached beneath the glove compartment. "Otherwise you might've been on your way to jail."

Evan took another long pull on the menthol, exhaled, and rubbed his aching temple. Exhaustion and disappointment pummeled him, but he wouldn't be intimidated.

"You got homo tendencies, kid?" Menard asked. Evan stared bullets at the back of his head but didn't respond. "Because this is a notorious homo hangout. You knew that, didn't you?"

Evan said nothing and smoked his cigarette. He had no idea the innocent place from his youth had become a secret man-on-man rendezvous point, just as he was unaware how homosexuals were converging on his neighborhood.

"It's in your best interest to talk to us," King said. "We could leave you to the vice squad, you know."

"Or you could spray me with BZ again." Evan barked out his contempt.

Now the other men in the car fell silent. None of them faced Evan.

"My mother was home at the time! What if she had come downstairs? Would you assholes have drugged her, too?"

The men in the front seat remained mum. Evan's hand shook with anger as he puffed on the cigarette. Harkess sat beside him with a stone face.

"Your mom was in no danger," Harkess said.

"Then you admit it!"

"It was SOP," Harkess said, using the military acronym for standard operating procedure. King and Menard turned to shoot daggers at Harkess in the backseat, barely bottling their betrayal. Harkess continued by saying, "They were acting in the interests of national security, and you interfered. They had to subdue you by whatever means necessary. Deal with it."

King and Menard faced forward and stewed. Evan wasn't sure if they were acting or genuinely pissed off at Harkess. "I *interfered*? In my own fucking house?"

"Calm down."

"My mother! My sister might've come home!"

"Nobody wants to harm civilians," Harkess said, "but sometimes things go haywire. So… where's the diary?"

"Who killed my brother?"

"I don't know what Patrick wrote or what you hallucinated while under the influence," Harkess said, "but your brother's killer is in San Quentin. Period! We – did – not – kill – him! Get that through your skull."

"This is simple, Mr. Dunne," King said. "Give us the diary and we go away."

Evan didn't know what to believe, but he swallowed hard and considered his options. If the diary was still somewhere inside the windmill, they would likely tear the structure apart in order to find it, and he still didn't want them to have it. On the other hand, intuition told him that someone had absconded with the book, in which case the agents weren't likely to find it anyway. Above all, though, fatigue overwhelmed him. Between the drug effects and lack of sleep, he was no longer himself. In defeat, he hung his head.

"The diary is gone."

King's brow narrowed in disbelief. Harkess tapped an ash out the window and asked, "Where'd it go?"

"I don't know. It was in the windmill. Now I can't find it."

King glared at him through the rear view mirror. He echoed with mocking skepticism. "In the windmill."

"What the hell was it doing in there?" Menard asked.

"That's where I put it. For safekeeping."

"In the fucking windmill?" Menard said. "Why?"

Evan felt no need to explain his reasons to them. If he had recounted the childhood tale of how he ran away from home and spent days living in the windmill, they would only have scoffed and considered him nuts. In hindsight, maybe he *was* nuts to leave anything of value in the rotting structure. Maybe the BZ had clouded his judgment. Every crazy notion for the past five days sprang from an altered mind. He said, "If you assholes hadn't drugged me, I might have made better decisions."

King huffed and said to Harkess, "Stay put. We'll check it out."

Then he motioned for Menard to get out of the sedan and join him. The trunk opened, then closed, and Evan saw two flashlight beams wander off into the darkness toward the windmill.

The police cruisers and the paddy wagon drove off with its payload of alleged offenders, leaving the black sedan alone in the dark behind the Plymouth. The ocean wind swayed trees and lulled Evan into a stupor. Cigarette ashes fell onto his dirty jeans. He wiped them away and cranked down the window to toss the remaining butt outside.

"Listen to me, Dunne," Harkess said. "You don't know what deep shit you're in. For your own sake, you have got to fork over the diary."

"I told you. It's gone."

"I'm trying to help, so don't play with me, goddamnit."

"It's not where I left it. Somebody must've taken it." When Harkess kept staring, Evan scowled and said, "Go see for yourself."

Harkess blew smoke out the window. "They don't look it, but these guys are mad dogs."

"And you sicced them on me."

"Not me. If I'd known fixers were involved..."

"Fixers?"

"They were already on your tail. About a week ago you tried to contact a reporter on the phone...?"

"Yeah."

"They knew Patrick had been in touch with the guy. What was his name? Bernstein?"

"Burnblad."

"So they monitored the reporter. Rerouted his calls to an answering service to intercept them. When you tried to contact him, the agency got wise to you. The AP editor who returned your call was CIA."

Evan's jaw hung open. He'd been duped from the very beginning. "The editor said Burnblad died."

"Probably to throw you off. Listen to me. King and Menard are assigned to clean things up. Dosing you with BZ was kind. They could've done worse."

"Why didn't you stop them?"

"I wasn't there, man!" Harkess said with bitterness. "My orders were to go to ground after Patrick's death. Until you showed up at my place, I was out of the loop."

Evan recalled how Harkess visited with the go-go girl just before they left the trailer park. "Your neighbor girl. You had her call these two."

"No, I had her call my agency cut-out. He called the fixers because they were already in the field looking for you. I never even met those two until after you left me stranded in Golden Gate Park."

Evan scowled with skepticism. "Why are you telling me all this?"

"Jesus, you stubborn mick. I'm trying to save your ass here."

Evan recalled what Patrick had written about Harkess and said, "You're only looking out for number one. You had no intention of talking to the press."

"That's right, but I came along anyway because I wanted to see the diary for myself."

"And destroy it."

"Damn straight. If that ever becomes public, the dam will burst. Look at the big picture, man. Society is teetering on the edge of rebellion. If the truth of our operation ever got loose, this country would explode with violence."

"Save the hyperbole," Evan said.

"You think I'm exaggerating? If newspapers ever print the facts about Shunpiker, watch what happens. We've already got riots all over the country. Race riots, war protests, open flaunting of authority. The hippies will burn down the Haight, it'll spread across the city like a virus, then to other cities, and then you'll have tanks and soldiers on every street corner. Marshal law in America. That's why it can't see the light of day. That diary is an atomic bomb."

"Maybe you guys should've thought of that before you got to Haight Street."

"I can dig it, man," Harkess said, "but the shave cream is already out of the can, and it ain't going back in… Now, please. Give up that diary."

Evan's head throbbed with anguish and exhaustion. He wished he could magically produce the damn book just so Harkess would shut up. If the diary was still in the structure somewhere, the agents would find it and Evan's weird misadventure would be all for naught. He could live with that now. He wished the book had never existed. Under the circumstances, the diary might never surface again. He wished it was just a phantom hallucination, but he knew otherwise.

"Patrick wrote something about you," Evan said. "He said you consider hippies the enemy. Do you actually believe that?"

With a straight face, Harkess replied, "They've been mounting a Marxist movement to subvert our way of life."

Evan scoffed. "They're just a bunch of wayward kids on drugs."

"Not to the Establishment," Harkess said. Then he took a long drag on his cigarette. "Youth culture is on the march. Nearly half the population is under thirty. Old-timers like King and Menard feel threatened. They know the times they are a-changing. Real fast. And the hippies are instigating change. The Establishment wants to neutralize them. In a war, you knock out the command structure, but the hippies don't have one. The only unifying threads are music and drugs. So that became the goal. Get and keep everybody high. Acid, speed, pot, heroin, and shit nobody ever heard of. Their so-called hippie utopia would fall apart in due time. And look what's happening."

Evan seethed. Harkess sounded detached from his own argument, as if he had no part in the youth culture, as if he lived in another America. Patrick's diary warned about his eccentric right-wing views, but hearing them in a cold, calculating voice sent electrical jolts of self-righteous anger through Evan.

Harkess exhaled a stream of gray that filled the car. He scratched the tip of his hooked nose. "Look, I'm juggling a lotta balls here, man. One day soon, I'll spell it all out for you. But for now, you've got to tell Laurel and Hardy where the diary is. If not, they're gonna hound you and make life miserable for your family until they find it."

Evan tilted his head back and sighed with anguish. "I'm telling the truth. The diary isn't where I left it. It's gone."

Flashlight beams bounced through the darkness as King and Menard returned to the sedan. Had they found the diary? Evan held his breath in anticipation. Then the men climbed into the vehicle empty-handed.

"Quite a hiding spot, I'll give you that," Menard said.

"Tell us what you did with it," King said.

Frustrated, Evan rubbed his hands across his head. "After you assholes drugged me, I took the diary out of the house so you'd never get your hands on it. Then I hid it in the windmill. I thought it would be safe in there, but…"

Evan said nothing more. The men all sat in callous silence. Harkess whipped out another cigarette, lit up, and filled his lungs. King was lost in thought and rubbed an earlobe. Evan sank into the seat and stared out the window. Just beyond the windmill and the trees, he saw the lights of Playland at the Beach glowing off the flowing fog. Despite the howling ocean wind, he could hear the bells and toots and rumbles from the amusement park as well as the distant shouts of glee from roller coaster riders. He tried to remember what glee felt like.

Then King said to Menard, "Give him his keys."

"What? We're collapsing the tent?" Menard asked.

"We're going to search the bushes," King said. "Give him the keys."

Menard dug into his coat pocket and then tossed the keys to the Plymouth over his shoulder. They landed in Evan's lap. He looked at King's eyes through the rear view mirror.

"He's of no concern," King said. "Records show that he was just released from San Francisco General on a drug overdose. Anything he says in public will be perceived as the ranting of a drugged-out hippie lunatic. He'll also be discredited for escaping from a homosexual raid. What's more, I believe he's due to report for basic training two days from now. So you see, this young man isn't going to cause any more static. Are you, Mr. Dunne?" King crooked a thumb to indicate he should get out of the sedan. "Good luck to you."

Evan's spirit dissipated like teakettle steam. He glanced at Harkess who wouldn't meet his gaze; his head was turned away as he blew smoke out the window. Then, with a pang of humiliation aching in his gut, Evan climbed out of the backseat. King and Menard got out of the sedan, too. Their flashlights came to life.

Evan pulled his jacket collar up to ward off the wind as he marched toward his Plymouth. He slid into the driver's seat, turned over the ignition, popped on the headlights, and sped away, kicking up gravel in his tires' wake.

Tears hindered his vision. He drove two blocks to Playland at the Beach, pulled into the mostly empty parking lot, and convulsed with sobs.

Lights from the Cliff House burned through the evening fog, as did the neon of the amusement park. Few people braved the chill winds and fog to attend Playland anymore. The arcade and rides were in disrepair and echoed another time, not the modern world of 1967. Fog swallowed the neglected relic. They should bulldoze this dump, he thought. On the off chance they found the diary in the bushes, they could destroy that, too. The damn book was a hex.

No, Evan thought, I'm the jinx.

Exhaustion and despair made him a zombie. All he could do was sit in the driver's seat, blubber, and stare at the mesmerizing arcade lights. Then he heard the familiar chortle of Laughing Sal, the ugly hag doll that greeted visitors atop the entrance to the Fun House. He always hated that strange mannequin and its weird cackle. Now it seemed to be laughing at him. Mocking. Taunting. Calling him a loser.

His head dipped. His chin hit his chest. He fought hard to stay awake, but sleep would not be denied.

28
Stony End

Sunlight barely penetrated the morning fog. Seven miles to the east in downtown San Francisco, blue sky greeted commuters, but not a hint of it showed at the seaside. Playland had not yet come to life for the day's business. Seagulls squawked and waddled about the parking lot in search of discarded popcorn and other amusement park garbage. Waves crashed against the beach.

Evan awoke curled on the front seat of his Plymouth. He sat up and shook the soot out of his mind. A weeks worth of stubble itched on his face. He ran a hand over his bristled blonde hair and wished for a shower. His mouth felt dry and tasted rancid. Evan climbed out of the vehicle and stretched his achy body. His brain craved coffee and a cigarette.

Then he spotted a pack of Chesterfields on the Plymouth's dashboard. He reached inside the car and retrieved the pack to find just two cigarettes remaining. They weren't his brand. Evan couldn't stand non-filtered cigarettes, and Chesterfields were notoriously strong. Where had they come from?

He hadn't noticed them before. Thinking little of it, he stashed the pack in his shirt pocket. If he got desperate, he might smoke one.

His bladder demanded relief. Golden Gate Park was within walking distance, but he spotted the blades of the north windmill and chose never to return to that old haunt. Instead, he strode across the parking lot to the Fun House entrance. After searching all about and convinced that no one would see, he unzipped his pants and pissed on the wall beneath silent, inanimate Laughing Sal. Then he skulked back to his car and sat on the hood with the wind at his back.

It was Friday. Patrick's ashes were to be spread onto the bay that afternoon. Alice and Dolores and Sandy would be expecting him to attend. What was there left to do but go home? What a giant snafu. Duped and drugged. Nearly busted by the vice squad. And the diary was gone. The game was lost.

A young hippie man approached. His hair was mussed up, and his grungy clothes spilled sand. He carried a sleeping bag under his arm and looked as if he'd spent the night sleeping on the beach. Not wise, given the tides and harsh winds.

"Hey, man," the hippie said. He looked no older than Evan. His beard grew out like wild brush. "Spare some change?"

Evan shrugged. "Sorry."

"Got a smoke?"

Evan reached into his breast pocket, extracted the Chesterfields, and handed over the pack without a word.

"Thanks," the scraggly hippie said. He removed the cigarettes, put one in his pocket, crumpled up the pack, and tossed it on the ground to be blown away by the ocean wind. Then he wandered through the mostly empty parking lot toward Fulton Avenue and Golden Gate Park.

Evan climbed into his Plymouth and contemplated what to do. The tarot card flashed through his mind – the Chariot. Just get in the car and drive, he thought. Put the Golden Gate Bridge in your rear view mirror and vanish. Then he recalled the Green Beret. The soldier left the Free Store, boarded the Muni train, and disappeared into the Carl Street tunnel. The passageway couldn't take him to the past, but maybe it led somewhere better. A free man. Evan had run away before, but that was the act of a guileless child. Better for him to return home and ask his family for forgiveness. Then he would pay last respects to his brother, get a good night's sleep in his own bed, and board the bus for Fort Ord. It was the proper thing to do. Yet he prayed for an alternative. Reason clashed with anguish to churn acid in his gut.

The car's engine was cold, so the ignition took three tries before kicking in. He revved the motor to let it warm up. Then he shifted into drive and left the desolate amusement park.

As he turned onto Fulton, he spotted a small commotion on the sidewalk. A panicky teenage girl and a middle-aged man crouched over a figure lying on the grass. A third man in a heavy coat and herringbone cap ran with purpose toward the amusement park. Evan saw the scraggly hippie who approached him moments earlier sprawled out on the ground. Curious, he parked his car at curbside, left the motor running, and rushed over to offer help. The hippie lay unconscious.

"What happened?" Evan asked.

"Don't know," the man answered. "I offered the guy a light, and he started coughing up a storm. Next thing you know, he just fainted."

"Should I call for help?" Evan asked.

"That other fella just went off to do so," the man said. "Probably drugs."

"I don't think so, Daddy," the teenager said. "I think he's sick."

"Something funny in those cigarettes, I bet," the man said.

A Chesterfield smoldered on the grass beside the young hippie. Thin wisps of smoke rose from the tip and dissipated in the wind. Evan stared at the butt until it dawned on him: the hippie had been smoking a cigarette he gave him and then fell ill. Evan trembled. Were the cigarettes to blame for whatever had befallen the man? If so, what was in those Chesterfields? He'd never seen the pack before. Not even his brand. Where had they come from? Did someone put them in his car? No one had been in his Plymouth—

Menard. The fixer had searched through the car for the diary. Had he planted the cigarettes? Were they intended for Evan?

Was the hippie poisoned?

Panic rippled through him. Bile surged up through his esophagus, and Evan gagged. But he repressed any vomit. Then he turned away and staggered back to his car.

His heart told him to stay and help. His mind said go. The cops would arrive soon. If the hippie awoke and pointed a finger at Evan as the person who gave him poison cigarettes... Maybe he was just being paranoid. Maybe he had it all wrong. But he couldn't afford to stick around and find out. Fear jolted him fully awake, and self-preservation made him flee.

He climbed back into his Plymouth and sped away.

July 12, 1967

I made it clear to SG that I want out. Take me off your roster, I said. This operation is a bust. The bruises mean nothing. I'll heal. But the point of the exercise is lost on me. SG understands my frustration, or so he says. Experiments fail more often than they succeed, he explained, but that doesn't mean they aren't worth pursuing. Tactics need to be reassessed. The canisters were never meant for riot control, just for personal protection during chaos. Now he tells me. As a matter of fact, the lab boys are creating a BZ bomb, just like a smoke bomb but with a more potent payload. Fine, I said, but do we get gas masks to go with it? Good idea, he told me, as if nobody had ever thought of protecting the ops. I complained how that was exactly the sort of shortsightedness I found frustrating. Half-baked ideas. SG told me to hang in there. We're only a month and a half into the summer, and there are more experiments to come. Then he hung up without letting me enter another complaint.

To hell with it. I'm laying low. Better yet, I'm going home to see my wife and kids.

July 13, 1967

Found that Associate Press reporter's card in my wallet. Carl Burnblad. I'm seriously considering contacting him about what CIA is doing in the Haight. Probably a bad move. The agency might learn that I'm the source of any information, and then there will be one major shit-storm to follow. But my conscience is burning, and I need to get some things off my chest. A shrink would be best for that, though. Not the press. I'm torn.

July 15, 1967

Saw the Newark riots on TV. What a nightmare. Thank God no one is burning down buildings in the Haight. At least, not yet. The cops will focus on the Fill-more district and Oakland. Race riots in the Haight are unlikely even though blacks are all over the neighborhood. But if riots erupt in the Fillmore, things could easily spread to the Haight. Not sure I want to be there when that bomb drops.

July 16, 1967

Does CIA have infiltrators like me in Newark? Perhaps a few black men are on the payroll. Could CIA be fomenting race riots? Can't imagine why, but then again I'd have never suspected Operation Shunpiker, either. Nobody in their right mind would. But CIA works in strange ways for dubious reasons.

July 17, 1967

Some asshole accosted me on the street. I went to the bank to make a deposit before heading home to the family, and a punk tried to rip off my valise. I grabbed it with both hands, hollered like a lion, and kicked him in the shin. He surrendered and ran away.

I wonder if J is somehow involved. How many people know that I carry cash in this case? Nobody but J. Supposing she told the punk to rob me... Hell, I'm getting too paranoid. Anyone could surmise what's in the case.

For safety's sake, I'm buying handcuffs to prevent theft. If somebody wants the valise, they'll have to pry it from my wrist.

29
When the Music's Over

Evan drove the Plymouth up Fulton Street along the full length of Golden Gate Park and then turned right onto Masonic Street. That would take him through the Haight up to 17th Street and then downhill to Eureka Valley. His heart pounded. Strange scenarios played out in his head. What if he had smoked the cigarette instead of giving it away? Would he be sprawled out on the ground now instead of the hippie? Maybe the guy had a seizure. Maybe his problem was unrelated to the cigarette. After all, the fellow already looked like a mess. Evan wondered if he was being paranoid or if his life was in danger. If so, was it wise to return home where the fixers could find him? Where else could he go?

As his car approached the corner of Haight and Masonic, traffic slowed to a stop. A mob of people blocked the intersection. Hundreds of hippies filled the street like cattle. The rally piqued Evan's curiosity. He parked his Plymouth in a fortuitously vacant spot and walked up the block to investigate. The marchers showed no concern for automobile traffic.

The street was theirs alone as evidenced by their disregard for blaring car horns. Gaiety abounded amongst the throng despite the fact that pallbearers carried a man in a casket. Smiles and laughter and singing contradicted the funereal sight. Two men held a large hand-painted banner that read Death of Hippie. The procession then began to move west along Haight Street. Barefoot hippies danced and marched behind and ahead of the casket. Tambourines and bongos were struck, and a young woman played a lively funeral dirge on trumpet. People along the route threw flowers. The man in the casket was only acting.

A bright-eyed brunette with peace symbols painted on her cheeks sidled up to Evan. Her smile was infectious. She slid her arm under his and tugged. "Hey, there. Join us."

Though reluctant, Evan gave in. The scene seemed strange but harmless.

"Who died?" he asked.

"Hippie," she said over the din. He frowned with confusion. "The hippie is a press phenomenon, and we won't be controlled by the mass media. So we're staging a funeral for hippies. This marks the birth of the free man!"

"Who organized this?" Evan asked.

"The Diggers, I think. Does it matter? Just be free, brother."

She took another stranger by the arm and pulled him into the moving crowd. After one block up Haight Street, the marchers grew in numbers. Photographers captured the scene. That's when Evan backed off. He didn't want to be photographed amidst a hippie throng. Instead, he slipped off to the sidewalk in front of the Drogstore Café as the mock funeral procession moved on.

Then he spotted the pixie girl who he'd met in that same location days earlier. She stood on the opposite side of the street watching the parade in front of a jewelry shop. Her short hair and acne-scarred face were unmistakable. She wore a man's corduroy suit jacket that was three sizes too large. A gangly man with a bird's nest of hair, presumably the jacket's owner, put his arm around her shoulder as they joined the procession. Evan jogged out into the street and followed. He wracked his memory for her name. Then he blurted out, "Genevieve!"

The pixie girl spun around in search of the person calling her name. Evan caught up to her and waved, but she showed no recognition and was less friendly. Her eyes were glassy. Even early in the morning, she was high.

"I'm Evan. I met you on the street. Tom-Tom's brother."

Still, her face was blank except for a stoned grin. He marched alongside on her left as her boyfriend, if that's what he was, walked on her right and still had his arm around her.

"I was the guy looking for Jane Corcoran," Evan said.

"Downtown," she said over the racket from the crowd. "The Tenderloin."

That surprised Evan. "What? Really? Do you know the address?"

"Some fleabag hotel on the corner of Turk and Leavenworth."

"What's she doing there?"

Genevieve eyed him with suspicion. "You're a friend, right?"

Evan hesitated. He could have lied and said yes in order to get the information. Instead, he said, "I'm Tom-Tom's brother."

She raised a hand to her mouth and frowned with pity. "Oh, I'm so sorry."

For whatever reason, probably because she was high, Genevieve showed no memory of having met him just days ago and having the same conversation. He said, "Tell me about Jane."

"I was coming from the bus station, and there she was standing up above me on a fire escape," Genevieve said, "and I said, What're you doing up there? And she just waved like she was tripping or zonked out on something. Then a man guided her back into the window, and I didn't see her again."

"She stood on a fire escape outside a fleabag hotel?"

"Yeah, corner of Turk and Leavenworth. I thought she might be in trouble. Will you check it out?"

"Yeah, sure."

She smiled with stoned eyes, held up a two-finger V-sign, and said, "Peace."

Then she and her boyfriend marched on with the 'Death of Hippie' parade as it surged down Haight Street and gathered gawkers and more demonstrators. Evan fell off from the crowd and walked back toward his parked Plymouth.

Finding Jane Corcoran didn't matter so much now that the diary was lost. She couldn't verify what he didn't possess. Besides, she might know nothing. Maybe she was just a stoned junkie. But Evan didn't dwell on it. For reasons he couldn't explain, even to himself, he felt compelled to find her.

Then he stopped dead in his tracks. According to Jane's mother, King and Menard had been searching for the black girl, too. She might be hiding from them. Why? Maybe she knew more than he realized. Evan ran to his car with heart thumping in anticipation of hopefully reaching Jane Corcoran at last. He prayed the fixers hadn't found her first.

July 23, 1967

Riots in Detroit. We saw it on TV. Sandy said she's thankful we don't live there or in Newark. I reminded her that the Black Panthers are based across the bay. Race riots could happen in Oakland or SF as easily as anywhere. Watching the news coverage made me nervous.

July 25, 1967

Detroit is burning. People have died. They called in federal troops. I can't believe this is the United States of America. Please, dear God, don't let that happen in this city.

30
Desolation Row

The Tenderloin was a seedy neighborhood sandwiched between City Hall and Union Square. Nob Hill residents looked down on the area, both literally and figuratively. While those locales sported modern shops and lavish buildings, the Tenderloin was one huge neglected tenement, a sordid reminder of the city's untamed Barbary Coast days. Prostitutes and rummies dominated the ten-block area. As a consequence, so did cops. Middle-class San Franciscans rarely ventured into the neighborhood. Not the law-abiding citizens, that is.

Evan found parking up the hill on Leavenworth and marched down to the corner of Turk. The stench of stale beer and urine rose from the sidewalk. Spent needles stood out among the sidewalk litter. A crazy man sat in a doorway. He wore tattered clothes, hadn't bathed in a decade, and hollered invectives at an imaginary companion. Evan marched past him to the ten-story building on the street corner.

The red brick hotel had all the charm of an outhouse; the sort of place the chamber of commerce would forbid from appearing on tourist maps. A last resort for indigents and welfare recipients. A wrought iron fire escape snaked up the side. No other building on the corner had one, so Evan felt assured he was in the right place.

The entrance on Turk was hard to find; a narrow, recessed doorway hidden from the street. That added to the creepy atmosphere. Evan tried to enter, but the door wouldn't budge. He yanked twice until a buzzer sounded. Then he pulled and the door gave way.

A tight hallway with one dim bulb overhead and torn linoleum tile on the floor led to an office the size of a tollbooth. A grizzled fat man with glaucoma in one eye sat listening to Motown music from a transistor radio. The man's labored breathing sounded like a leaking radiator, and his abuse of aftershave curled Evan's nose hairs.

Evan pulled out the worn photograph of Jane that had spent too long in his jacket pocket and was now bent and wrinkled. He smoothed it out and displayed it to the fat man. "I'm looking for this girl."

The fat man glanced at the picture and then at Evan. "And?"

"Is she here?"

"We don't give out private information about our guests."

Evan glared at the man's damaged eye, which unnerved him. He hesitated and then said, "I need to know she's safe."

"What are you implying?" the fat man said. "That our guests aren't safe? We've got certification from the board of health." He pointed a flabby finger at an archaic, yellowy paper certificate taped to the wall behind him.

"Her name is Jane Corcoran. Just tell me she's here."

The fat man shook his head. "Never heard of her."

"You're sure?"

The fat man grabbed a registry book from a shelf and flipped it open. He then held it out for Evan to see. Names were listed on lined pages. "You see her name anywhere?"

Then he slammed the book shut and jammed it back onto the shelf.

"Has anyone else come here looking for her?"

The fat man huffed. "How many ways do I have to say it? She's not here."

Evan pulled a twenty-dollar bill from his wallet, the last large bill he had on him. He held it out to the obese innkeeper. "Just tell me whether or not anyone else has been here searching for a black girl. Two men. Older."

The fat man snatched the twenty and said, "No."

That wasn't worth losing twenty bucks over, but Evan had asked for it. When no other course of action came to his mind, he turned around and marched down the dirty hallway to the sidewalk outside.

From across Leavenworth, he looked at the building and the fire escape that ran up the side. Most windows were closed against the autumn chill, and most blinds were drawn even at mid-morning. Somewhere up there, he reckoned, was the girl who had answers. Then again, maybe she knew nothing. According to the diary, Patrick had kicked her out of his apartment shortly before his death. Maybe she wasn't even in the rattrap hotel. Maybe she finally returned home to San Leandro.

"Jane!" Evan hollered. He cupped his hands around his mouth to amplify his voice. "Jane Corcoran!"

His yells barely penetrated traffic noise. Normally, raising his voice would be a cause for embarrassment, but in the Tenderloin, with crazies talking to themselves all day, hollers and screams didn't draw any stares from passersby. His eyes darted from window to window up and down the building. No one drew up a blind. He called out again.

"Jane! Jane Corcoran! Jane Corcoran!"

Then she appeared.

Three stories up, a blind rose. A young black woman appeared at the window and scanned the street for the source of the hollering. Evan's breathing stopped. Was it her? The woman was slender. Her hair was trimmed short, not a bushy

Afro like in the photograph. Her age and height couldn't be determined from a distance. He waved his arms to draw her attention.

"Jane Corcoran?"

She stared down at him with furrowed brow as if straining to recall his identity. Then she raised her hand in a confused greeting, and he knew he'd found her.

She moved away from the window as if pulled by force, and a hand pulled down the shade.

Was that really Jane? Who was up there with her? Was she being held against her will? Evan had to know. He counted the stories; she was on the third floor on the south-eastern corner of the building.

He ran back to the Turk Street entrance and banged on the hotel door. As soon as he heard the buzz, Evan yanked open the door and raced up the hallway. The fat man's glazed eyes widened with surprise, but he was too slow to keep Evan from running past the booth.

"Hey!" the fat man called out.

Evan ignored him, ran past a dilapidated elevator, and flew up a flight of stairs. The steps creaked under his footfalls, and he feared he might fall through a couple of weak steps. He passed a hypodermic needle in the dirty staircase and kept climbing. The smell of garbage assaulted his nostrils. He sucked stale air as he ran up to the third floor. Then he stopped, leaned against the wall, and caught his breath.

The elevator whirred beside him, and Evan wondered if the fat innkeeper was on his way up to intercept him. He leaned his back against the wall and waited for the elevator door to slide open. When it did, the fat man came out brandishing a snub-nose revolver.

Impulse took over. In one motion, Evan leapt forward and kneed the fat man in the groin while reaching both hands for the gun. The fat man's wrist cracked as it made contact with the edge of the elevator door, and the weapon fell to the floor without discharging. Then Evan jammed his elbow into the man's soft, fleshy neck below the double chin. The fat fellow's windpipe wasn't crushed, but his breaths came in gasps. The fat man then clutched at his injured wrist as he fell backward into the elevator. Evan punched the button for the first floor, stepped out, and the door slid closed. The elevator whirred and descended.

Then Evan grabbed the revolver that had fallen to the floor and skulked down the hallway. The noise hadn't alerted any tenants. Maybe few people were home. Maybe the sounds of violence were too common for neighbors to check out. They were wise to ignore it.

Evan kept the gun to his side and aimed at the floor. He had no experience with firearms, and holding it made him nervous. Nothing in the Boy Scout manual prepared him for this. The safety was on, so he released it, although he wasn't sure why, just something he saw in a movie. But this wasn't Hollywood. This was the Tenderloin where real danger lurked.

He crept along the filthy carpet runner to the window at the hall's end. Through it, he saw the fire escape. Leavenworth Street was directly below, and the intersection with Turk was visible. That meant that the window from which he'd spotted Jane was inside the apartment to his right. The door was closed. He pondered knocking. Maybe he should bust it down like a movie cop. Instead, he stood close to the door and listened.

Music played. A record skipped as Aretha Franklin sang about respect. Underneath the music, a man spoke in a halting, one-way conversation, which Evan presumed was a telephone call.

"Yeah, right outside. He was callin' out her name... Whatcha want me to do?... Yeah, my cousin's place... Shotwell... Can't remember the address, but I'll call you once I... Hey, man, be cool. I got it covered."

The phone receiver clacked against the plastic cradle. The music ended as a needle scratched across the record. Then came an unintelligible conversation between the man and a whining woman.

This was the moment to break in. The girl was in there and possibly being held hostage. Evan's heart pounded. Fear tingled in a wave across his skin. He took three deep, heaving breaths in preparation. Then he held the revolver out before him and prepared to kick in the door.

The door swung open to reveal Jane and a black man behind her. They froze and stared with shock at the gun in Evan's outstretched hand. Jane gasped but didn't scream.

Unsure what to do, Evan acted on instinct. He took the girl by the forearm, yanked her out into the hallway, and shielded her from harm while keeping the revolver trained on the man in the doorway. He was around thirty, medium build, with bloodshot eyes and a leather jacket, and he raised his hands to chest height. The smell of marijuana wafted out the doorway, and the man's dilated eyes suggested he'd been toking. Evan couldn't decide what to do. His impulse was to take the girl and flee. The fat man would return soon, and he probably wouldn't come alone.

"Stay cool," the black man said. He stared at the gun, not at Evan. "Whatever you want, you got it. You want dope? I got some. You want the girl? Take her. She ain't worth me gettin' my nuts blowed off."

Evan turned to her. "Jane Corcoran?"

Her eyes widened with fright, yet she remained still except for a slight nod. Her lean frame made her seem tall when in fact she stood two inches shorter than Evan. She wore no make-up but, aside from acne on her cheeks and chin, the girl could have passed for a Ronette or a Supreme. Up close, her youth showed. Barely out of her teens. She wore the same clothes as in the photograph; a cowgirl leather jacket with fringed sleeves, tattered blue jeans, and knee-high black boots. Short curly hair had replaced the Afro seen in the Polaroid. Her perfectly set large brown eyes hypnotized, yet both were bloodshot. And her tummy bulged a little.

"Are you being held here against your will?" Evan asked.

She nodded.

"Grab your things. You're coming with me."

After a moment of hesitation, she spoke in a sweet soprano voice. "I don't have anything."

She carried no purse, no backpack, no personal items at all besides the clothes on her back. Either she'd been robbed of all she had or Jane lived the hippie lifestyle, free of possessions. Or the life of a runaway.

Evan took her by the hand, moved backward down the hall, and kept the weapon trained on the doorway. The black man made no effort to follow and backed into his apartment. Evan broke into a sprint and practically dragged the girl along. Her boots clomped on the floor. They raced to the stairs and descended. Jane tried to wrench free her hand from his grasp, but Evan wouldn't let go. She staggered along and nearly tripped on the stairs.

"Where are you taking me?" she asked.

"To safety. How do we get out of here?"

"I don't know."

He stared at her for a moment. "Are you high?"

"Yeah."

Down the filthy staircase they scurried. Between being stoned and clomping in her big boots, Jane slowed their escape. Evan practically had to yank her down each flight. At the second floor, she stopped to catch her breath. When she nearly fell over from dizziness, he grabbed her around the waist to prop her up and encouraged her to keep moving. When they reached the bottom floor, Evan grabbed her wrist and pulled her through the narrow hall.

With no other exit in sight, Evan decided to risk running right past the reception booth to the front door. As they did, the fat man appeared. He stood behind his post with a telephone against his ear. Evan aimed the revolver at him.

The fat man showed no fear of the weapon. In a voice made hoarse by the blow to the throat, he said, "It isn't loaded, dipshit."

That surprised Evan and made him rush for the door. With Jane in tow, he ran out onto Turk Street. Police sirens

blared blocks away. He tossed the pistol into a garbage can.
They then turned the corner onto Leavenworth and raced up
the hill to where Evan's Plymouth was parked. He fumbled in
his pockets for car keys. Then he unlocked and opened the
passenger door. But Jane wouldn't get in. She gasped for
breath and stared at him in a drug daze.

"Come on!" Evan said. Sirens grew closer.

"Who are you?" she asked without budging.

"I'm Evan Dunne." When that admission didn't change
her vacant expression, he added, "Patrick's brother."

Jane's face was a blank wall. Evan froze with confusion. Was this the wrong person? Had the pixie girl in the
Haight given him false information? Had he wasted his effort?
He pulled the Polaroid from his pocket and held it out for her
to see.

"Is this you?" he asked.

She frowned with suspicion but then nodded. Was she
so stoned that she couldn't think straight? Then it dawned on
him – she didn't know Patrick's real name.

"My brother... You called him Tom-Tom."

Her dark eyes widened and moistened, and a hand
went to her mouth. Then he guided her into the passenger seat
and closed the door. As police sirens grew louder, Evan
climbed into the driver's seat and revved the engine.

The Plymouth shot up Leavenworth to Nob Hill. In
minutes they were out of the Tenderloin and driving blindly
around San Francisco because Evan had no idea where to go
next. Nowhere seemed safe.

July 29, 1967

J needs to get away from here. The Haight is no
place for teenage girls. Damn it, she's a sweet kid, and I
can't help feeling I'm just fucking her up. Drugs are her
own trip, and while I let her go unchecked to fulfill my
cover I can't stand seeing her so messed up anymore. She
has sworn off acid, or so she says, and I won't let her touch

heroin, but she smokes pot like a damn chimney, and who knows what else she might experiment with. Probably anything she's given, knowing J. I realize why, of course. She's psychologically still escaping from her stepfather's clutches. When she's really stoned she will occasionally cut loose on the horrid things he did to her. Whether or not she's telling the truth, I don't know for sure. If not, she's got a vivid imagination. Poking her with a soda bottle sounded too sick to be fake. Plus, she's so matter of fact when she discusses it, as if it's just a rite of passage for teenage girls. But then she pours out other sick stuff, like being forced to live for days in the attic when she got sassy. I can appreciate that fathers do twisted things. My old man used to beat me just for being late for dinner. I'm not sure if J's tales are truth. But if they are, she's not doing herself any favors by escaping from the real world through drugs. Especially not if she's pregnant. Leaving her abusive family makes sense, but she needs to build a new foundation based in reality. Wish there was some way to facilitate that but, hell, I've got commitments at home. Maybe the only thing to do is put J on a dinghy, set her adrift, and hope she learns to paddle.

August 1, 1967

I'm practically bawling as I write these words. J just told me another sad tale of home. I asked why she stuck around her parents' house if her stepdad abused her. She said that adopted kids put up with all sorts of crap just so they won't be rejected and returned to the system. Even a shitty home, she said, was better than no home. She needed to belong and be wanted. So she gave up her body and never complained. She needed some semblance of family life that badly. Now, she says, she's found a family in the Haight. She thinks this collection of misfits is her new tribe. God, that's pathetic.

Then I asked why she ran away if she craved family life that much. One night, she said, her stepfather got too rough. She claims she bit his cock hard enough to draw blood. Then the stepmother comforted him while chastising J. She wisely bolted. Running was the right thing to do. Why stay in a dangerous situation? She could have wound up dead. Self-preservation has to take priority. She was no coward to run. Poor kid.

If I were the heroic type, I'd do something for her. But what? Someone will take her away from here. A Samaritan will carry her off. At least, I hope so.

31
Badge

The Plymouth zipped toward the Embarcadero Free-way. The bridges were to be avoided as one-way traps. Driving to Highway 101 South and the expanse of the peninsula opened up escape routes, presuming they needed to make a getaway. Evan wasn't even sure if anyone was after them, but he had strong suspicions. His blood pulsed.

"Who was that guy in the apartment?" Evan asked.

"Jimmy. Don't know his last name. Just Jimmy." She slurred her words, and her bloodshot eyes rested at half-mast. She slumped into the car seat as mellow as a housecat.

"He was holding you hostage?"

"Well, not like that. But I haven't left that dump for weeks except to get my hair done, and I need to get the hell out. I'm not some animal in a cage." Her voice, as soft as velour, tantalized him. "Got a cigarette?"

"Fresh out. Why were you being kept there?"

"For my own protection, if you believe Billy's bullshit. Which I don't anymore. Where are we going?"

"Where would you feel safe?"

"In the Haight."

Evan didn't approve. Taking her there would only lead to trouble, he believed. On the other hand, she probably had connections and friends in the neighborhood. "Do you have a place to stay?"

"Sure. Drop me at Haight and Masonic, okay?"

The Plymouth rolled up the ramp and onto the elevated Embarcadero Freeway past downtown San Francisco's looming skyscrapers on one side and the bay on the other. "Let's talk first. What are you on right now?"

"Nothing heavy. Just pot. What's your name again?"

"Evan Dunne. Did my brother ever talk about me?"

"No." She rolled down the passenger window just enough to let fresh air in.

"He told you about his wife and kids, though, didn't he?"

She sighed and looked out the window. "I really need a cigarette."

"Wait a minute." Evan's eyes widened as a thought popped into his mind. "You said Billy was keeping you safe. Billy who?"

"Tom's friend. Billy Batson."

Stunned, Evan slammed the brake pedal in time to prevent a collision with the car in front of him. The brakes screeched, the tires squealed, and the Plymouth fishtailed.

"Jesus," Jane said. "Be careful."

Evan couldn't believe his ears. Billy Batson; the street name used by Gil Harkess. "What was he protecting you from?"

"From the guy who killed Tom."

"From Pulasko?"

"Is that his name? I called him Lurch. Tall guy. Speed freak."

"He was a biker," Evan said. "They called him Curious Jack."

She cocked her head at him. "What? No, not him. I know Jack. He's a bulky guy, shorter."

"That's who they convicted."

Jane twisted her face in confusion. "What are you talking about?"

"Don't you read the papers? Curious Jack is in San Quentin right now for murdering my brother."

Jane's face dropped with the news. "What the hell...? He wasn't even there. And why was Billy...? What the hell is going on here?"

"I was hoping you could tell me."

She looked askance at him. "You've got your facts all wrong."

"It was reported in the newspapers. Didn't you read about it?"

A faraway look set into her eyes. "Jimmy didn't get the newspaper. Didn't even have a TV. We just played music and smoked pot."

Driving had become distracting. Following instincts, Evan had merged onto the highway maze that would take them south toward the peninsula, but now he took the Ninth Avenue exit that deposited them in the South of Market warehouse district. Then he turned onto Brannan and parked the car in front of a vacant auto body shop. He rubbed his temples and tried to ferret out the details.

"You were Patrick's – Tom's girl. Right?"

She shook her head. "No possession. We were too groovy for that. Free love, okay? But it was love, for sure. We just don't believe in... you know, he was free."

"He was married."

Jane rolled her eyes. "You don't get it. We were soul mates. Both Geminis. Both from abusive fathers."

Evan flinched at the last remark. Is that how Patrick portrayed their dad? Given the combativeness between father and son, it wasn't a stretch. "Did you know he was with the CIA?"

"Who? Tom?" Perfect white teeth flashed at him when she broke into a high-pitched, marijuana-induced cackle. She looked askance at Evan as if he were the one who was high. "You serious with that shit?"

Revealing that information, he realized, was a mistake. Harkess hadn't told her a speck of truth, and telling her now might only endanger Jane. Evan tried to backpedal. "I don't mean— Never mind that for now—"

"Oh, please." She waved him off and tugged at the door handle. "Let me out here."

"Wait," he said as he reached out for her arm. Telling her too much detail would probably only confuse things further. Instead, he wanted to learn what she knew. "I really need to know about the murder."

"It's still a mystery to me," Jane said. "All I know is that Billy wants me to lay low till the smoke clears. But you say they threw Jack in the slammer?"

"Weeks ago. He confessed." The conversation was zigzagging, so Evan tried to steer it straight. "Just before the murder, Tom kicked you out of his place, right?"

She bowed her head. The comment hurt. "He didn't kick me out. I left. It was mutual. When you're not wanted, you move on."

"Where did you go?"

"Different places. A couch here, a floor there. The street if necessary. I was sleeping in a doorway two doors down from Tom's place on the night he died. That's how I saw Lurch."

"Who?"

"That's what I call him. You know. From the Addam's Family. Ever see that show? The tall butler guy...?"

"What exactly did you see?"

Jane fell silent, either because recounting that night's events left a pall over her life or she was too stoned. "I was jacked on speed, so I was pretty awake most of the night. Just wandered the Haight with a girlfriend. But then she split and I started to crash. I stopped in the nearest doorway to sleep it off." She caught Evan's sympathetic frown. "Don't give me that pitying look, man. That's life in the Haight. I've done it many times. You crash wherever you find shelter. No big thing. I just happened to be near Tom's pad, so… Okay, maybe that wasn't a coincidence. Maybe I wanted to go back to him. You think fucked up thoughts when you're high. Whatever. I'm no shrink. Anyway… All of a sudden, there's this big, tall guy coming out of the building. Not a hippie, but definitely a speed freak. You could tell real easy. All jittery and bug eyes darting around and mumbling to himself. It was hard to see in the dark, but when he rushed past me he held out his hands palms up as if he had blood on them."

"Did he see you?"

"I think so, but he ran off. I was crashing, so I didn't even really pay that much attention to him. He was just another stoned junkie in the Haight, you know? Anyway, sometime later, I woke up and there's Billy's van double-parked in front of Tom's building. So I walked over and got inside. Fell asleep on the passenger seat. I mean, I was out of it. Next thing I know, Billy's nudging me. He said, What're you doing here? I said, I need a place to crash. Is Tom up? Then, with no explanation, Billy drove off."

"You stayed behind?"

She shook her head. "I was still in the van. He took me to his pad and told me to sleep it off. The next day, he drilled me about what I was doing on the street last night and all that. I told him I had crashed in the doorway. Then he asked if I saw anything weird. I said I saw Lurch coming out of Tom's pad. That's when Billy told me Tom was dead." Her voice broke on the last word, but she composed herself. Showing emotion wasn't her style. "Can we get some cigarettes somewhere?"

"In a minute. Did you see Curious Jack that night?"

"No. Billy explained it like this. Lurch had gone to Tom's pad to kill him for selling bad drugs to his friend. Then Billy was tipped off and went by to check it out."

"Billy said this guy Lurch was the killer?"

"Yeah."

Evan's face twisted with confusion. Nothing she had said jibed with what Harkess had told him. "Why were you being kept in that hotel?"

"I was a witness, man."

Evan's brow dipped. "But you didn't see anything."

"I saw Lurch leave the scene, and he probably saw me. When I asked Billy if my life was in danger, he said maybe, but not as long as I stayed underground, cleaned up my act, got off speed and other shit, and let him deal with the situation. In a few more weeks, he said, the coast would be clear. But he never says when or how. And Jimmy doesn't know shit. He just keeps rolling joints and tries to get into my pants."

"Then he *was* holding you against your will."

"Well, yes but no. I mean... Jimmy is just some guy Billy hired to be my guardian. To protect me from the killer and to keep me off acid and speed. Go figure. A drug dealer wants me to go straight. But I guess it was Tom's dying wish, so..."

"His dying wish?"

"Billy said Tom made him promise to keep me out of trouble." Again, her throat constricted as if she were struggling to repress emotion. Then she regained composure and changed the subject. "I'm... I'm pregnant, is what it is."

Evan glanced at her belly. Only the slightest bulge appeared. He knew from the diary that she was carrying his brother's child.

"Wait a second," Evan said. "If you were a witness, why didn't you go to the police? You wanted them to catch the killer, didn't you?"

She shrugged. "Billy said no. To tell the truth, I think he was hiding me so the cops wouldn't get to him."

"Get to him for what?"

Jane lowered her brow at him as if it was an ignorant question. "He's a pusher."

"Do you think he had anything to do with my brother's death?"

She dropped her chin to her chest. "That crossed my mind. I've been kinda scared about it…" With her defenses finally torn down, Jane turned her head away to prevent him from seeing her tears. She fought hard to suppress her emotions.

"This guy you call Lurch," Evan said. "Who was he?"

"I don't know, but I overheard Billy on the phone with Jimmy. They called the guy Mel."

Evan blanched. Dizziness spiraled through him as if his soul whooshed down a drain. He couldn't breathe. His throat tightened. Every muscle stiffened. The Lurch image burned into his brain. The sunken eyes, the height, the broad shoulders. The portrayal fit. He knew. As surely as he could recite his own name, he knew the man's identity. He couldn't fathom the reason, it made no sense, it couldn't be true, but he knew whom she meant.

She had described Sandy's brother. Patrick's own brother-in-law.

"Mel Capp?" he asked.

"I don't know." Then in a stoned haze, Jane said, "Now how about driving me to the Haight?"

32
I Can See For Miles

The Plymouth screeched to a halt on the street in front of Sandy's house. It was broad daylight at early afternoon, but Evan no longer felt any need to skulk about the premises or hide from strangers. He leapt out of the car and jogged to the front door with purpose. He rang the doorbell twice to no answer. Then he peered in a window. No one appeared to be home. Finally, Evan tried the back door, which hadn't been locked. He didn't feel he was trespassing; it was his brother's house, after all. And he wanted answers.

"Sandy!" Evan's voice echoed in the kitchen. No other sounds emanated from the small house. Sandy and her boys were away. Evan glanced at the wall clock, which displayed the time as quarter past twelve. Where would they be on a Friday afternoon? Then he slapped his forehead with realization: Patrick's ceremony. They were scheduled to pour his ashes into the bay in less than two hours. Sandy had probably taken the kids to the Dunne house by cross-town bus or subway train. A phone call to his mother's house would let him know if he was right. He had a barrage of serious questions for Sandy.

Just as he crossed the room to make the call, Sandy's phone rang. Evan wasn't in the habit of answering someone else's telephone, so he waited for the ringing to cease before he placed his call. But the phone rang and rang and rang. Over one minute passed. His impatience burned until he finally lifted the receiver and pressed it to his ear.

Evan didn't speak. Neither did the person on the other end. Evan was about to hang up when a voice grumbled over the line.

"Dunne?"

The gruff male voice sounded familiar, but Evan couldn't tell for sure.

"Hello?" Evan said.

"Where's Jane?"

Now he was certain. It was Harkess.

"What the hell...?"

"Where's Jane?"

"How did you know I would be here?"

"I saw you go in—"

"What's happened to Sandy?"

"Christ, take it easy. I saw her leave with the kids half an hour ago. I'm at a payphone on West Portal Avenue. Meet me at Happy Donuts." He hung up.

August 12, 1967

Everything's turned to shit. Can hardly bring myself to write about it.

Went back to the streets. GH received the new BZ device from TSS. Rumor spread that a riot was planned for that evening, which meant we had to test the new unit. But the bastards didn't send us any gas masks. I balked. GH told me to calm down. Our instructions are to plant the device and split. Cool, but how are we supposed to record the results if we're not around? GH insisted once again that we're not the only ops on the street. Maybe he's right. I don't know. Do they have gas masks?

But no riot occurred. The Hell's Angels sent word out to the neighborhood – any rioters would face the bikers' wrath. That practically cleared the street. GH was disappointed he never got to employ his new toy.

The very idea of using it so haphazardly still shocks me. Are we supposed to alert SFPD about the nerve gas? Should we warn them to bring masks? Or do we just let them get dosed, too? What about innocent bystanders? How about infants and the elderly who live in the neighborhood? People walking their dogs? Tourists?

My conscience kept me up all night. Something has to be done about this absurd operation before it becomes a catastrophe.

The next morning I phoned Carl Burnblad. The reporter didn't remember me, and why should he? But I told him I had a story to tell about CIA infiltration of the drug trade in the Haight Ashbury. He perked up at that and wanted to hear more. Not over the phone. I arranged to meet him across town at Red's Java House by the piers at 11 p.m.

I never made it.

That searing look in Sandy's eyes will be forever burned into my mind. How she found me on Haight Street, I don't know. Maybe she followed me. Maybe one of her girlfriends saw me on the street and informed her. Doesn't really matter.

I stood in my usual spot beside the bank on Belvedere. Banging my tom-tom. Time was about 3:30. I'd just sold a lid to a couple of chicks, pocketed the cash, and looked up. There was Sandy staring laser beams of hate at me. The ache in the pit of my stomach hasn't left me since. She glanced at the valise handcuffed to my wrist. Can't imagine what she thought of that.

She ran, I followed. Our car was parked on Page. I tried to stop her, she almost ran me over. I raced back to my crash pad, dumped the valise in the safe, and took Muni buses across town to our house.

By the time I arrived home an hour later, a lock-smith was already changing our door locks. Christ, that was fast. I paid the guy $200 to go away and leave the locks untouched. He didn't have to be asked twice.

Sandy was tossing my belongings out of the house. Everything she could get her hands on, she flung out the window. Matt & Andy were stunned. I told the boys to stay calm. Mommy was just upset. Matty cried. I told Andy to look after his little brother.

God, the fury. She's been that mad before, but not for such a prolonged period. She kept ranting well past sundown. I begged her to calm down for the boys' sake. Nothing worked. Finally, Mrs. Whetfield from next door offered to take Matt & Andy for a few hours. She must've heard the yelling. Sandy let me have it both barrels. She refused to believe that I'm working for Naval intelligence, and I can't blame her. Sounds crazy. If I admitted that I'm actually with CIA, that would sound even nuttier. I just had to grit my teeth and take her wrath. Let me speak to your commanding officer, she said. I tried to explain that talking to him was out of the question. She went hysterical and called me a liar. Can't blame her. I wracked my brain to come up with some way to convince her without di-vulging operational details, but I came up blank. All I could do was stand there and take the abuse.

When she ran out of steam, I collected all my be-longings and temporarily placed everything in the garage. Andy watched from the neighbor's house and then volun-teered to help even though his mom hollered at him not to. Sandy tried to get me to leave, go wherever I go during the week, just go. I refused. She slammed doors. For the boys' sake, I left.

Back in the Haight, J was passed out. An empty bottle of cheap wine on the floor beside the mattress. GH had come to the apartment and left a note. 'We need to talk asap.' Very odd. He rarely comes by. Called but no answer. I hit the sack.

Friday morning, J tells me she's having my baby. This blows my mind. <u>My</u> baby? I thought she'd been raped. She was, but the rapist used a rubber. That's crazy. She insists it's true. Well, I don't want a baby with her. J refuses an abortion because it's immoral. Stupid girl, your whole life is immoral. The drugs, the sex, running away from home, you name it. That sent her into tears. I told her to deal with it because I've got serious problems to solve.

Then GH comes by unannounced. He's all cloak and dagger, hopes he wasn't followed. Says Gervin, one of my regulars, found GH on the street. He brought with him a newspaper reporter who was trying to track me down. Burnblad, I assume. I played dumb. Harkess gave me the evil eye. Asked if I was talking to the press. Absolutely not. Give me a lie detector test. I'd pass it hands down.

He then tells me SG and the TSS thinktankers are under pressure after the anarchy in Detroit. They need us to test the BZ device pronto. We're ordered to foment a riot this weekend using whatever means available and use the new weapon. I blurt out, No. Have them use it in Detroit where the real riots are. Orders are orders, he says. I'm not testing that thing without safeguards. GH explains how it works on a delay. We set it and split. But how are we supposed to instigate a riot? He knows it will be difficult, but he has a few ideas. We need to brainstorm and implement asap.

No, I tell him. I need to go home. My marriage is crumbling. My wife saw me on the street. My cover could already be blown.

GH's eyes go dead. No emotion, impossible to read his mind. He sits in silence for two minutes, then rises from the chair. All he says is, Good luck with that. Then he splits.

I removed my valise from the safe. Took out seven hundred bucks and gave it to J. Told her to take care of herself and that I didn't expect to see her when I returned. She turned to stone, didn't shed a tear, no emotion at all. Then I split for home.

Got back home last night. Sandy had the locks changed again. Andy let me in. Got the silent treatment from then on. She won't even look at me. Explanations are useless. I don't know what else to do. My mind has gone numb.

It's Saturday midnight and everyone's asleep but me. Slept on the sofa but haven't been able to close my eyes. Until now, that is. I've hit a wall. Exhausted physically, emotionally, and spiritually.

God, please release me from this hell.

The donut shop didn't appear to be a trap. The storefront had ceiling-high windows offering a direct view of the busy avenue, and there sat Harkess on a stool ten feet from the doorway staring out at the street. Evan saw no other patrons, just a sleepy-eyed proprietor behind the cash register. He parked his Plymouth in a metered spot, got out, and peered up and down the avenue. Nothing alarming on the street, just workaday San Franciscans going about their lives. Evan entered the donut shop and sat on the nearest stool. Harkess already had a cup of coffee awaiting him.

"Don't tell me you stuck Jane in that goddamn windmill," Harkess muttered.

Evan smirked. "No."

Harkess removed a pack of cigarettes from his shirt pocket and offered one to Evan. He declined with a suspicious glare. Harkess lit up and sucked deeply, letting the smoke relieve his nerves. "You've really screwed up my magic act, Boy Scout. There I was pulling rabbits out of hats, total misdirection, keeping everybody dazzled, and then you came along threatening to show how the trick is done."

Evan asked, "Who killed my brother?"

Harkess glanced over his shoulder to be certain the donut shop proprietor, the only other person in the place, didn't overhear. Then he spoke in a hushed, gravelly voice. "Here's the deal. I'll clear the air, but you have to promise, fucking scout's honor, that you will bury everything I tell you."

Evan scowled. "Why should I trust you to tell me the truth?"

"Swear to me on your father's grave," Harkess said with conviction, "that you will let this matter rest."

Evan hesitated. "My brother—"

"You're not listening," Harkess said. "Patrick ain't coming back. A biker went down for the crime. And that has to be the end of it."

"Did the CIA kill him?"

Harkess peered over his shoulder but the donut shop owner had slipped into the back room, so he couldn't hear the conversation. "No, the agency didn't do it. Wipe that crazy notion off your slate."

"Was it Mel Capp?" Evan asked.

Harkess shot him a surprised glance.

"Jane's description, a perfect fit." Although he was afraid of the answer, Evan asked again, "Was it Sandy's brother?"

Harkess gave a sad nod.

Tears of rage welled in Evan's eyes. "Don't bullshit me."

"No bullshit," Harkess spoke in a soft, pitying voice.

Evan's lower lip trembled, his breathing quickened, and his chest felt ready to collapse. Bile rose in his esophagus, and he wanted to retch. Even though he'd hoped for a more sinister conspiracy, something toward which he could direct his righteous anger, he sensed it was true. Mel murdered Patrick. He rested his arms on the countertop, buried his head, and sobbed.

Minutes passed. Neither man spoke. Customers wandered in and out of the shop to purchase fattening fried dough. Harkess smoked in silence. Evan regained his composure, wiping away snot with a paper napkin. Once the rush of customers passed, Evan continued.

"If Mel did it, why is Pulasko in prison?"

"I'm talking under one condition. You tell me where Jane is."

The arrangement only made Evan angry, but he wanted answers, so he gritted his teeth and nodded his consent.

"It happened on a Sunday night," Harkess began. "I was stoned sky high on pot brownies. We were listening to records—"

"Who's we?"

"My guy Jimmy. Not important. I got a phone call from Patrick. Just checking in. He had been agitated and had a lot on his mind. His wife had spotted him selling on the street. As I was talking, somebody came to his door. Patrick put down the phone while I was still on the line and let the guy in. I heard shouting in the background, cursing, a man with a deep voice calling him a dirty nigger lover. Hollered it real clear. Patrick tried to talk but kept getting shouted down. I was afraid of a drug deal gone sour, you know, a disgruntled customer, so I rushed out the door and drove right over. I walked in and found the big man standing over Patrick's body. I met Mel once before and recognized him right away. Kind of a hard guy to forget." Harkess ran his hand through his bushy hair.

"It's weird, y'know. Every guy sees himself as Steve McQueen, cool in a crisis. But I freaked. I was stoned, and Patrick was lying there... All that blood... The arm... And there's Mel in total shock, blubbering. Told me he didn't mean to do it. Only meant to beat the crap out of him for dishonoring Sandy. But I guess Mel lost his cool. Found a butcher knife in the kitchen. I didn't ask for any more details. The blubbering idiot begged forgiveness over your brother's body, and then ran off in a panic. Then I called—"

"Didn't you go after him?"

"Believe me, I wanted to strangle the motherfucker right then and there! But that would only make matters worse, and I knew the agency would deal with him eventually. Besides, man, I was in shock and stoned out of my gourd. I called my contact and asked for help. He said that since the cops might trace Patrick and me back to the agency, I needed to cover up the damage at all costs and, as soon as that was done, go to ground. So I got the hell outta there." Harkess sucked on his cigarette. Trembling fingers belied his guilt. "When I got out to my van, there was Janey passed out in the passenger seat. Like I needed her to complicate things. I drove her to my pad, put Jimmy in charge of her, and I paced around trying to conjure up a miracle cure. It didn't help that I'd eaten, like, seven pot brownies. Paranoia city, man.

"Then it hit me. I'd left my prints all over the crime scene. Once the cops investigated, they'd come for me, and the agency would disavow my employment. It was a potential shitstorm, and I had to act quick. Grabbed a bunch of rags. Didn't want anyone to grab my license plate number, so I raced back on foot. Wiped everything down as best I could. Took all the rags and dumped them in the trunk of Patrick's car. I wanted to remove his body, but it was impossible. So I created a diversion, a red herring to throw the cops off. I stuffed the arm into the briefcase and took off with it."

Evan's face contorted with angst and he slammed his palms against his forehead. "That's fucking crazy!"

Harkess glared daggers at him. "Of course it was! I was higher than Saturn!"

"That doesn't even make any sense! Where's the logic?"

"You want logic? Study algebra! But don't expect logic in the condition I was in! Not in the Haight!"

Evan buried his head in his hands. Harkess's story sounded mad yet, given all he'd read in the diary and all he'd lived through in recent days, he believed it. Utterly mad, thoroughly irrational, drug-addled surrealist derangement. But possible.

Harkess stubbed out his cigarette into a tin ashtray and, with quivering hands, lit up another. "So I drove into the park, dumped the bloody rags in a trash barrel, and set 'em on fire. Then along comes this scumbag Pulasko. He's stumbling along, jabbering nonsense, even higher than me. A plan popped into my head. A crazy, stoned improvisation, but it worked. I put Pulasko into the backseat of Patrick's car, where he passed out, and drove off to the beach in Pacifica. Left him there with the dead arm in the briefcase. Wiped down my prints. For good measure, I sprayed him with BZ. Then I bolted. Later, I called in the murder from a payphone. A Narco agent intervened, the cops backed off, and the fixers stepped in. In no time, the cops found their killer, and Pulasko, thank God, was in no position to fight the charge. Case closed."

"You framed an innocent man."

"The hell he was. Pulasko came out of the womb guilty."

"But the real killer went scot free."

Harkess shook his head. "The agency took care of Mel. Shipped him straight off to the front lines. And he said thank you. Said he was ready to give his life for his country. Kinda batshit, if you ask me. Look, it turned out a win-win situation. A bad ass went to prison like he deserved, your family got some kind of justice, and everybody can get on with their lives."

"That's insane."

"That's reality."

"No, it isn't!"

"It is now."

A beefy woman in a pillbox hat entered the shop to purchase a baker's dozen. Both men sat in silence while the proprietor served her. Three minutes later, she exited and the conversation continued in hushed tones.

"Why are you telling me all this?" Evan asked.

"You've been fighting for answers. I can dig that. Here

they are. Happy birthday." Harkess took a sip of coffee. "Besides, you heard what King said. Anything I say, if you repeat it, means you'll be crowned an acidhead conspiracy nut. And a homo to boot."

"Not if the diary surfaces."

"It did." Harkess blew out a plume. "King and Menard found it."

Evan gasped. "How? Where?"

"Near your crazy windmill. They destroyed it immediately."

Blood filled Evan's face so that he felt dizzy. He had let his brother down so miserably. He wanted to bolt down the street in a mad howl and tear something apart with his bare hands, anything at all. Then his anger gave way to self-loathing. All Evan wanted was justice for Patrick, yet he'd blundered monumentally. He wished for some way to make amends. He wished it was all a hallucination. He wished he were dead.

Harkess sucked his cigarette. Then he said. "Let me give you some advice, Dunne. Don't pick a fight with the United States Government. You'll only dig your own grave. If you go public, the agency will refute every syllable you utter, assassinate your character, and flush your soul down the crapper. Give it up. Nothing you do is going to bring Patrick back, and nobody's giving you any more merit badges. My advice? If you wanna play hero, go do it in Vietnam."

"You mean like the asshole who killed my brother?" Evan said in a voice jagged with sarcasm. A minute passed as his anger steeped. His mind throbbed from the insanity. Then he asked, "Why were you hiding Jane?"

"You don't need to know," Harkess said. "Just tell me where she is."

"She said Patrick had a deathbed request that you take care of her. But you just said Patrick was dead when you arrived."

Harkess shrugged. "I told her fairy tales so she wouldn't freak out."

"Is Jane in danger?"

Harkess offered no response. He stared out the window and smoked.

"She thinks Patrick's killer is after her. Did you tell her that for her own protection?"

Harkess said nothing.

"Who are you hiding her from? Not from Mel or Pulasko. The fixers? They searched for her in San Leandro."

Harkess said, "Tell me where she is."

"Why do you care about her?"

"I've told you everything, Boy Scout."

"Stop calling me that! Why were you keeping her off drugs? Because she's pregnant?"

Harkess took another sip of coffee.

"Why do you care?" Evan asked. "It's Patrick's baby, isn't it?"

Harkess flinched. His lower lip quivered and he blinked. A moment passed, and Evan realized everything.

"Oh my God," Evan whispered. "You're the father."

Harkess sucked cigarette smoke. The red ember burned like his conscience, and the cigarette trembled in his hand. Then his eyes softened, and the man shrugged.

Evan sat upright on the stool and arched his back. The revelation surprised him, and he empathized with the odd man.

"You've been hiding her so the fixers won't get to her," Evan said. "You know they're going to kill her, so you're protecting your child."

In a hushed voice, Harkess said, "Just tell me where she is."

"My life is in danger, too, isn't it? Those cigarettes on my dashboard. Did you know about them?"

"Not until after the fact. Swear to God."

"Poison?"

Harkess hung his head. "I don't know."

"I gave them to some hippie kid, and now he's probably—"

"You agreed to give up Jane."

Evan's gaze turned to steel and he asked, "What are you going to do with her?"

"Goddamnit, Dunne."

Evan pointed at the man's chest and said, "Tell me there's a conscience in there."

Neither man spoke as more customers entered the shop. Two minutes passed, during which the angry tension in Harkess's body made him vibrate. Then his shoulders sagged and he rubbed his calloused hands over his bearded face and hooked nose. Then the surly man stubbed out his cigarette and sighed.

"I hoped she could stay in San Francisco after the flak died down," Harkess said, "but it's not gonna shake out as I planned. I realize now that as long as she's here, they'll find her. I need to get Jane out of San Francisco, out of the state, and convince her to never come back."

For the first time, Harkess lowered his defenses, and Evan believed what he said. A spark of humanity glowed in the surly man. A heart beat beneath his concrete shell.

"What about your child?"

Harkess shrugged. "It might be mine, it might be Patrick's. Who can say?"

"Don't the fixers know she's pregnant? They wouldn't hurt her if…"

Harkess arched an eyebrow at Evan. "What do you think?"

Evan shuddered. "You'll go with her?"

Harkess's shoulders slumped. "I thought about disappearing with her, going underground, but I've got this situation you can't just walk away from. If I vanish, they come after me and I'm as good as dead. Forget it. I'll stay put. But I'm going to give her cash and put her on a bus."

Several seconds passed and then Evan said, "What about me?"

"Sorry," Harkess said. "Get your ass into uniform and be a model soldier. That's the best chance you have."

Then Evan said, "That's not what I meant."

✧

Minutes later, after the conversation concluded, Evan strode out of the donut shop, climbed into his Plymouth, revved the engine, and pulled out of the parking spot.

As he drove, his mind drifted. He pondered how events had so mightily changed. Since leaving Loyola University to visit Italy, Evan's life had plunged into a cosmic sinkhole. If only he had stayed in college instead of chasing after *la dolce vita*, he might never have been sucked into the miasma. One poor decision fostered a chain reaction that altered his fate. Reality had produced a cancerous tumor in his soul.

If you don't like reality, change it.

With his spirit plumbed to its darkest depth, with the vision of his future never cloudier, with the oppressive truth revealed as madness, and with righteous anger welling inside him, Evan plotted a new course. Another noble goal lay before him, and he vowed not to screw this one up.

33
We're Going Wrong

Evan's car sped up Eureka Street. Uncle Stu's Brougham was parked in his mother's driveway. As Evan double-parked across the street, Sandy and her sons exited Alice's house and walked down her front steps. The boys were dressed in smart suits, and Sandy wore a black mourning dress and sunglasses beneath a pillbox hat and veil. Dolores, dressed in a black skirt with a dark coat and black silk gloves, followed with an urn the size of a large coffeepot. Then came Alice in the same black dress and veil she'd worn at her husband's funeral years earlier. At the top of the steps, Uncle Stu stood in his outgrown policeman's uniform. Evan cut the engine and climbed out. The old cop dropped a blistering scowl on him. Dolores glanced at him with wordless pity. Evan beelined toward Sandy but stopped short at the sight of his nephews' sad eyes.

"We need to talk," Evan said.

Sandy stared at him through her sunglasses. "Good, you're here. Now we won't need a cab. Can you drive your mother?"

Evan couldn't cause a scene in front of Matt and Andy, but neither could he bottle his emotions. He blurted out, "I know what happened."

Sandy looked him up and down, taking in the filthy, wrinkled clothes he'd worn for days, and said, "Please go in and change."

Dolores wrinkled her nose with revulsion and said, "Some cologne, too."

"I know about Mel," he said.

Sandy gave a vacuous stare. Either she had no idea what he was talking about or she had the acting talent of Elizabeth Taylor or she was so deep in denial that she wouldn't acknowledge his words. She clucked her tongue and shuffled the kids into the backseat of the Brougham. Dolores also ignored the comment and carried the urn to the car.

Alice stood paralyzed at the bottom of the steps and stared at Evan. Her face went stiff with fear. Instant sobriety flashed through her.

Uncle Stu waddled down the steps, which taxed his ailing lungs, and took Alice by the arm to lead her back up into the house. Then he motioned for Evan to join them and said, "Excuse us for a moment, girls."

"We're already running late," Dolores groaned.

"Give us one minute," Stu said. Then he and stunned Alice entered the house with Evan right behind them.

Uncle Stu closed the door and spoke with quiet intensity. "Your family has been worried sick about you—"

"It was Mel," Evan said without emotion and then waited for a reaction.

"That's crazy," Uncle Stu said. "Stop this nonsense."

Alice hesitated and quivered with shock. Evan had seen that look in his mother before; she was on the verge of collapse. Then she raised her hands to her face and burst into tears. Uncle Stu's breathing grew more laborious, his face reddened, and he gave Alice a pitying glance. His emphysema forced him into the nearest chair. Evan wasn't sure how to interpret their reactions. Neither of them asked him to explain what he meant. Did they have any idea what he was talking about? Did they just assume he was still on drugs? Evan felt confused.

Then, through her sobs, Alice whimpered, "He didn't mean to."

Her words whooshed through Evan's mind and left him feeling faint. When he stopped breathing, electrons danced before his eyes. Then he sucked air as if recovering from a blow to the solar plexus, and burning anger surged through him to set his heart on fire. His voice rose an octave as he said, "You knew? You knew?"

Alice clasped her hands together in prayer and stared to Heaven. Tears fell in streams along the wrinkles on her face. Without meeting Evan's fiery gaze, she said, "God, forgive me."

Then she ran to the hallway bathroom and locked herself in. Evan stood in shock and then followed. He banged at the door, but she refused to open it.

"Mom!"

Through the closed door, Alice repeated over and over in a tiny whimper, "Forgive me, forgive me, forgive me..."

"Mom, come out here!"

Uncle Stu ambled into the hallway. "You weren't supposed to find out. Nobody was."

"What the hell happened?" Evan asked.

"You don't want to know—"

"Don't patronize me!"

From inside the bathroom, Alice sobbed and muttered scripture.

"Mom!"

While gasping for breath, Uncle Stu held out a hand for Evan to stop. Then the old man slunk into a hallway chair and said, "Mel called your mother from Vietnam and... He was crazy drunk."

"What did he say, Mom?"

In the bathroom, Alice wept without replying.

"He confessed," Uncle Stu said.

"Why?" Evan hollered. "Why did he do it?"

"Let it go, Evan."

"Was it because Patrick had a black girlfriend?" When his mother wailed and Uncle Stu flinched, Evan banged on the bathroom door. "Is that why he killed him?"

"Drop it, son."

Evan clenched his jaw so tightly he could have chipped his teeth. "Tell me!"

Uncle Stu sucked air as best his failing lungs could manage and said, "Mel said there was a black girl, a junkie. That's how low Patrick had stooped."

"How did Mel find out about her?"

Uncle Stu shrugged. "Who knows?"

Evan balled his fists and hollered, "You knew all along what Patrick was doing!"

"I did, but your mother didn't." Uncle Stu jabbed a finger at him. "And I warned you not to poke the hornet's nest."

"The wrong man is in prison!"

"A buddy on the force admitted the murder was mysterious. But, he said, even if Pulasko was framed, the Feds and the DA couldn't care less. The case is tied off, sewn shut, and off limits."

Evan pounded the door again. "Why didn't you tell me, Mom?"

"I told Alice not to tell anyone. For your sakes. It's the government, Evan. You just don't mess with them. What's done can't be undone. I warned you to steer clear."

"You were a cop! What about justice?"

Uncle Stu sucked air and said, "The biker is in prison. That's all the justice we're likely to—"

"Two men broke into this house and drugged me so they could squash the truth! Now I find out my own family – my own goddamn family! You kept the truth from me, too!" Evan banged at the bathroom door with both fists. He hurled curses. He wanted to smash things. He glared and burned and stewed and shouted. "Nothing but lies!"

"Lies can protect," Uncle Stu said with a straight face.

The condescension set Evan further ablaze. "Fuck you!"

Uncle Stu ignored the curse. "Look what the truth has done to you, son. Look at your mother. The truth would crush Sandy and her parents. She and Dolores and the kids don't need to know. Think about it, Evan. It's better this way."

"Her brother killed my brother!"

"What do you expect, revenge?" Uncle Stu said. "From who? From a grieving widow and her fatherless kids?"

"I want the truth to be told!"

"At what cost, son? At what cost? Hasn't this family suffered enough?"

Dolores entered the front door and said, "What's all the yelling about?"

"Please wait outside, dear," Uncle Stu said.

"The boat isn't going to wait for us," Dolores griped. "Is Mom in the bathroom?"

Furious, Evan raced past Dolores and up the stairs to his bedroom. He ripped open drawers full of socks, underwear, jeans, slacks, and shirts and dumped everything onto the bedspread. Then he rushed to the closet, yanked shirts and slacks off of hangers, and tossed them onto the bed, too. Two pairs of shoes were pulled out from under the bed frame and added to the pile. He then took a final scan of the room and saw nothing else worthwhile. Then he grabbed the four corners of the bedspread, folded them into the center, and tied off the ends to create a huge hobo's bundle. Evan hoisted the pack onto his back and hauled it down the stairs.

Déjà vu hit him. He'd done this before; leaving the house with a pack of clothes. When he was a boy. When he ran away from home. The first time he went chasing windmills.

Dolores was no longer at the front door. Evan looked over his shoulder to see a tableau of his sister giving solace to their weeping mother in the kitchen. From the hallway chair, Uncle Stu stared at him with concern. The old cop's face had turned a shade of blue to match his uniform. His faltering lungs prevented him from speaking, and Evan didn't give him a chance. Out the door he fled.

Sandy sat in the backseat of the Brougham with her sons. She stared off at some distant vision and barely noticed Evan. Then she looked up at him with the vacant eyes of an ivory statuette. Evan stood frozen with his mouth open, but no words escaped. Their eyes locked, but he couldn't read whatever thoughts lay behind hers. Nor could he discern any emotion. How could the truth harm Sandy, he wondered, when she had already turned into a pillar of salt? Yet he couldn't bring himself to speak. Not when two innocent boys could overhear. He marched away with the heavy bundle.

Let my mother and uncle bear the weight of truth and lies, Evan thought. He absolved himself of all that. He had new goals.

After shoving the bundle into the backseat of his Plymouth, he took a last glance around the old neighborhood. Gray clouds mottled the sun and exposed the dirt and disrepair of the neighbors' homes. Two thin, mustachioed young men walked down the street. Both had perfectly coiffed hair, crisply ironed slacks, and one wore an ascot. They grinned and winked at one another, and Evan thought of the stranger inside the windmill. He took a mental snapshot of the neighborhood and sensed that the reality of the place was likely to change before he ever saw it again. *If* he ever saw it again. Then he climbed behind the wheel and sped away without looking back.

August 13, 1967

This breaks my vow of never writing when I'm high, but screw it. This will be my final entry. Keeping this diary was probably a huge mistake in the first place, but I intend to turn it over to the press asap. Until then, it's not safe with me. I've got to hide it. Somewhere temporary until I can get back in touch with Burnblad. Damn, I wish he'd answer. Why didn't I get an address from him? Stupid. I suppose I could mail it to someone I trust who can hold it for me. Somewhere I can retrieve it within a few days. It's not safe here at my pad. I'm not even safe here. Not at home. Not here. Maybe nowhere on earth. If I were one of those astronauts, maybe I'd be safe in space.

Shouldn't write when I'm stoned.

I can't overcome a sense of impending doom. That's not just drug paranoia talking. I wish I could just walk away, go to ground, pack Sandy and the boys into the car and go into hiding. No, bad choice. Can't drag my wife and kids down with me. Got to keep them out of it. I doubt she'd go with me anyway. Not now. Maybe never again.

As I see it, I've got only one shot at redemption. I need to spill my guts to the press. Once I tell the world the truth, my family will see me as a hero. At least, I hope so. Then Mom can put my photo up there on the wall beside Evan's.

This is all assuming I don't get killed, of course. The information I want to make public might put me in some assassin's riflescope. Or I'll be labeled a traitor and hung.

Maybe I should run. Get the hell out of here. Said the joker to the thief.

I'm torn. I'm stoned. But I'll think of something.

Problem is, I get the craziest thoughts when I'm high. Absurd notions lead to weird actions. Probably true for everyone, stoned or straight.

Come to think of it, who needs drugs when reality is the ultimate absurdity? The universe is preposterous, and God is daft.

Aren't you, Old Man?

34
Tomorrow Never Knows

At the crest of Market Street at Portola, Evan stood beside his Plymouth and stared down at the city. Fog blocked the
scenery. Nothing to see but a wall of gray. If he could have
waited until noon, the fog would burn off and he'd have one
last view of San Francisco. But not on this Saturday morning.

He smoked a cigarette and contemplated what lay
ahead. So many emotions stirred within him that they all
served to negate one another. In two more hours, the Army
would officially designate him a draft dodger. He didn't care
how that would reflect on his family. Instead, he focused on
plans. A new path lay before him, even if he didn't know
where it would lead. The goal was concise; the way would be
improvised. Convincing Jane to join him took all night. Explanations were complicated but she understood. It helped that
she was finally straight and lucid. She showed no fear of
jumping into a void, and he admired her for it.

The fog only seemed to grow thicker. There was nothing to see anyway. Nothing he hadn't seen one hundred times before. The time had come for fresh vistas.

Up and over the peaks he drove, past sleepy neighborhoods to the corner of Carl and Cole. He parked the Plymouth at curbside, grabbed his vehicle registration from the glove compartment, and entered the Free Store.

The tall, bearded hippie in a dashiki stood at the center of the room. Evan approached him. "Billy sent me."

"Cool," the hippie said. He pointed through the window to a blue Volkswagen Beetle parked outside.

"A bug?" Evan said with disapproval.

"In perfect working condition," the hippie said. "New brakes, new carburetor, and an oil change."

"What year?"

"It's a '63."

"It's not a stick shift, is it?"

"Best I could do on short notice, man."

Evan sighed. He wished for an automatic transmission and a car with more room and more horsepower. Under the circumstances, he had little choice. There was no time to haggle. "Who was the previous owner?"

"Does it matter? She's giving the car to whoever needs it. Just like you're giving yours. The barter system. No money. It's beautiful, man."

"Okay, what do I need to do?"

"Just sign your pink slip. Where's your car?"

"The Plymouth Valiant parked right outside."

The hippie peered out the window, nodded, and offered a ballpoint. Then Evan penned his signature on the registration. He doubted the legality of what he was doing but he didn't care.

"What about the documents?" Evan asked.

"Billy has them."

"What do I owe you?" Evan asked, even though he already guessed the answer.

The hippie flashed two fingers and said, "Peace."

"Thank you," Evan said with humility. His cheeks reddened. He bowed his head and shuffled his feet and didn't know what to do with his arms. He struggled to find more to say, but instead extended his hand, shook, and repeated, "Thank you."

Then Evan strode outside to the Beetle. As a precaution, he scanned each street for King and Menard's black sedan but saw no sign of it. After climbing in, he revved the engine, which grumbled louder than a motorcycle, pushed the clutch, grinded the gears, and, in herky-jerky fashion, drove away.

Three blocks later, he pulled the blue Beetle into the driveway on Waller Street. Evan scanned the street but saw no sign of the black sedan. Then he rushed up the stairs and entered the always-open doorway into the house. Robby sauntered out of the kitchen and met Evan in the middle of the long hallway.

"How's she doing?" Evan asked.

"The girl's got a hell of an appetite all of a sudden," Robby said, unaware of the facts.

"Thanks for looking after her," Evan said.

"Hey, man, Janey is one of us."

Evan followed him down the hallway to the dirty kitchen. There sat Jane at a rickety card table before a plate of rice and beans. Her tender brown eyes conveyed sobriety. One day without pot seemed to create an entirely new personality.

With trepidation and a smile, Evan asked, "Ready?"

She nodded. With that, Evan marched down the hall and up the stairs to a bedroom. His bundle of clothes had been folded into neat piles and placed in two plastic trash bags. He grabbed the bags and the bedspread and carried them downstairs to the front door. Then he looked up with surprise.

Gil Harkess stood in the living room.

He had disguised himself as best he could in drab suit, glasses, and a panama hat, but his hooked nose gave him away. "Did the hippie come through with your wheels?"

"Yeah," Evan said.

"Good," Harkess said. "They'll be looking for that Plymouth." He held out two fake IDs and a pair of passports.

"Passports, too?" Evan said as he admired the handiwork. "Where'd you get them?"

"Connections," Harkess said. "Those guys at the Free Store are amateurs. Rely on the passports."

"Thanks," Evan said as he pocketed the paperwork. Then he pointed to a leather satchel at Harkess' feet. "I thought you were staying put."

"Consider it a going-away present," Harkess said as he pushed the satchel with his foot. "Remember, this is no half-assed measure. You've got to commit."

"I get it."

"She can survive on the lam," Harkess said. "Can you?"

"Well, if everything goes according to plan and you never hear about me again," Evan replied, "then you'll know the answer is yes."

Harkess nodded. They stood in wooden silence for five full seconds. Then, without even a hint of sentimentality or a farewell, Harkess walked toward the door.

"Aren't you going to say goodbye to Jane?" Evan asked.

Harkess stopped in the doorway, turned around, and considered the idea. His cheek twitched, the closest thing to emotion he would show. Then he spun and marched out the door and down the steps. Out on the street, his go-go dancer neighbor sat behind the wheel of her blue Camaro. After he climbed into the passenger seat, she gunned the engine, burned rubber, and peeled off down Waller Street.

Evan grabbed the leather satchel and opened it. To his astonishment, it was stuffed with loose bills – fifties and hundreds and twenties that probably amounted to tens of thousands of dollars. He guessed it was drug money Harkess had accumulated while working Haight Street. At the donut shop, Harkess had agreed to finance the getaway, but Evan didn't realize how much money the man would pony up. He wished he could thank the guy, but he doubted he'd ever see him again. If all went well, he never would.

"You're free to do whatever you want, Janey," Robby said as he and Jane strolled out of the kitchen and down the hall. "Stay here if the spirit moves you."

Jane put on her leather cowgirl jacket with the fringed sleeves. "Thanks, Robby, but I need to ramble."

"Alright then," Robby said with a shrug. Jane hugged him. "Be cool, baby."

She then followed Evan out the open doorway. Jane left with no possessions except what she wore. Evan carried his plastic bags to the Volkswagen and stuffed them in the trunk, which was at the front of the vehicle. He placed the leather satchel behind the driver's seat.

"It's a different car," she said. "Stolen?"

"No. A trade. This is our chariot now."

They climbed in and Evan turned over the ignition. Smoke belched out the exhaust pipe and the engine backfired. Jane waved to Robby at the top of the steps, and then they were on their way out of the Haight.

While Evan drove, Jane gently rubbed her belly. Then she tuned the AM radio. The strongest signal played big band swing music.

"It's gonna be a crappy ride if these are the only tunes we get," she griped.

"There's always conversation," Evan said.

"Yeah," she said as she switched off the radio. "Ever been to a commune?"

"Nope."

"Supposed to be some up in Mendocino, Napa, places like that."

Evan looked askance at her. "We're going to have to go a lot farther north, you know."

"Yeah, but we could stop along the way. Say hello to some of the Diggers."

As he drove the Beetle to Park Presidio Boulevard and then north to the Golden Gate Bridge, Jane chattered away about people she had met in the Haight, music she loved, adventures she had taken, politics, astrology, and finally about Patrick.

"You remind me of him," she said. "The same eyes, the same chin. Different style, though. You're an Aries, right?"

"I guess."

"Patrick was a Gemini. The twins. Dual personalities. That fits, doesn't it?"

Her lulling, sexy voice mesmerized Evan. Her patter reminded him of soft jazz vocals, and all he wanted to do was listen, even if the content ran the gamut. He could get used to hearing that sweet voice, he thought, just as he once believed he would learn to love Italian.

Within minutes, the Volkswagen was on the huge red bridge, which the fog enveloped so completely that the towers were obscured even when the car was right beneath them. Once they were across the Golden Gate's span, he had to press the accelerator to the floor to ascend the grade on the Marin side. All Evan could see through his rear view mirrors were gray wisps whipped by the ocean wind. Jane turned in her seat to wave goodbye to fog-enshrouded San Francisco.

"So long, city," she said with sadness. "It's gonna be cold up there, isn't it?"

"Come wintertime, yes. But I hear Vancouver doesn't get that much snow."

"I've never really been in snow before. I mean, not like Santa Claus snow."

Evan said, "Me neither."

"I've always wanted to, though," Jane said.

"Do you think you could get used to it?" Evan asked.

"I suppose," Jane said as she rested her hands on her bulging belly, "but I'm a California girl."

Evan grinned as he recalled Harkess saying, I wish they all could be California girls.

They drove through the dark Waldo Tunnel, built into a hill, and came out the Marin side into brilliant sunlight. The edges of the blanketing fog cut off just outside the tunnel at the crest of the Marin Headlands. The hills formed a natural break wall to protect Sausalito from the gloom. The winding highway climbed further up and then descended sharply down the hillside. He shifted the Volkswagen into neutral and coasted downhill like a carnival ride. In a scant ten seconds, gray fog had given way to vibrant colors; blue sky and green pine trees and brown earth drenched in sunshine. The bay waters were glassy smooth. Two hawks floated overhead like a welcoming committee. Locals knew how drastic the change in weather could be from one side of the Waldo Tunnel to the other, from dense fog to vivid daylight, and although Evan had driven the route many times before the simple splendor of it never struck him until that moment. It felt like passing through time or being reborn.

Evan took it as a good omen.

Novels by Dan Spencer

MYSTERIES

Going to the Sun

HISTORICAL FICTION

Rule of Existence

Loop the Loop

All Eyes Skyward

Four Wheels Good

SATIRE

Be Now, Buddy What

Jack of Bilge

Nothing the Fish Talker